To
Doug & Pat,
with many

Frederick A. Read

A Beach Party

The Adventures of John Grey
Book Five

Frederick A. Read

A *Guaranteed* Book

First Published in 2009 by
Guaranteed Books

an imprint of Pendragon Press, Po Box 12, Maesteg
Mid Glamorgan, South Wales, CF34 0XG, UK

Copyright © 1998, 2009 by Frederick A Read
Cover Illustration Copyright © 2009 by Gareth Evans
This Edition Copyright © 2009 by Pendragon Press

All Rights Reserved, in Accordance with the
Copyright, Designs & Patents Act 1988

No part of this publication shall be reproduced in *any form*
without the *express written consent* of the publisher.

Frederick A Read asserts his moral right to be identified
as the owner of this work.

ISBN 978 1 906864 02 6

Typeset by Christopher Teague

Printed and Bound in Wales by
Print Evolution
www.print-evolution.com

www.guaranteedbooks.net

Chapters

1. *Volunteered* — 1
2. *Trials* — 10
3. *Typical* — 14
4. *Daly Report* — 21
5. *A Red Light* — 26
6. *Say Hello Again* — 32
7. *Delighted* — 36
8. *Ship Shape* — 45
9. *Panama Plates* — 52
10. *The Phatts* — 66
11. *Shields* — 77
12. *Stan* — 83
13. *The Usual* — 93
14. *Clever Stuff* — 103
15. *A Proper Fix* — 109
16. *Take a Seat* — 117
17. *A Stuffed Pig* — 127
18. *Delivery Boy* — 134
19. *Underground* — 147
20. *Floating Islands* — 162
21. *Au Naturel* — 168
22. *The Big Turn On* — 175
23. *Nice and Crisp* — 181
24. *Surfing* — 190
25. *Geronimo* — 197
26. *Recovery* — 213
27. *Saving Graces* — 219
28. *Blazing Torches* — 226
29. *Chief Taster* — 230
30. *Sausages and Pies* — 237
31. *Choices* — 245
32. *So Long* — 250

Foreword

This is about a ship that sailed to the other side of the world to reach her destination, which was a small group of islands seemingly enjoying the lifestyle found in paradise, and only to be found in the middle of the biggest ocean of the world, the Pacific, where the East meets the West.

These islands of paradise have a terrible secret that only the Islanders know about, and for those who visit these shores to experience life there, could also cost them their lives.

At the time of John Grey's visit, which was to set up a cold storage area for the islanders to have a continuous supply of fresh food, the island was devastated by not just one Tsunami but two, with the second being a MEGA TSUNAMI.

How will these small islands survive such a massive wave, and what would the islanders do when their newly arrived fresh provisions got destroyed in such a destructive manner?

How would their Monarch find the food to provide a special BEACH PARTY?

A Beach Party

Chapter I
Volunteered

The clock in the HQ foyer rang the required number for the hour, just as John looked at his fob watch to check its timing against that used by the company, before putting it back into his waistcoat pocket.

"No wonder I was given a company timepiece. It's spot on as usual." John said quietly, buttoning up his coat again.

He entered the despatch room where the ships' officers go, to find out where, if and when they had another ship to join. He looked at the large grid chart on the wall, which indicated the ships available, Its type, size, tonnage, crew compliment, its present port, intended voyage, who were on it at that time and who were to join it.

"Not a mention anywhere of me, but I see Andy is berthed." he whispered to himself, looking at another list of ships on an adjacent wall that had a pencilled notice drawn above them:

<u>**VOLUNTEERS WANTED**</u>
CURRENT TRADE CERTIFICATES NEEDED, BUT MUST AGREE TO UNDERGO SPECIAL TRAINING, WHICH WILL ATTRACT A SPECIAL BONUS ON TOP OF NORMAL PAY SCALES. See Despatch clerk for details.

"Extra training and a pay rise at the end of it, that's for me." he added quietly, but had a reply from behind him.

"You really must stop talking to yourself John, or men in white coats will take you away to the funny farm." Larter chuckled, placing his hand on John's shoulder.

"Hello Bruce. Have a nice time off? Sold off those little stones I gave you?" John replied unabashed, and turned to greet his friend[*].

---

[*] See *Fresh Water*.

1

"From what your letter told me, I was robbed by some conniving jeweller. How was I to know that the pink and lemon stones were rare diamonds. He offered me a couple of hundred quid for the lot, yet according to your letter that arrived too late, I could have got ten times that amount. Still, I managed to help my family out of a difficult patch but I could have done with my retainer as well. It always arrives late and has left me in the lurch on several occasions, and as always I'm skint again. The compensation Belverley owes us, which is about several hundreds of pounds each should get me back on an even keel again. In the meantime, let's hope they'll give us a decent lucrative contract this time, John."

"Yes, the stones I gave you and Andy were worth several hundreds of pounds. I've kept a couple for a rainy day, but even I splashed out on my family just like you did. I also had a great couple of weeks with Helena and her family, so I know what you speak about. I gave my biggest ones to her father to sell for me, except the one the size of a chestnut which according to him should be worth several hundreds on its own, even before it's been graded and polished.' As you've spent all your proceeds, I take it that you've got some special gold mine somewhere to fund your eventual retirement, whenever or wherever you decide to finally hang up your hat?"

"Not me John! Andy is almost the same as me, and unlike you, we're not known for saving up. I always spend it as it comes along, and I'll worry about my pension when the time comes."

"There's no answer to that Bruce, but for your sake I suggest that you really must start now to save for your retirement before it's too late." John concluded.

"Well whatever! Anyway, what's the score on this board for you to be found muttering to yourself once more?"

"These notices have caught my eye. One asking for volunteers and one with Andy's name down for the *FarmLea*, but it has been scratched off. Maybe he's still to come along and see, or perhaps waiting to see what we're doing."

A Beach Party

"Well it says something about special training, which means it will be some sort of a trials ship. There's not much they can teach me about my job as a radio officer, but if it means extra pay then I'm all for it."

"As for me, I've still got a lot to pick up, so I'm going for it too. Come on Bruce, let's see the man and see what the score is." John led the way into the despatch office and spoke to a surly looking man behind a desk.

"I've come to volunteer my services for the good of the company."

"Who are you and what papers have you got?" demanded the angry looking man.

"I've got the Belfast Telegraph if that's any good!" Larter quipped, which made the man look even angrier.

"Who asked you? I was talking to this officer here, so shut up and wait your turn." he retorted.

John produced his Officers Booklet and his folder with all his trade certificates neatly tucked inside it.

The despatch clerk looked up from reading John's papers and frowned.

"Hmm! I'll have to speak to the SRF office. But for now, just put your name under the ship of your choice, and wait here." the clerk said truculently, then went and made his phone call.

"Bruce, there's no name put down for radio officers yet. Quick, put it down before he comes back."

Larter looked at the blank entry and entered his name into it.

"There! Let's hope Andy spots it and joins us. It would be nice to keep our partnership going even for another voyage." Larter said, signing his name with a flourish.

"Yes, that would be good for the three of us." John agreed.

"I'll say. Almost being like the Three Musketeers and all that. Mind you, as long as we stay away from that infernal sand, as it gets into any place and everywhere." Larter said with a smile, scratching his groin quickly to emphasise the word 'everywhere.'

The clerk came back and spoke in a bumptious manner.

"Engineer Grey! You are to report to the SRF's engineering officer when you get there, here is your documentation back. Sign here for your ship embarkation card." He said, stamping John's booklet with a large rubber stamp that proclaimed John had been accepted.

He looked down at the book and saw that Larter had signed it too and grunted his displeasure, but told him same and carried out the same officious jobs worth ritual to Larter's book.

John and Larter left the building and made their way down towards the Ships Repair Facility, where John had been sometime before.

"Last time I was here I joined the SFD2, Bruce." John stated, showing Larter the streets they went down to reach their destination.•

"At least, we get to see some dear old faces again." Larter said with mild sarcasm, which made John groan.

"I can face anybody except that mad bastard Cresswell, let alone his shipmate Trewarthy. They were in charge last time, so let's hope they've both gone home and given someone else a chance."

"We're joining a ship not the SRF, that way at least, they can't be on both at the same time. So cheer up John." Larter said cheerfully.

Both men walked in through the wrought iron gates that marked the home of the SRF, and over the cobble stoned pathway before they reached the impressive facade of a low lying building and entered its revolving doorway.

"Here we are Bruce! Keep close eye in case Cresswell ambushes us from over there. Look there's Trewarthys' office next to it." John whispered, as he pointed to two frosted glass doors with the words 'SRF COMMODORE Trewarthy' and 'S.R.F. CHIEF ENGINEER Cresswell' inscribed in gold letters on them.

• See *A Fatal Encounter*.

A Beach Party

"Hello you two. Come to join us then?"

John spun around and saw Day coming from a corridor doorway.

"Hello Happy! Pleased to meet you again." John greeted cheerfully, shaking hands with his former chief.

"Hello chief! Got room in your classroom for two more suckers?" Larter asked, also shaking hands with Day.

"Which ship did you sign up for John?" Day asked politely.

"Why, the very one I saw your name on, of course!"

And me chief!"

"God help us all then." Day chuckled, and looked piously to the ceiling.

"What's the score on these ships Happy? Special trials? How long on trials?" John asked in quick succession, which made Day chuckle even more.

"There you go again John. Full of questions as usual. But never mind, all will become clear when we get you both down to the classroom area. So if you follow me please." Day responded, and the two friends followed Day down the corridor.

"Here we are John, just like last time. So find yourselves a seat and have a cigarette if you like. There's a drinks machine if you want a tea or coffee, but make yourselves at home as I'll be along shortly when the rest of the volunteers arrive." Day prompted, and left them.

John and Larter were greeted with sheep sounds from the several other officers who were waiting in the room.

"Oh well, at least we're all sheep and get sheared together." Larter said with a grin at the mild banter from them.

"I'm 3rd engineer Grey, this is radio officer Larter." John said as his introduction to the group.

Each man stood up in turn and introduced themselves to John and Larter, before they joined the ranks and sat down to a cup of tea and a cigarette.

The room went quiet as a group of newcomers arrived; who performed the same courtesy of introducing themselves. By the time that was done, Day had entered the room with a couple of other men behind him.

"Good morning gentlemen! It's nice to see so many happy and eager faces that answered the call." Day greeted, introducing the other men that came in with him.

"You have volunteered to undertake a five day instruction period. It's all free and gratis, and you even get a special payment at the end of it, providing you pass the practical tests that is.

This room will be your main room where you will meet every day before and after going on to your own tutorial rooms.

You will have your own instructor for your trade or discipline until the week is over. For you engineers, you will be meeting your own chief engineer before joining the ship that you signed up for at the despatch office.

As for the rest of you, your instructor will advise you on what comes next. Should any of you have any problems or difficulty in keeping up with your instructor, you will be asked to return to the despatch office and be re- assigned.

This type of course is not for the money grabbers or for those looking for a free handout, but for the hard workers that the company needs to keep the sea-lanes open as befitting a seafaring nation. You are warned on that score, so be professional and get through the course. I will now hand you over to your own instructors." Day announced civilly.

The instructors took a list of their 'students' before they had them file out to go to their own tutorial rooms. This left John with five other engineers along with Day.

"Now we've got rid of the odds and sods, let's get down to some real instructions." Day said with a smile, and clapped his hands together, drawing everybody's attention to him.

As each day of instructions and lectures were completed, the number of volunteers were getting fewer and fewer in each tutorial class, and by the end of the week there were only two in John's class, with just Larter in his.

A Beach Party

This caused great concern back at HQ and Belverley came to see for himself just what had happened, especially as both Trewarthy and Cresswell were away on other company business.

"Chief engineer Day. As you're the acting chief instructor, I wish to know just what went wrong with this very costly scheme." Belverley demanded crossly and in front of the remaining volunteers.

Day replied that the devised scheme as approved by the board was strictly adhered to. Those who were left were the genuine volunteers and would eventually become the next generation of instructors for the company.

He also stated that the input and feedback from the volunteers was such that a better and perhaps a harder course should be given, or at least be introduced during the initial training courses for each discipline.

Belverley and his advisors listened quietly, taking notes as Day and the other instructors went through their assessments of the course, until he was satisfied with what he heard.

"Thank you for your candid and forthright accounts gentlemen, at least we got rid of the pretenders and time wasters, even though we still have the odd purloiners of patents. They shall be dealt with through normal company discipline procedures, as I don't want such people let alone the slackers and shirkers in this shipping line.

The problem we had to address, was more of an engineering one, but at least the other departments will benefit from this experience. Who was the person who suggested this type of instructional course should be incorporated in basic core skills training?"

Before Day could mention the person's name, Belverly answered it for him.

"I see engineer Grey is among the last few. Now if I didn't know any better, I'll bet it was him."

"That's not all. He's come up with a few 'extras' that might help any engineering problem discovered during the course." Day agreed proudly about his former junior engineer.

"But of course he would, he's that kind of engineer who thinks he can keep his ideas to himself. Which points out to us that maybe we need to breed if not recruit good company engineers who will work for the good of the company and not line their own pockets, chief." Belverley said sarcastically, but more for the benefit of his advisors than to Day.

"Just as long as we don't go round shooting Arabs again, Mr Belverley!" Larter riposted.

"Et Tu Brute!" Belverley replied angrily, rising from his seat to make his way out again.

"I will congratulate each of you for completing your course and well done to your instructors, they might end up as our full time instructors after all. Mr Brooks, see that these men have the weekend off with pay and have them report on board their respective ships by 0700 Monday morning. Good luck to all of you!

Chief Day! Chief Cresswell will be back by then, so after you've handed back over to him, you will join your own ship again. Thank you again chief for your time in taking charge of this course, it's been a good pilot exercise all round despite the outcome." Belverley said finally, and left the room with his entourage.

"John, you have the weekend off, but I'm afraid I need you on board, sorry and all that." Day advised, when John and Larter were about to leave the SRF building.

John looked at Larter in puzzlement but turned to Day and said.

"If you need me Happy then who am I to complain? But a weekend at home with Bruce here really would be better."

"I can't agree more with you John, but needs must on this occasion." Day replied then turned to Larter.

"I feel sure you appreciate the inconvenience Bruce, given that you're the head of your own department anyway. Maybe the next time around?"

A Beach Party

"Yes John, you've had a torrid time learning all that guff about refrigeration and such like. Perhaps a swift hands-on experience before we sail would be more beneficial to you than us two painting the town red again. Besides I can always catch the Liverpool ferry over for the weekend, so don't worry about me, I'll see you on board first thing Monday morning." Larter agreed diplomatically.

"I was hoping that you and Happy here would have the chance of visiting my home before we sailed. But as you've just said, 'if needs must'." John replied stoically.

"That's the spirit John. See you Monday morning then." Larter replied and bade them farewell.

"You've made an excellent choice John, and the right one, which I knew you would make anyway. But I had to ask rather than demand, if you understand what I mean." Day said softly, as both engineers left the building.

"So if I'm not going home then where will I be berthed Happy? What's on the agenda? Do I get my trade certificates before we sail?"

"There you go again John. All will be revealed just as soon as we get on board." Day said and smiled at his junior officer.

Chapter II
Trials

For all of that day and most of the next, Day took John around the ship just like he had during his first time on board the *Brooklea,* posing various leading questions to John, who answered more or less what Day needed to hear. By the time they had finished the grand tour, John had several notes and a pile of diagrams and technical drawings to read through.

"This certainly is a lot of bumf to wade through Happy. Isn't there an easier way around all this? I mean, maybe I could learn it as we go along, so to speak." John asked, flicking through it all. Day looked at his wad of instructional material and shook his head slowly.

"This subject is far more in depth than the run of the mill air conditioning and ventilation control.

The thing is John, the reason why you did that intensive training course, and fortunately for both of us you passed, is because you need to be qualified to operate the different installations. Not only in a mechanical sense, but also be conversant with the understanding of certain basic biological principles involved, let alone the principal of thermo dynamics. You will be required to advise the captain on his planning to carry various cargoes, especially refrigerated and general. Don't forget the first rule of Thermo Dynamics whereby no calorie is lost in maintaining your cargoes. Anyway I have already given you the main factors causing food spoilage and the necessary refrigeration required in containing it. In other words, you are to see that the cargo does rot whilst in transit, which would be a financial disaster to all concerned. Remember to ascertain the type of foodstuffs, as each one requires their own special handling, be it 'live' or 'dead'.

So I suggest that we go and have our lunch now, then get some 'simulation' practice in before the day is over. We load up tomorrow afternoon, so we must have our systems checked in

A Beach Party

case of a last minute catastrophe. From then on you'll be on your own, but you'll have an assistant assigned to help you in your duties. However, I'll always be available to advise you should you need me, although knowing you as I do, that would be on a very rare occasion, John. Do this and you'll have yet another feather in your cap and one experience that you will be able to use on future voyages."

"Thank you for your support Happy but I can only do my best." John said humbly as both engineers entered the dining saloon.

"John Grey! We meet again but on a much bigger tub this time." a voice came from seemingly nowhere, when John was finishing his after meal cigarette.

John looked around to see whom the almost familiar voce belonged to, before he recognised who it was.

"Joe Tomlinson, er, captain Tomlinson." John said falteringly, remembering his ships' protocol and manners.
Tomlinson gave a throaty laugh and held out his hand in greeting.

"Whatever! What are you doing on board John?" he asked, then turned to Day and asked.

"I hope this engineer is one of ours chief? We could do with his sort on this vessel."

Day smiled and confirmed that John was the second 3rd but was to take sole charge of the experimental refrigeration units on board for this particular round trip.

"Good for you John, glad to have you on board. I have a million and one things to do just now, so I'll see you later for our pre-voyage briefing. Engines, I would like a briefing from you some time tomorrow afternoon concerning this experimental ship before I'm happy to take it to sea. I'll be on the bridge or in the bridge cabin all day tomorrow, so see you about 14.00 okay?"
Day agreed with Tomlinson but told him he had to make sure that John had enough practical knowledge to back up his very recent intensive course on refrigeration.

"John and I were on the SFD2 together when we took it down to the Falklands, so I've got no qualms about him. As his chief,

I feel sure that he will no doubt live up to your expectations too." Tomlinson said without patronising them, nodding his head and left the two engineers.

"He's a good captain, just as you're a good engineer Happy. I feel at home already." John said quietly, but saw Day smiling at him.

"I've said it before and I'll say it again. You'll make a good chief engineer one of these days John. Now lets go and see what mischief we can get up to." Day concluded, as they left the dining saloon and clambered back down into the bowels of the ship.

"Because this ship is the trial ship for long haul freight, we will monitor the differences between the cold brine circulation system using the 'Grid system' in the for'ard hold and the 'Air Battery' system in the aft hold. So we've got to sort out our acceptance temperatures, the fresh air ventilation and methods of dunnage and avoidance of mixing cargoes in the same hatch space. That's why we've got a variety of systems to experiment on, and why you've got a helper to keep a good monitoring system. We'll come to that later, but for now, we must check the insulation material, as this ship is only 'single skinned' but has been specially fitted with both cork and rock wool panels in each hold respectively. We'll check the Co_2 absorption units and bottle supply whilst we're at it." Day explained.

"I've already started on a monitoring system, based on the maintenance schedules I devised and used on my last three vessels. It keeps me fully aware on the state of each auxiliary machine on board." John said, showing Day his maintenance log. Day looked through the logbook and was satisfied with what he saw.

"These are just what you need, John. Keep on that vein of thought, as you will need to devise a separate set of temperature logs for each type of cargo and storage spaces. Plus a separate log to be kept on the amount of Co_2 amassed or used, but your indicators and gauges will assist you in that.

However, you can get your assistant to keep them updated, but you must be aware personally of any potential problem or

A Beach Party

mishap that might occur in both systems. If in doubt, give me a shout." he instructed, handing the books back again.

"With all this paperwork perhaps I need a scribe too, Happy." John said in jest.

"Don't even think about it John. My work is mostly paperwork and I'm supposed to be a chief engineer not a pen pusher. That goes with the territory John, so beware if you're thinking of becoming a chief in this outfit." Day moaned.

"No harm asking him Happy, seeing as this is a trial ship anyway. A stoker with a gifted pen would be great, as at least we don't have to take the time explaining the technical jargon to him." John replied hopefully.

Day looked at John and laughed heartily.

"You certainly like sailing close to the wind John. It's a fair enough request, so I'll see what I can do." He said after he had finished laughing.

Chapter III
Typical

"**G**ood morning gentlemen. We have a few items on the agenda to go through before we sail on our special trials voyage, so listen up. I shall stop half way through for a fifteen minute refreshment period, but any questions you may have will be answered right at the end of this meeting." Tomlinson said in a polite but authoritative tone of voice, then commenced to wade through his pile of documents.

He spoke in an up-beat manner, pausing from time to time to recap on what he had said, explaining various diagrams, charts and other pamphlets he had, before he gave his question and answer session.

John usually asked direct questions on various points but on this occasion he said nothing, which was a surprise even to Day. This was because Day had given John a problem that had cropped up, and which John needed to get his head around and come up with a workable solution prior to the ship's departure.

"Okay then gentlemen, once our quota of passengers have embarked, we sail for Barbados." Tomlinson concluded, as he and Day left the rest of the officers to get themselves ready and sorted for their voyage.

"Looking forward to your voyage then Bruce?" John asked, when Larter joined him.

"Actually John, I'm supposed to be sailing on the *Waterlea* with Andy tomorrow, but my relief hasn't shown up."

"Oh! Where is she going to?"

"She's one of the trial ships earmarked for the Argentina beef runs, as the *Downlea* is earmarked for the Caribbean fruit runs, but you're going to the Pacific and on a much more technical trial run than that."

"I was hoping that all three of us would make this trip, so I might be on my own then." John replied glumly.

"It happens John. Mind you, it's good you know and get on

A Beach Party

well with the captain and engineer this time. According to my radio schedule, at least we should meet up in Barbados for a run ashore. Now that will be fun." Larter said cheerfully

John frowned at the very thought.

"Yes it will. Perhaps we can dispense with the courtroom dramas this time, Bruce."

"That I can guarantee John." Larter said with a grin, patting John's shoulder gently.

"Oh well then, that will be nice to look forward to anyway. Must go and see to my helpers Bruce. If I don't see you at lunch then I'll know you've been relieved. By the way, who's your relief?"

"It should be a 'Tyke' by the name of Pete Trevitt. He's slightly taller than you and several years older too. I met up with him a few years ago during a training course at Marconi's and appeared to be a decent chap if my memory serves me correct. His assistant is a 'Brummie' from Smethwick called Dave Evans. Say hello to both of them for me won't you."

"Well Bruce. Here's to it. Take care and say hello to Andy for me." John said, and shook his friend's hand in farewell.

The SS *Inverlogie* sailed out of Belfast Lough but without 3rd engineer Grey standing at his customary place on the foc'sle. He was busy with his helper down in the cargo holds, sorting out the routine for recording details from the various sources and setting up a maintenance routine, for them to follow.

"That's all we can do for now. You know what the score is, so if you've any questions now is the time to speak up, not when there's a crisis on our hands. We will keep a special monitoring watch to record each detail as I've shown you until we get to Barbados. As I shall be busy troubleshooting the systems, I'm relying on you for accuracy and a high level of professionalism. If all is okay by the time we get to the other side of the Panama canal then we'll keep a relaxed but timetabled schedule until we reach our first round of cargo pick-ups."

As there were no questions for him to answer, John concluded by saying.

"Remember, I'm always around if you need me. If you've got a problem and can't locate me, then for God's sake speak to the chief. In the meantime I intend for us to have a good voyage, so let's work on one together. As you missed the course, you will do the second watch but with me in attendance, and until such times as I feel you're okay on your own. Had you done the course like I did then you'd be on a ship of your own. But look on the bright side, at least you'll get an 'Air conditioning' certificate at the end of the voyage, which is a good halfway towards a full certification." John said breezily.

"I've already got one of them 3rd, that's why I volunteered for the course. I was two days late for the course due to a family bereavement, so that's why I took the chance of teaming up with you for this voyage." Blackmore said glumly, looking at the ream of instructions and temperature tables.

"Chief Day didn't tell me you've got one of them. In that case, we're halfway there already. What else should I know about you other than being a 4th engineer?" John asked with surprise.

"I got stood over from my 3rd engineers exam board last month." He said, but got cut off by John.

"I know the score on that one, so you've no need to pain yourself again. As I've said to you earlier, if you've got a problem, come only to see me, or failing that, Chief Day. I say 'only' because you and I are independent from the rest of the ships' officers and we are only on board for this special trials voyage."

"Glad you said that as I thought the 2nd engineer had the instructional duties on board. But why chief Day as well as yourself?"

"Day was the course instructor for this trial, and as it happens, a friend of mine going way back to the days of the *Brooklea*. You've probably seen her alongside at one point, but she was my first ship and Day, the 2nd engineer before he was promoted to

A Beach Party

chief. Anyway, it's a long story but remind me to tell you sometime."

"So it is you. You're the engineer we've all been hearing about in our engineering college. Wait 'till I tell my friends about this." Blackmore said with glee.

John looked at the delighted face of his younger charge and even though he was only a few years older than Blackmore, he realised that life had moved on considerably since his own early days.

He also realised that this was a moment in time where life catches up with you in the form of someone who is probably just like you were at that time. Young, eager, and very keen to get on. "Yes, I am he. But don't get too carried away, so get yourself back to ground level. We have a busy schedule to operate, and I'll be expecting you to be at your best if you wish to join the ranks of 3rd engineers." John said quietly, which suppressed the rising curiosity that Blackmore was displaying.

"That's fair enough 3rd. But you do know I'm only on board until we reach Barbados as I'm supposed to be joining one of the 'Bay' tankers, the *'Tobermory Bay'* I think."

John was surprised yet again at this information, as he was promised a helper all the way throughout the entire voyage and trials.

"Yet another shining example of the typical strokes that are played on the ships officers and crew, by this company" John muttered to himself, as Blackmore was looking elsewhere.

"Thank you for that info 4th. That puts a different perspective to the workload facing me from there on. We'll leave that subject for now and head back to civilisation as we've got a meeting with the chief after lunch, so lets get ourselves smartened up to join the rest of the passengers." John replied, and led the way up and out of the cargo holds.

"Afternoon Happy. I've come early to our meeting to discuss certain items only revealed to me just before lunch." John announced, as he knocked the door of and entered Day's cabin.

"Hello John! What is the problem?" Day asked politely, pointing to a seat for John to use.

John told Day what Blackmore had revealed about himself earlier, and commented on what changes would have to be implemented to conduct all the experiments and trials.

Day listened quietly but spoke only to confirm certain details before making his comments known.

"That was decent of Blackmore to tell us, and it certainly does make all the difference to what the company has planned for us. Must speak to the captain about all this, but after we have our meeting. I have 1 hour to spend with you John before I go down the engine room, so lets make it a good one." Day advised, when Blackmore finally entered the room.

"Good, now we can start the ball rolling." Day said breezily, with Blackmore sitting next to John.

The meeting was conducted in such a manner, that it was over sooner than was anticipated, which delighted Day.

"I have a good team in you two and feel happy, no pun intended. As I've said to you earlier John, you're virtually on your own and this is your passport for better things. Any real problems that you come across try and sort them out before calling for me as I'm only your last resort. Good luck to both of you. Now I really must get below to the engine room." Day concluded.

As the engineers left Day's cabin, John said that he would speak to the captain and let him know of the outcome.

Day merely nodded but reminded John that as he was in charge, he would conduct his own affairs and independently from Day. John thanked him again and left with Blackmore.

"C'mon 4th. Let's do our first round of monitoring. The more we do this side of Barbados the better chance we stand in gaining a good trials report." John said, and led Blackmore down to the monitoring station.

The first session took longer than John had envisaged and over-ran into the scheduled next one.

A Beach Party

"We'll do this one together to set the pattern, 4th. But you will do the rest, as I've got a few mechanical problems already to sort out. Once we've done a full 24hour cycle we can send off our first trial's report from the radio shack. Are you happy with that?" John asked politely as the two men wrote down the various figures and notations for the trials log.

"Yes, ecstatic 3rd!" Blackmore replied sarcastically but with a forced grin on his face.

"Thought so 4th! 62.5%. +5 degrees, -2 degrees, 95%." John replied with his own grin, and commenced to read off the gauges and dials.

When the second monitoring session was over, both men stowed their logbooks and made their way through the motor room where the electricians were attending their electrical switchboards and power circuits.

"Make way for two boffins! Don't forget your slide rulers or you'll never find your way out again." An electrician said sarcastically, using a brush and pretending to sweep the deck before John could walk on it.

"Why thank you, here's your tip!" John said politely, just as he was about to step through the watertight hatchway into the engine room compartment.

The electrician held his hand out, fully expecting a gratuity for his sarcasm, but got the nicotine stained end of John's last cigarette as John pressed it into the man's hand.

The electrician looked at it incredulously, then cursed loudly before he threw it back at John, and for the other electricians to laugh at the practical joke John had played on the man.

"You'd better sweep that up before the chief sees it." a stoker said crossly when the offending cigarette butt landed in front of him, which made the electrician scowl even more at his fellow watchkeepers.

"You certainly turned the tables on him 3rd." Blackmore chuckled, as both men finally reached the accommodation area.

"Just goes to show what happens if your crew don't know

who you are and especially when you're in overalls. We are separate from the rest of the officers and crew, so if you put them in the picture next time you go down that should be the end of it." John replied with a grin.

"Anyway 4th, I'm going up to the radio shack to make arrangements for our first report. I'll see you in the saloon for a beer later." He concluded.

A Beach Party

Chapter IV
Daily Report

The *Inverlogie* sailed out of the choppy waters of the Irish Sea and headed Southwest towards the deep and vast open oceanic waterscape of the North Atlantic, on the 3000mile first leg of her voyage.

Everybody on board had settled down to their own little rhythm of life, with the hope that all would go well during their watery transit.

Depending on the type of ship, and taking the *Inverlogie* as an example, she has three human elements that make up her society on board.

If you are a passenger, your life revolves around the daily chore of finding what next to do just to fight off the boredom, whilst idling around squabbling about some abstract thing or other in a mind numbing existence. If you're part of the crew, your life has some purpose even if you perform your duties in robotic fashion and without using one atom of your brain.

However, if at the other end of the spectrum and in the third element as an officer, you would be on a daily ration of sorting out the myriad of things to do. The golden rule for remembering as to who does the problem solving and has the burden of worry, is how far up the promotion ladder the officer is, no matter if he was an engineer or deck officer. Thus the last stop and final words made on board would go to the captain of the ship.

"Good morning Joe! May I come in?" John asked politely, knocking on Tomlinson's day cabin door.

"Hello John! Yes you may. How's your show so far, all right I take it?" Tomlinson asked with a smile, raising his head up from reading a chart.

"Not too bad at the moment Joe. Here is my first radio report for you to sanction, and for you to see for yourself. Although I dread to think what's going to happen after we leave Barbados."

"Oh?   Why is that?" Tomlinson asked, quickly reading through the radio report.

"Given the present level of activity required to produce my daily radio report, it takes two engineers to compile. What would my instructions be when my helper 4th engineer Blackmore leaves us at Barbados?"

"Who's leaving at Barbados?"

"4th engineer Blackmore. He's to join the *'Tobermory Bay'*, which according to the radio officer will already be there and will sail before we do."

"Is he by jove. What does the chief have to say on that?"

"Happy, er, I mean the chief, is acting only as my unofficial overseer. This is my show as it was on the SFD2, but I need backing from you to ensure that I complete this project as per company directives."

Tomlinson read through the report again before replying.

"I know exactly where you are coming from John.   If something should happen during the trials, not only would I lose my cargo but also put a question mark on the entire company project of getting their fleet of fridge ships on the move. I might be captain of this ship, but am not part of the 'Lines' personnel department and policy makers. The only consolation I can offer you at present are for me to request that Blackmore remain on board, or at least you be given another helper. It is yet another occasion where you find yourself between a rock and a hard place, so to speak." He said, shaking his head slowly.

"As your cargo is stable, and all equipment is in good working order at present, I cannot guarantee these idyllic conditions to be correct even 12hours from now. This ship is virtually a new one so hopefully it will not arise, but all it would take is a mechanical or electrical breakdown, which if not sorted within a few hours, would cause a melt down and a distinct stench coming from each hold. I've told Happy Day all of this, as he is a friend of mine, just as I'm telling you Joe. If there's nothing you can do for me,

A Beach Party

then at least would you kindly enter this meeting in your narrative log." John said quietly.

"Yes John, it's good as done. Here, I'm satisfied with your report and signed it for transmission. You don't need to get my signature for any future reports, just so long as I get a copy of it." Tomlinson said, handing back the trials report, then added.

"I have the entire rules and regulations governing these trials, and have been given the right to interpret them as I deem judicious and for the good of the company. Yours is by far the biggest part of these stack of books you see in front of you, but I have a couple of my own that would dovetail into yours. Let me see if I can come up with something. It will take us about ten days to get to Barbados, so hopefully we will have your problem solved by the time we get there. In the meantime John, keep up with the good work."

John stood and thanked Tomlinson before he left the cabin.

"It's good to know who your friends are, as you once told me Joe. Glad that Happy and you are among mine."

Tomlinson nodded his head and smiled.

"You and me both John."

"Morning gentlemen. Here is the first report signed by the captain. He tells me that I can just bring it up to you for typing as long as he gets a copy." John greeted when he walked into the radio shack..

"Morning 3rd. Let's have a look at it then." Trevitt said politely, taking the sheets of paper from John, and starting to read through them.

John sat down in an empty chair and looked around the neatly kept office, waiting for Trevitt to give his verdict on it.

"Phew! That is some report 3rd." Trevitt whistled.

"It will take me about two hours to get off. Am I to take it that each one will be just as long? The thing is, you'll have to give it to Dave Evans here to transmit, as he's on board specially for your trials." Trevitt asked, when he finished assessing the report.

"More or less. If it's too wordy then I'll try to cut it down a bit, but the format really is down to basic facts as it is now."

"Dave is otherwise engaged at the moment which means I'm on my own for a while. So I'll have to send it after my next radio schedule when it gets a bit quiet. That is of course if you're in no hurry to get it off?"

"No hurry, just as long as Belfast gets it by 1600 every day."

Trevitt looked at the clock, which displayed GMT also known as 'Zulu' time. This is the internationally recognised time that is used by all radio operators when working in their wireless offices or radio shacks.

"In that case, I'd better get it ready for transmission now. If you come back say after tea time, I'll have it ready for you to collect again."

"Thanks Pete. I'll leave you to get on then." John said, leaving the radio shack for a breath of fresh air on deck.

"3rd engineer Grey?" a voice came from the side of him.

John looked around to see a tall, almost beanpole like, but well tanned man standing near him.

"Who's asking?"

"I'm the outside engineer, 3rd engineer Langley. Can I have a word with you?" the man asked civilly.

"What can I do for you Langley?"

"I have a problem with the crews ventilation system, and am wondering if you could come and help me with it."

John looked at this man and shook his head.

"Sorry 3rd, but I've got my own set of problems to deal with. Suggest you go and see your 2nd or even the chief, they won't mind. Before you take umbrage at what I've just said, you must realise that I'm not part of the crew, but on special duties as 'Trials officer'. That being so, I'm not allowed to assist in normal ship's duties."

Langley sighed and mumbled his apologies and left.

'Strange to have an outside engineer who's not conversant with the ship's machinery. I wonder what Happy will say to him.' John mused,

A Beach Party

flicking the last of his cigarette over the side of the ship and watched it tumble down into the creamy foam of the ships' wake.

Chapter V
A Red Light

As the days merged into each other in a seemingly endless time zone, so did the trials monitoring system. It also meant that it became easier for the two engineers to be able to feel confident that they had finally got on top of their tasks.

"It will be a different story each time we get a different cargo, as different cargoes have a different method of handling as is the different method of refrigeration. So just remember the 'differences' and you can't go wrong." John stated, finishing yet another days report ready for transmission.

"This all good stuff for me 3rd, but I'll probably forget it all when I come off the tanker. Speaking of which, what equipment have we got here that would be used on board the *Tobermory Bay*?"

"I don't rightly know 4th. I should imagine it would all depend on the various machinery and equipment it has. It would be mostly valves, suction or discharge pumps, sluices and flow meters on deck. But one thing is for certain; it won't have all this palaver to deal with. You'd probably only deal with its air conditioning or even the ships main food stores and fridge spaces."

"I should imagine that as the tankers spend more sea time during transits than freighters, it would have a bigger storage space to keep their frozen foodstuffs in."

"Yes 4th, that would fit the scenarios perfectly. Anyway, that's enough for now. Take the daily report up to the radio shack and report back to me in my cabin when you've done so."

"See you then 3rd!" Blackmore said with a cheeky grin, and left hurriedly.

As John was leaving his little domain that was the 'Trials office' he noticed a red light flickering on the electric switchboard that indicated the electricity power supply to various parts of the ship.

"Why is that light showing red? What part of the ship is it from?" John asked with concern to an electrician who had his feet up on a desk and reading a girlie magazine.

A Beach Party

The electrician looked up from his book and shrugged his shoulders with unconcern.

"Don't know boffin. Maybe when the electrical officer comes back he'll tell you. I'm only here to look after the turbine to make sure it doesn't stop. Come back in couple of hours or so." the man said lazily, and cast his eyes back down to his book.

John walked swiftly over to the man and kicked his tilted chair over so that the man fell backwards with a heavy thump onto the steel deck plates.

"I want answers from you now not next week. Get me the electrical officer now!" John snarled, as the man started to pick himself up from the deck.

"Just who the fuck are you to demand anything. You're only a fuckin' passenger fiddling around with a few dials. Unless you get out of this compartment right now, I'll fuckin' well throw you out." He said angrily, rubbing the back of this head.

John sighed and went through the watertight hatchway that separated the motor room with the engine room and saw Day standing on his inspection platform.

"Happy, there is a red light showing on the grid panel in the motor room, but I've got an electrician who simply does not understand nor wants to know who I am on board this vessel. Would you do the honours and enlighten this man and maybe get him to remain on watch for at least until he can explain the function of the grid panel." John shouted into Day's ear.

Day looked at John with surprise, but swiftly climbed down and marched into the motor room where he found the electrician still reading his book.

"You, get yourself off your fat arse and phone for the electrical officer to report down here right now!" Day screamed into the electrician's ear.

The surprised electrician fell off his stool again and almost crawled across the deck to the telephone.

"4th! The chief wants to see you right away. For gawd's sake come now!" he croaked before slamming the receiver back down

27

into its cradle.

John was examining the panel, trying to trace where the red light might be connected up to, when the electrical officer arrived panting and gasping for breath.

"You sent for me chief?" the man asked between breaths.

"I have the Trials officer here, who is a fully qualified 3rd engineer, and wants to know why there is a red light on your grid panel. Now unless you can satisfy his questions, you and the rest of your men will be watch on stop on until his demands are met in full. Is that clear 4th?" Day shouted so that he would be heard over the noise of all the various machinery.

The 4th engineer looked at John with surprise and started to offer his apologies, but got short shrift from John.

"That excuse for an electrician you've got behind you will remain on watch until I say so. He will eat, shit, and sleep here until he is fully conversant with the importance of such expensive equipment that is supposed to be part of his job." John said vehemently, cutting into the 4ths mumbling apologies.

The hapless electrician was still rubbing his neck and shoulder when he discovered who John was, and was almost begging forgiveness as he heard his fate.

"So just what area does that red light serve, 4th?" John asked angrily.

"It tells me that there is an electrical shortage somewhere for'ard."

"Okay 4th! Take your time and tell me exactly just where for'ard?" John persisted.

"Not sure where 3rd. It just tells me there is a short circuit, that's all."

"So what do you do about it 4th? How long does it take you to remedy it?" Day asked coldly.

"We go round checking the circuit from the ships' circuitry drawings. That takes a team of men about four hours before we discover the fault. Then depending on my watch system and the

A Beach Party

parts available, add an extra two hours or so, depending on the type of repair needed."

John looked at Day with deep concern.

"Six hours to repair a faulty circuit? How long has this light been showing red? Have you got a buzzer alarm to tell you there's a red light on?" John snapped.

"Yes we have, but we disconnected the buzzer on account it was disturbing my men's concentration on their other watch-keeping duties." the 4th replied defensively.

John was usually a calm and collected man, but when it came to a show of incompetence and downright laziness from a so-called professional man, and especially from his own trade, he finally lost his temper.

"Now look here. I came into this compartment to find a man propped up in a chair, reading a book. This light was on for probably god knows how long. Do you mean to tell me that the warning buzzer was disconnected just so that your watch-keeper can read his magazine in peace? Do you mean to tell me that you, an electrical officer cannot keep on top of his departmental duties? What do you suppose is different from this ship and say an ordinary freighter? Do you understand the reason why this is a special voyage, and why I am on board as special 'Trials officer'? Do you realise how important it is that the ships' electrical grid system is kept active at all times during this special trial?" John shouted, whilst poking his forefinger into the taller mans chest on each question, forcing him backwards and against the control panels.

Day interceded by pulling John gently away from the 4th in case John had the notion of thumping the man.

"Gently does it John. I'll start the ball rolling this end to find the fault and get it repaired. Suggest that you go and check through your figures and test results and compare them with the present readings given off."

"But that will take longer than this stupid lot will take to repair the fault, that is if they can find it." John replied with indignation, pushing his victim away from him.

"If you remember John, we carried out a simulation exercise to combat such an eventuality. Just make sure that you shut down the whole system and lock all gangways to prevent any crewman entering the holds. I'll let you know when the problem has been fixed." Day said soothingly.

"Both me and my 4th have been here for the last four hours, and as you know that we have a maximum limit of a 12hour power failure gap, Happy. After that, then the captain will have to be told why his cargo is starting to stink and why he has to jettison it all." John said with feeling, but was starting to calm down under Day's calming influence.

"Yes John, you're right on that score. But hopefully it won't come to that, so give me a chance to sort out my end of the matter before you make your report."

John looked at the terrified 4th engineer and the electrician watch-keeper, then turned back to Day.

"You are a good friend of mine Happy, and that's why I agree to your request. Although I feel there is no need for it but it's what I call payback time." John said earnestly, then looked at the flashing light on the power grid board and added.

"I think you'll find that the problem is in the for'ard hold. If I'm correct then we're in big trouble." John said quietly, and backing away from the confrontation left the motor room to Day.

"Now look here you stupid excuse for an electrical officer…" John heard Day shout, as he went out of earshot.

"The electrical officer finally found the fault, which was in the for'ard hold as you suspected. It is now repaired so we can have the rest of the voyage in peace, yes?" Day announced, and sat down next to John in the saloon.

"We have yet another problem there Happy, and it's a problem that I have been concentrating for a while now, but I seem to come up with the same answer. I have concluded that it's the axial fans currently installed in the for'ard hold. They are of the single type, but in fact they should be of the double type."

A Beach Party

John replied before he went on to explain his theories and remedies to the situation.

Day listened intently, examining John's diagrams and analysis of the situation before he too responded.

"From what you've said and shown me John, I think you've got it figured out. I can't see their lordships doing anything about the changes until the ship gets to some decent ship repair yard. If we are going into the Pacific, then the nearest one to us would be Georgetown B.G. before resuming our route. The next one would be the Kiwi naval base at Christchurch, failing that then Brisbane. But by then, most of the cargo would have long since perished, so they'd just ask us to make do and mend as the situation occurs."

"The statistics contained in the daily report should have alerted them on this problem, so maybe they will send me a considered reply and instruction as to what gets done next. We're about 36hours off Barbados, and unless we can sort this out while I still have my assistant, then forget it after we've sailed for the Panama."

"Yes John, I had forgotten that. Stick that into your next report and demand an urgent reply to it. If we don't succeed then I'll try and get a suitable replacement from somebody on board."

"Just as long as it's not that stupid electrical officer or any of his gang, Happy. I need somebody with at least one iota of gumption to get this trial to a decent end result."

Day smiled at John and concluded by saying.

"See what we can do in Barbados, as there'll be at least three of our ships there during our stay."

"Thanks for that anyway Happy." John responded as Day left.

Chapter VI
Say Hello Again

John was having a breather on the boat deck as the ship docked alongside the harbour wall.

'Let's hope this visit will be an improvement to the last one, I don't feel like another round of courtroom dramas. Just a plain good old run ashore to stretch my legs will do me. Judging by the amount of company ships I see that are already in harbour, it should be interesting if not a bit of fun. Let's hope Bruce and Andy are here at least.' John muttered to himself, as he watched the hustle and bustle of the workers on the dockside.

"John, we've just received your reply to the last daily trials report." Evans said, coming over to John with the signal pad in his hand.

"Hello Dave! My last one? But I'm still waiting for the reply from my first one." John said with surprise, taking the signal off Evans and began to read it.

"It seems that I'm on my own, but I get to receive a couple of extra pieces of equipment that I'm to install by the time we reach the Pacific." John said aloud, when he finished reading the signal.

"When you're ready Dave, please make a copy out for the chief engineer too as he's got a keen interest in this project."
Evans nodded his head and returned to the wireless office, as the ships' 3rd engineer approached John.

"Engineer Grey! I need a favour off you before you shoot ashore for the day." the 3rd asked apologetically.

"Still got ventilation and air conditioning problems 3rd?" John asked gently, in anticipation as to why this engineer needed this favour.

"Of sorts, yes. But I need some info from you to verify if my solution to the problem is correct."

"Very well 3rd, fire away."

The engineer described his problems and his intentions to overcome them, with John listening carefully to what was being said. "It seems that you are suffering from the same sort of

A Beach Party

problem as me, 3rd. Perhaps if we tackle this together whilst we're still in harbour, then maybe both of us can get some peace from it. When you make your report to the captain, and especially to the chief, tell them of our discussion and that we'll endeavour to sort these nagging problems out together. I say this because I'm not supposed to interfere with the ships' internal matters. However, as we both have the same problems then it makes sense to join up and sort them out together, two heads instead of one so to speak." John said at length.

"Thanks Grey! I'll see you later on this morning, once I've made out my maintenance report." the engineer said gratefully.
John looked at the grubby piece of paper that the 3rd held in his hand and asked off handedly.

"If that is your report, how long have you had it? How often do you make them?"

"Yes, it's my latest. I only make one out at the start and end of each leg of a voyage. That way the chief engineer gets to know what I've done during my time on board." The 3rd said proudly, but much to John's surprise.

"One report per lap of the voyage? What about progress reports, planned maintenance schedules, and contingency plans to cover emergencies? In fact how long have you been a 3rd?"

The 3rd shook his head slowly and repeated his words.

"Nothing like that Grey. It's just as I've said, one report per lap. I've been a 3rd in this company now for nearly ten years now and have discovered that is all I'm required to submit, so that's all I give them. Why do you ask?"

"Oh nothing, forget I asked. I'll see you tomorrow morning instead." John replied with a sneer, and left the 3rd without a further word.

'No wonder he's still a 3rd.' he muttered to himself in disgust, when he saw Larter walk swiftly over the gangway.

"Bruce! Up here!" John shouted and waved to his friend.

"There you are John!" Larter greeted, when he met up with John.

"Been in Bridgetown long, Bruce?"

"We arrived here about 3am, and inboard of the *Forest Lea*. How did you find Pete Trevitt and Dave Evans?"

"Pete Trevitt is a good man, and it's a shame he was taken to the sick bay suffering from malaria that he contacted some years ago. Therefore Dave has been almost run off his feet these last few days in trying to cope. The doc is sending Pete back to Blighty, but I don't know if Dave can cope with my transmissions and that of the ship, he's only an assistant radio officer. A bit like me as a 3rd trying to do the chief's job as well, sort of."

"That's the second reason why I came on board, with you being the first, John. Once I've signed my papers with the purser I'll come back to you and we'll have a run ashore."

"That sounds good to me Bruce, but where's Andy?"

"He's been here a couple of days now, and is already ashore. He says to meet him in the Yacht club later, about 2pm. Tell you about it when I come back. Give me about 15 minutes" Larter said, then rushed away.

John and Larter strolled into the luxurious setting of the yacht club and made their way to the cocktail bar to where Sinclair was sitting at a table surrounded by other people.

"Hello Bruce, glad you found John! Come and sit with us." Sinclair invited, and drew two empty chairs towards the table.

"Folks! You remember Bruce Larter and John Grey from the *Brooklea*?" Sinclair asked, introducing them.

John looked at each face around the table and recognised most of them, as he said hello to them.

Once the initial introductions were completed and a fresh round of drinks arrived, John had a chance to catch up with some of those faces and he expressed his delight in meeting them once more.

"We appear eager to meet up with you all, but please accept our sincere condolences on the demise of Nanny Stock. I remember her smile at the look Dr Whitcombe gave me when I brought her to the hospital. Sorry he's no longer on the island

A Beach Party

for me to say hello again. But as for Nanny Stock, to me she seemed to be a proud yet humble woman, and everybody was fortunate to have known her, Andy." John said with sincerity, with Larter nodding his head in agreement.

Sinclair thanked him and Larter, as did the rest of his family, before the party broke up and the people to leave.

"They still remember your trial John as if it was only yesterday. You did a wicked thing to those people, but nothing more than they deserved. My Uncle and Aunt hope that Bruce and you, will come and visit them before you sail away again." Sinclair said softly.

John nodded in agreement, but his mind was racing over the events that happened during his last visit to this jewel in the Caribbean.

"Just as long as we don't have another 'bash' in this place Andy. A quiet run ashore is all I need this time around." John replied.

"Well, must be getting back to the home farm estate. Got some things to sort out, so I'll see you both on board tomorrow." Sinclair said then waved them goodbye before climbing into a black limousine, driven by a man dressed in a white livery.

'T*here's that black and white, again.*' John whispered but was overheard by Larter.

"That's a good idea John, never mind the Dimple, lets have a good snort of the old Black and White down at Harry's bar."
John nodded his head as both men left the building and wandered down the wide palm lined avenue towards the familiar part of town where the crews were making merry and other things that took their fancy.

Chapter VII
Delighted

"**M**ornin' Happy! Have a good run ashore, or is 8 o'clock in the morning a bit early for you?" John greeted, meeting Day coming over the gangway.

"Hello John! Yes I did, as a matter of fact. Mind you it was not a patch on our last visit, but at least it was peaceful and productive." Day said amiably, holding up a heavy looking object for John to see.

"That looks nasty, Happy. What's that when it's at home?"

"A new motor for the outside engineer to play around with. Maybe you can pop by and see me in my cabin in about one hour so that I can go through it with you. As my schedule is tight please don't be."

"I know, adrift!" John said aloud, finishing Day's sentence for him.

"That's the one John. See you then." Day chuckled, and disappeared out of sight.

'That reminds me, I've got the 3rd to meet in a few minutes, so better get him organised to see the chief at the same time' John said quietly, making his way towards the accommodation area of the ship.

"Hello Grey! I was just about to come looking for you as you promised to help me out with my confounded problem." the 3rd said truculently, when he met up with John.

"Right then. I've just spoken to the chief, who has a new motor for you. So if you've finished with your morning deck rounds, perhaps you'll meet me in his cabin in about half an hour from now." John said civilly, even though he had a distinct dislike for this slovenly man.

"What deck rounds are those Grey? What has a meeting with the chief got to do with us sorting out our mutual problem?"

A Beach Party

John sighed and turned his head away in disbelief at this apparent disregard to normal engineering practice, that he had always set his standards by, and one that had always stood him in good stead.

"Meet me in the chief's cabin by 0830. Bring all your maintenance books and your daily report log, as the chief will want to see them. If not, then our joint meeting will be a total waste of time and effort on his and certainly my behalf." was John's terse reply, before he climbed up the companionway ladder towards the bridge.

"What a beautiful morning! The sun is shining, and we've got another day in port, yet you've got a face like a thunder cloud, John." Sinclair greeted him jovially, as John walked into the bridge.

"It's that stupid 3rd engineer. No wonder everything is up the creek on this supposedly new ship. The old *Brooklea* was better looked after than this one, even though I do say it myself." John moaned.

"Well never mind him, as the buzz from the stokers mess has it that he's on his way home on the *Waterlea*. Him and the electrical officer, along with that poor radio officer Trevitt."

"Well, whatever. Just as long as I keep my helper to finish the trials that's all I need worry about.

Anyway, what's this new toy you've got to play around with?" Sinclair pulled a canvas cover off a small grey box that looked like a small screen with a roll of paper coming from the bottom of it.

"This is an echo sounder, John. It records the depth of water under the ship by making a pen mark onto the roll of paper you see dangling from it. We switch it on for several hours at a time, and then keep the roll of paper until the Admiralty wants it. Look, we passed the 100 fathom mark when we left the continental shelf to cross the Atlantic." Sinclair explained, unrolling the paper from its little holding tray.

John looked at the trace and noted the various depths recorded on the graphs, and asked if Sinclair could describe how the machine actually works.

"Well from what Bruce has told me, it works on the same principle as radar, as both use a device that bounces sound off an area, then gets recorded on the radar screen as a blip to show how far away it is. In this case, a line tracer on the paper to record the depth of water the ship has just passed over. From what he said, it's a new way of helping the captain to navigate his way through uncharted waters on the one hand, and to make a new survey of the oceans on the other."

"Sounds simple enough to me Andy. So we can now rely on you not to let us go aground anymore."

"Just as long as the skipper realises that a ship with a 3 fathom draught, can't sail through a 2 fathom channel, as many a skipper has discovered when his ship is sinking from below him." Sinclair laughed and put the cover back onto the machine.

John smiled at the basic logic that Sinclair had stated.

"Oh well Andy, must go now. I'm seeing Happy Day in a few minutes, as he's the chief on this trip. So maybe I'll see you later on for a run ashore." John concluded, with Sinclair giving a mock salute in reply.

The meeting with Day proved to be a small watershed for the ship's engineering department, as Day informed them that the 3rd engineer and the electrical officer were to return to the UK for discharge. John's helper Blackmore would be taking over the duties of both men, as they needed someone with a more professional attitude. This meant that John was on his own from that time onwards.

This news of both the 3rd and the electrical officers departure was a mixture of surprise and relief, to John and even Blackmore, who was happy to receive such an undertaking. John mentioned in a very diplomatic way that he'd rather conduct the remainder of the trials on his own. He also added that Day would understand the reasons why, given the present circumstances prevailing on board concerning the ventilation and air conditioning problems.

A Beach Party

When the meeting finished, John remained in the cabin with Day and for the 3rd to leave the office mentioning that he had loads of work to do.

"Happy, it appears that man hasn't a clue as to what is required of him. How he became a 3rd I'll never know, and as for Blackmore, I think it was a good decision to use him instead."

"The reason why he was made up was because he is a relative of Cresswell. A very poor example of the Cresswell mould I grant you, but never the less, it's one that we've had to put up with until now. I personally would prefer the two roles be reversed if only to preserve the ships' officer compliment. But Company rules dictate that I can't have the luxury of two 3rd engineers on board, although you are making the single and unique exception to the rules to make it three."

Both men talked shop for a little while before John decided that he had a myriad of jobs to be getting on with.

"I've come up with a plan to sort out our electrical problems Happy. When I'm ready, and hopefully before we sail tomorrow, I'll give you a nod."

"In that case, I'm already looking forward to you giving me a trial run." Day concluded, for John to leave Day's cabin.

John found Blackmore in the motor room giving the electricians a severe lecture on ships' husbandry and how he wanted the department to work. He sat down and listened quietly to all that Blackmore said and noticed the truculence and petulant looks that were coming from the men. When it was all over, Blackmore clapped his hands twice, and ordered the men to have a 15minute break before all the work was tackled.

"Remember men! The sooner you get the work done, the sooner we all get a run ashore. No work, no shore time, that's the deal!" he said with a smile.

The men mumbled and grumbled to themselves and trooped out of the compartment, leaving John with Blackmore.

"Whew Blackie! That was some speech that I haven't heard the like of since meeting a chief engineer Cresswell, some way back now." John greeted with a smile, offering the man a cigarette.

"Thanks, er John, if I can call you that, now I'm also a 3rd. I had to get the men thinking straight and for me to set out my rules what to expect from me, especially as I'm also the outside engineer."

"You may call me that. Anyway everything now is just as it should be!" John replied as he walked over to the little space at the back of the motor room where his own tiny workspace was situated.

"I've come up with a plan to combat this electrical fault finding problem, and need you to help me prove it works. If all goes well and I can give a practical demo to the chief, then both of us will have a quieter time on board than of late. Mind you, that electrical officer who's just left and you are replacing, will be sick as a parrot when he finds out that his problems were solved even before he had time to pack his bags.

I won't say anymore in case I look just as sick if my plan doesn't work. What about it Blackie?"

"If it means cutting down on a heck of a load of work then yes I'm all for it, John. Give me a shout when you're ready, as I've got some backlog of work to sort out before tomorrow." Blackmore said enthusiastically then left John to his own devices. John sat down and calculated out what he required, before he got the bits and pieces assembled and ready for testing.

He opened one of the electrical conduits and by using his probes, he saw the light bulb at the end of his pieces of wire, light up. He then went over to a cooling fan that was switched off and did the same test, to find that the light bulb did not light up.

'Bingo! One electric tester ready for patenting. Must get the drawing and the method of operation written out and sent off to Fergus, before it becomes known by Cresswell and co.' he mused with satisfaction, double checking his test and the diagrams he made.

A Beach Party

Blackmore had arrived back into the motor room to see John sitting at his desk with a big grin on his face.

"Judging by that look on your face John, it must be the proverbial 'EUREKA' moment. Knowing you, albeit only lately, you've come up with another one of your inventions. If it's the one you've spoken about then let's get a demo laid on for the chief. Just tell me what you require and it shall be done." Blackmore said with increasing excitement.

John smiled, putting his pen down onto the pile of papers on his desk.

"Okay Blackie, I'll give you a small, quick demo, but need to test my other theories for yet another set of inventions. Are you ready?" John replied, then showed the Heath Robinson contraption before doing the test on the electric fan."

"Observe the light Blackie. If there's a current flowing through the wires, then the bulb will light up. Conversely, if not then it won't, if you get my meaning."

Blackmore nodded his head eagerly, watching John perform his little demo.

"See Blackie? It means that we have a live wire tester that we can use anywhere on the ship. So if there's an electrical breakdown, all we do is attach it to any wiring or electric system. This way we can pinpoint where the fault will be found or what is causing it.

Its simple, if the bulb lights up, the length of wire is sound. If not, then there is a break in the wiring at that point to cause the malfunction. The other diagram I have is of a possible wiring circuit of a ship that would make this device of mine come even more into its own." John declared with simple modesty.
Blackmore asked for a go and was delighted to find that it worked for him too.

"No wonder, we've been told about you, John. I wish I could be as clever, as I'd be a 3rd by now just like you."

"Be that as it may Blackie, but we've got to rig up a suitable demo for the chief, which will be before we demonstrate it to the captain.

As both officers are good friends of mine, then I have no worries concerning patent rights and patent pilfering that seems to go on in this shipping line." John said quietly.

"Yes, I've experienced some of that too, so don't worry about me. I'll be only too happy to be the first electrical officer to enjoy the privilege of having such a tool on board to help me in my work." Blackmore said candidly, playing with the contraption.

"I've got to tidy it up a bit to make it more, shall we say, pleasing to the eye. But we'll find out for definite if it works for real on the rest of the ship. Are you ready Blackie?"

John knocked on Day's cabin door and was pleasantly surprised to find Tomlinson there having a chat about ship matters.

"Hello John, do come in. What can I do for you?" Day invited cheerfully.

"Glad you're here too, Joe. I have worked out and tested my theory that I spoke to you about earlier on, Happy. As you are here together I can save time and give you both the same demo." John said quietly.

"If I know you John, it's probably in that little bag you're carrying. But do carry on, what is it that you want us to see?" Day asked with a big smile.

"Yes John, what's the secret you've got to keep until it gets let out of that bag?" Tomlinson chuckled.

John took his contraption out of the bag and explained the basics of how it worked. He then switched off the electric fan that was keeping them cool, before he did his first half of his demo. The fan was switched back on, and John was able to show that the light was glowing from the bulb whereas it wasn't when there was no power to the fan.

Both Day and Tomlinson looked totally amazed at what they saw and followed John eagerly down into a cargo hold where it was explained that Blackmore would be part of the experiment.

After a couple more demonstrations and in various parts of the ship, John concluded the experiment and the demo. During all this time,

A Beach Party

both Day and Tomlinson became more and more delighted and convinced that the simple but awkward looking device was a brilliant invention.

When they got back into Day's cabin, Day reached into the drawer of his desk and pulled out a bottle of brandy, and brought out three glasses saying.

"I don't know about you Joe, but this calls for a little drink."

"Yes Happy! I think our 3rd here just about deserves one." Tomlinson said with a wicked smile, as all three raised their glasses in a toast.

"Here's to engineer John Grey. May his light shine all through his career." Day said, with their glasses clinking together gently, before they downed their drink in one go.

Tomlinson took the contraption off John and examined it again.

"We will keep this under our hats until we reach our destination port. That way, John can register his patent on it. If anybody from HQ finds out about it before then, we can just tell them it's yet another experiment that needed a full scale trial before it could be accepted by the company." Tomlinson informed, handing it back to John.

Day smiled and nodded his agreement before he filled their glasses again.

"If this demo and the work John has been doing lately comes up trumps, there is no reason why he can't be recommended for his acting 2nd rank. What do you say Joe?" Day asked pleasantly.

"Given his professional performance there's no reason why not. Both you and I would grant him that, no problem. However, he's got a growing number of disgruntled people ganging up on him back at HQ. No names no kitbags, but a certain couple of lords spring to mind."

John stood quietly, basking in the genuine praise that the top two men on the ship were sending his way.

The little celebratory drinking session ended with all three men going their own separate ways, John going straight down to the motor room and shaking Blackmore's hand in delight.

He told Blackmore what Day and Tomlinson had said about keeping the lid on it until the ship arrived at the other end of the voyage.

Blackmore, in turn, was just as excited and thankful to John, for he knew that John's little gadget would save a lot of man hours in fault-finding the numerous electric power cuts that occur on board.

A Beach Party

Chapter VIII
Ship Shape

An early morning breeze that blew over the land had come from far-away out in the watery wastes of the Atlantic. It seemed deliciously cool to John, as he sat on a borrowed deck chair on the boat deck looking out over the harbour wall to see the sun painting a kaleidoscope of colours on a sea-wrinkled canvas. When he drew on his a pre-breakfast cigarette he remembered his last such moments here that seemed a lifetime away.

His thoughts were miles away when he sensed somebody approaching him, who turned out to be Larter, on his way to his radio shack.

"What a lovely morning John, it looks like another scorcher here today, pity we're sailing in a couple of hours time." Larter whispered, then stopped and looked out to seaward.

"Yes it is. I always come up here in the early morning especially after my deck rounds, because sometimes I'm too busy to enjoy it later on when I'm stuck down the workshop repairing something or other." John replied after some moments.

"We've had some outings since leaving here the last time, John. Let's hope this leg of the voyage to the canal is just as peaceful as the one getting here."

"Glad we were fortunate to be here to support Andy during his bereavement. His family certainly took to the both of us."

The slow moving conversation was gentle as the morning silence of the sunrise that cast its hypnotic spell over them

The spell was eventually and brutally broken when they heard the metallic sound of the tannoy whistling and screeching before a Scottish voice announced that the shore electrical and water supply would be disconnected shortly.

"That's Andy telling us that we're preparing for sea. So I'd better be setting my radio watch now John. See you later at the captains briefing."

"Yes right, and I need some breakfast before I set up my next monitoring schedule." John replied, folding up his deckchair and stowing it away in a deck locker, before going below to the dining room.

"Morning John, all set for your next set of trials?" Blackmore asked politely, sitting down next to John at the breakfast table.

"Hello Blackie! Yes, I'm all set. Mind you, the signal I got back from HQ yesterday states that once we get to the Panama I can stop the trials until we're on our way back again. So basically, I'm going to have a nice cruise around the Pacific until then."

"Well isn't that just my luck. If those two bloody engineers had've done their job properly, I would be joining you, you lucky bastard." Blackmore stated enviously.

"Not to worry Blackie, as there is a silver lining in all of this. You're now picking up a 3rd's pay, and on top of that I'll be able to give you a hand just like you did me."

Blackmore nodded his head slowly in recognition of what John said, which changed his glum face to something like a smile.

"There you are, I knew you'd understand. I must be off now, but probably see you during the captains briefing." John concluded, leaving Blackmore to his repast.

Tomlinson and Day arrived together for the briefing, which to John, seemed to be a gentle affair compared to the fire and brimstone ones he'd experienced on previous ships.

"We have special passengers on board, namely the King and Queen and their retinue of their Atoll, some scientists and a small contingent of specialist construction engineers. You may ask as to why he's not on board a luxury liner to take him home, or even flying by one of the excellent flying boats that cover that area. It seems that it is his ancient tradition to travel the ocean, 'the long swim' his nation calls it, therefore he travels by sea and by any long voyage vessel he deems fit. As it happens, he has chartered this ship to, shall we say, deliver his groceries. In the meantime, for those of you who have been conducting special

A Beach Party

experiments and trials, it means the following. If we can prove our claim to be able to deliver his 'shopping list' just as if it came from the shop, then we, the shipping company that is, will get his royal crest and have his shipping franchise. In other words, we are the pathfinders to pave the way of what could be a good little number for those coming behind us, as the Pacific side of the voyage will be almost like a first class cruise. So let's show the ship owners that we're up to the job and secure that future for us all. Our illustrious passenger had been enjoying a state visit and had just come back from meeting our Queen, and has a new constitution given to him by our parliamentary mandarins. In with his retinue, are his bodyguards, his chief of police and other senior members of his new Government. So we will give him and his retinue the continued respect despite their looks and mannerisms. Due to his majesty being a religious man, nobody will consume alcohol or swear in the saloon during his presence. Whilst he appreciates the needs of any 'outsider' such as you and me, he will limit his time per visit to the saloon. We have a special cordoned off area which you will see that no-one in your departments wanders into, ships duties excepted." Tomlinson said in an upbeat manner, before he broached the subject of stores and other ship needs.

Because there were no specific orders for John save that of the continuation of the trails, and because the rest of the officers had already been primed up for the next leg anyway, the meeting came to an early end.

"Blackie, my first monitoring session will not be until about 1400, so I would appreciate it if you'd let me take your place on deck when we leave. I'll even do the for'ard rounds for you if need be." John asked politely.

"Yes of course you can John, but there's no need for the rounds, as I've already done them. In fact that is a good idea, as I can get on with a few other jobs that that bastard lousy 4th left me with."

"Oh, what has he left you?"

"He's only gone and left the switchboard circuitry like a plate of spaghetti. No wonder it took him hours to sort out what he was to do next. Still, with that gadget of yours, it won't take me long to re string them into their proper conduits."

"If that's the way you feel Blackie, then between us we've got a good deal going. You get your 3rd engineer rank and pay and with luck I'll end up as acting 2nd engineer. How about it Blackie?"

Blackmore almost grabbed John's hand before he shook it sealing their mutual working relationship.

"I knew I was right in volunteering to join up with you John." Blackmore said gleefully as John left to get himself prepared for his stint on the foc'sle.

The hairs on John's neck started to bristle, then he felt a succession of shivers and warmth coursing through his body that seemed to cause an instant rash of goose bumps all over him. He stood on his customary spot on the deck as if transfixed, but his mind was far away. Only his eyes seem to register everything when the ship slipped from its berth and left the harbour to make her way back out into the open ocean again.

His faraway look and mind was gently brought back to the here and now on hearing someone quietly coughing beside him.

"We're all secured for sea now 3rd, if you want to make your report." the 2nd mate suggested.

John turned slowly towards the man and thanked him, before both left the foc'sle to the flying fishes and the occasional sea spray that kept the decks cool from the burning sun.

"Excuse me but are you the 3rd engineer? Any chance of seeing to the sound telephone on the starboard side of the bridge, as it doesn't sound off when I turn the handle?" the helmsman asked when John came onto the bridge to make his report.

"No! 3rd engineer Blackmore is, but if you've got a problem then I'll deal with it for you in a minute." John responded quickly, before he made his short but concise report to Tomlinson.

A Beach Party

"Thank you for standing in for Blackmore. I understand from the chief that you and Blackmore will dovetail your duties once we get to Panama City?"

"Yes Joe. The chief seems to be and pardon the pun, 'happy', for me to do so, as the last outside engineer and the electrical officer left the ship in pretty poor shape. It would be unfair of me letting Blackmore work himself into an early grave whilst I'm lazing on the upper deck. I hate twiddling my thumbs as you well know." John affirmed.

"Very well John, have a good voyage. Keep in touch." Tomlinson replied, dismissing John, before he started to work on his sea chart again.

For the next few days of the 1700mile second leg of the voyage between Barbados and the Panama Canal, both John and Blackmore worked together as a team to sort out the legacy left by the two engineers who were taken off in Barbados.

They worked hard and methodically until both were satisfied with things, before they finally made their reports to both the chief engineer and the captain at a joint meeting in the captain's day cabin.

"We have read your interim reports and are happy with what you both have achieved since leaving Barbados. The ship is in a much better shape now, as is the health of my cargoes. As far as we're concerned, both of you can take it easy until we reach our outward destination, mechanical demands permitting, of course." Tomlinson said cheerfully, with Day nodding his head in agreement.

"What about my 3rd monitoring phase, when does that kick in, captain?" John asked with concern.

"It appears that your little bag of tricks have pre-empted the need to conduct any further trials until we get a fresh cargo on board. However, that won't be until we pick up our return cargoes, and even then on a limited scale."

John looked at Tomlinson and smiled before replying to that good piece of news.

"In that case, I'll move my things into the passengers accommodation, and just call me Mr Grey until we get there."

"Now there's a thing. Happy to oblige and all that, but maybe you could find the time to supplement the engine room watchkeeping roster. That way we all get a quiet voyage out of it." Day said with a smile.

"Besides, it's not very often we get two good 3rds on board the same ship, excepting large liners that is."

John and Blackmore looked at each other and laughed at the thought.

"Hold on now chief! You'll be getting us to take over the ship whilst you're at it." Blackmore responded.

"It had crossed our minds the way you two have conducted yourselves these past few days. The passengers were wondering if you both had a double on board, as they were seeing you in all sorts of places and seemingly all at the same time." Tomlinson joked, before he concluded the meeting.

"Before you both go, just be careful not to get too lazy or involved too much with the passengers. As I said during my briefing, we have a special group of passengers on board and the ship is full of their cargo. Now you will understand why we had to have officers that were up to the job to satisfy not only our passengers but also the occupants at No 10 Downing Street. We've already sent the bad ones packing although we got no replacements to cover them, hence our request for you to help out John. I have had a special notice put on the board to remind all officers of the need to maintain personal standards and protocol, and try to steer clear of our passengers to circumvent any, shall we say, diplomatic incident.

I dare say that both of us will still want to kept up to date with any developments that may occur in the forthcoming two weeks or so. But if you're too bored, then we can certainly concoct something that will keep you busy, if only to get your next promotion papers ready for signing. That will be all gentlemen, as I've lots to do now." Tomlinson said with a grin and a wave of his hand and dismissed them.

A Beach Party

John and Blackmore thanked the two officers and left the cabin in a jubilant mood.

"I told you it would work Blackie. Now we can have a quiet cruise across the Pacific, maybe stop by and get us a couple of dusky maidens wearing grass skirts to serve our cooled beer." John said jovially.

"No such luck for me John, I've still got a lot of 'schoolboys' in the motor room to sort out." Blackmore replied sadly.

"Still? Have you tried getting them working as a team?" John asked with surprise.

"They hate each others guts let alone working as a team. Must be something they're eating."

"Pair them up and give each pair a project to do, such as something that needs doing, or even something that you've got designs on, that you need to see if it works."

Blackmore thought hard for a moment and shook his head.

"Nothing that springs to mind."

"As it happens, I have a special project of my own to re-create. I shall be looking to you, or at least, to your men, whom I shall be asking to help me at some stage or other. When I've completed the paperwork and I'm ready, I'll give you a shout."

"Sounds interesting whatever it is, John. Lucky for you anyway, at least it should keep you occupied during our next long and boring voyage." Blackmore concluded, and left John's company.

Chapter IX
Panama Plates

The coast of Panama appeared over the horizon, as Tomlinson had his ship steered towards the narrowest part of the already narrow Isthmus between North and South America. There you will find a 57mile long, man-made waterway that ranks as one of the most vital canals of the world, and known as the Panama Canal.

It was the brainchild of a French engineer in the 1870's, who discovered that if this canal were built, it would cut the enormous and perhaps perilous voyage time going around the southern half of the Americas. It was a bold scheme that most shipping companies welcomed, as did the financial backers of the industrial trading nations between east and west. But after his demise, and as always with such great schemes, it was abandoned as a lost cause, much to the delight of the long established fraternity of the 'Cape Horners'.

Fortunately a few wealthy entrepreneurs of the day got together and had the work restarted, which was finally completed in time for the inaugural opening in 1904, and the first ship finally made the historic passage directly between the two largest oceans, the Atlantic and the bigger Pacific.

It is a very impressive feat of engineering, as it was cut through solid rock, and links up to the two major cities, of the now independent state of Panama, with Colon on the Atlantic side and Panama City on the Pacific side. Most local canals had horses to tow the barges along, but this one has powerful engines that run on a track, and are called 'mules'. These special tow engines are part of this marvel as they can tow, with ease, anything from the mightiest battleship all the way down to the humble tramp steamer or coastal vessel. Once his ship was hitched to these mules, the helmsman would enjoy the 12-hour ride through the system of locks, without touching his helm.

A Beach Party

But the deck party would be fully employed in case of the odd bump or nudge as the ship floated along its restricted waterway.

The ship arrived at its marshalling point and dropped its anchor waiting to be sorted into size and given a convoy transit number, whilst the ships themselves were getting prepared to receive the special towing equipment.

"We need Panama plates fitted on all four of our for'ard fairlees, 3rd. Either you get them bolted on or have them welded, but the Transit Officer will advise you on that." Tomlinson ordered.

"We have special clamps on board that will suffice, captain. I'll get them rigged right away." John informed Tomlinson, who merely nodded his head.

"Before you go 3rd. Make sure there's plenty of power to the capstans, as I may need them to stop me from astern or just maybe winch me up the lock a few cables. We've got a good 12-hour transit ahead of us, so just be available for the 2nd mate who's up on the foc'sle.

The idea is that I don't want to rely on the mules to stop me if there's a breakdown just when a solid rock is bearing down on my bow, if you catch my drift."

"Aye aye captain." John responded, then swiftly left the bridge.

"Bosun. Ask the chief engineer to see me in my cabin. First mate, you're now officer on the bridge. We're in a temporary anchorage and holding area, so let me know as soon as the Transit Officer arrives on the bridge." Tomlinson ordered.

Sinclair repeated his order, as did the First mate, before Tomlinson was satisfied to leave the bridge.

John was on the foc'sle working with the 3rd mate, fitting the special plates over the fairlees.

"If we're secured to those tugs, why do we need these things, Grey?"

"I'm not familiar with this type of canal, but I should imagine that at some point the bow will be much lower in the lock than the towing engine. If there were no baffle plates to stop the towrope from slipping up through the fairlees, then the rope would just slip up through the gap and away, so the tug would not be able to tow anything. I should imagine it would be the reverse when we're towering above it, how would it tow us given the same situation. All we've got to do is make certain that these baffle plates, known as 'Panama plates' are kept secured until we clear the canal."

"Thank you for telling me Grey as I failed to explain the reason why, to my deck crew."

"Glad you asked me. But don't forget, it's your part of the ship as a deck officer, and as such it's your problem, not one for an engineer. So do us both a favour and find out the real reason. Let me know the answer when you've made your report. In the meantime, I must leave you as I've got a man's work to do." John replied with irritation, as his mind was elsewhere other than answering fool questions that perhaps any seaman was able to reply to.

John decided to go up to the boat deck and see his friend Larter, when he met Sinclair.

"Hello Andy, how's your voyage getting on?" John asked cheerfully.

"Just the thing John. Glad I've bumped into you, 'cause I'm wondering if you've a mind to set up that, er, STAN, I think you called it. Only, once we've set our course from the Panama we've got a good 12 days on a steady course that would bore the pants off you if you were to just stand at the wheel doing virtually nothing."

"That's a good idea Andy, apart from the fact that I've still got a few niggling problems to sort out from the last time. Leave it to me for now, at least until we're clear of the canal."

"Fair enough John. I know that you're friends with the skipper and the chief engineer, so let's hope they will sanction your trials, as opposed to keeping it all a covert operation."

A Beach Party

"Ah yes Andy, you're right there, as long as you remember the wartime adage in case, '*Loose lips sink ships*'. But in our case, '*Loose lips maketh the company rich*' from our efforts." John replied, crossing his lips with his forefinger.

Sinclair nodded his recognition.

"Now we're getting somewhere John. Must go now, so see you later." Sinclair smiled, and gave John a mock salute, as he hurried away.

"Hello Bruce. How's 'Macaroni' land?" John asked jovially, on entering the radio shack, but seeing both radio officers fully busy with their radio sets, he decided to sit down on a vacant chair to have a smoke whilst waiting for them to finish.

After some minutes Larter finished tapping on his morse key and taking his headphones off, looked up to acknowledge John's presence.

"Hello John, what brings you to our little world of dots and dashes?"

"Just came up to see if all was well with your ACU, that and maybe sneak a few glances onto the master chart to see where we'll be going once we've come out the other side of this canal."

Larter chuckled at the real reason and pointed to a large map neatly attached onto a bulkhead behind him.

"We've still got problems with the ship supply John, which means that it's still on the blink. This means that for now we're using the standby generator and sweating our knackers off in the process. Unless we get a regular supply of ice cubes, then our equipment will be rendered U/S, due to the overheating of the transmitters and so on. Insofar as the chart is concerned, that red line on the chart you see is our transit course. The green one tells us of the sea current and the white lines tells us of the air streams. The dirty great black line indicates the predicted El Niño effect due up this year, which does not bear well not only to us seafarers but also those poor countries affected by the devastating forces that Mother Nature will unleash upon them."

"By the sound of you, you're in a miserable mood Bruce.

I'll fix your mechanical problem for you right away, but I'm not held responsible for dear old Mother Nature."

"That at least will soothe our troubled brows, John." Larter responded offering John a cigarette.

Evans had just finished his own transmissions and completed his operator's log before he too was given a cigarette.

"I've just received our exit permits from the canal dispersal area and orders for us to pick up our forwarded mail. Which means Bruce, we've both got to go ashore on the launch to pick it all up. Maybe we'll get a final short run ashore, whilst the ship is getting refuelled."

"Oh Dave? What is there that needs the two of us?" Larter asked in amazement.

"It seems that our illustrious passengers have several bags of sea mail and a rather large diplomatic bag to collect. I fancy that we'll need one of our stores launches to cope with it as they're quoting at least a couple of tons worth." Evans said nonchalantly.

"A couple of tons? What the bleeding hell is he fetching this time. He's already got the whole ship loaded to the gunnels with his cargo."

"Well maybe it's just a few 'rabbits' for his missus."

"His missus Dave? Bloody hell mate, where's your eyes these days? She's already on board, looking like a stranded whale. Him too, comes to that!"

"Oh so that's who those two great barrels of lard are. Then all the other barrels of lard must be belonging to him too. Still, I suppose they can be as big as they like, as he appears to be the top Injun and she his top squaw. King and Queen of the FAT ARSE tribes no doubt."

"That's not all Dave, we had to bring a shipwright and his carpenter with us, earmarked for you when you arrived in Bridgetown. They had to reinforce all the cabin furniture, and even widen a few doors so our passengers can get about on the ship. The poor buggers had a dozen men to help, and even they

A Beach Party

had to work all through our stay at Bridgetown. Mind you, it beggars belief on what they had to do to all the starboard lifeboats as well. They look like the old ironclad dreadnoughts of WW1"

John chuckled at the cross dialogue between Larter and Evans, but was more interested on the X that marked the end of their voyage, as it seemed to be right in the middle of absolutely nowhere. It was just an X in the middle of the Pacific that seemed to be chosen at random from all the other places the ship could be sailing to.

"We'll be tying up alongside one of those refuelling jetties over there 3rd, so kindly get those plates removed now as we're finished with them until we come back again." The 2nd mate called to John as he and Blackmore were getting the refuelling gear on deck and ready for use.

"All in hand 2nd." John shouted back.

"Blackie, our radio officers are still having problems with their power supply. I've just fixed their ACU again, but it really needs a new motor. If you can't trace the fault from that bunch of spaghetti down your end, then suggest that you get a good supply of diesel for their generator."

"As you've just said John, it's all in hand. Although I have to admit, it really is a bunch of bastards, as the 'spaghetti' as you call it is proving a lot more scrambled than that. It really is causing me no end of headaches, and the only solution I can come up with is to almost rewire the whole flippin' ship. For instance, I have a main cable with the ID tally for the galley, but in fact was traced to and connected up to the bridge area switchboard. The main cable ID'd for the wireless office in fact is one of the cables for the laundry room, and vice versa.

I've promised the chief that it will all be sorted by the time we reach our next port of call. Which, by all accounts will be in about two weeks from now." Blackmore moaned.

"All the same Blackie, you must provide some reserve power

up to the wireless office, as it is part of the bridge control system. It would be in your own interest to get a couple of drums of diesel up there whilst you're performing your miracles. I'll keep my eye on the rest of it for you, that's all I can advise."

"Yes I think you're right, and thanks for your help." Blackmore said with a smile, as both men finished their task.

"I must go now John, but I'll send one of the junior engineers up to take charge of the refuelling. If you're remaining on deck, would you ensure that he conducts all the fire and safety procedures."

"No problem Blackie. I'll set him up and brief him accordingly." John said, flicking the last of his cigarette over the side of the ship.

The familiar little bump that the ship gave told John that the ship had now arrived alongside, and was the cue for him to leave his familiar spot on the foc'sle and take charge of the junior engineer.

"Okay then 5th, I've shown you what to do and what to look out for. Shut down the valves and drain the hoses before disconnecting them. So stay on top of your duties or you'll be spending the next few hours cleaning up the mess. Once you've completed your refuelling, and all is neat and tidy, you can take down your hazard warning signs. Any questions?" John instructed.

"Yes 3rd. Where is my fire fighting equipment?"

"Your hazard flag is up and the announcement has been made, and the deck area is cordoned off; you have a suction pump already primed up to take water from over the side, and two drums of powder to create your foam. You also have those two stokers over there, standing by the pump and who are your fire-watchers but you must be alert and on the lookout for any stupid crewmen or passengers who might come up on deck with a lighted cigarette. Anything else?"

"I think that's all, thanks 3rd." the 5th said hesitatingly, as he fidgeted with his watch.

A Beach Party

"Well if you're not sure, contact the engine room at once. Don't forget the yellow valve is the furnace fuel oil (F.F.O.) and as it's a shore side meter, it measures its discharge in metric litres, but our gauge in the engine room measures in Imperial gallons. We need 200 tons, which should take you about two hours. The green valve is diesel and is measured in the same way, but you only need 1 ton of that, which will take about half an hour. Be careful in your calculations and conversions from metric to imperial. Right then 5th, it's all yours, have you got all that?" John asked to see if the 5th was okay with his instructions.

"Yes 3rd!" was the emphatic reply.

"Good! I'm off." John stated and left him.

John had just completed his daily check on the cargo fridge systems when he decided to come up on deck for a breather. He looked at his watch and calculated that the refuelling had been completed and looked to the flag mast to see if the hazard flag had been lowered, which meant that it was safe to smoke on deck again.

The flag was still up, and he found that the cordon around the fuelling area on deck was still in place. There was a distinct smell of stinking fuel oil in the air, which made him move swiftly towards the smell and found the 5th engineer was covered with and standing in a pool of fuel oil and diesel oil was running all over the deck.

"What the hell have you done here 5th?" John asked angrily.

"Well you did say 200 tons of fuel oil and 1ton of diesel 3rd!" The 5th replied in a state of panic.

John shook his head in disbelief at what he was witnessing.

He shouted over to the two stokers and got them to hose down the decks, whilst he went and checked the two main fuel valves on the jetty. When he came back he saw that the 5th was still standing in his own pool of oil, and shouted to him to get himself hosed down from one of the deck fire hydrants.

John sealed off the barrels and the main refuelling connections before the fuel hoses were taken off, then grabbed another hosepipe and aimed it right at the 5th engineer

He turned the water valve full on which sent a solid bore of water straight at the man, which literally lifted him off his feet and sent him sliding along the deck.

John kept flushing the man around the deck like a rag doll, before the man finally clung onto the rungs of a ladder.

"Better leave him now John. He's had enough now or you'll end up drowning him." Blackmore said gently in John's ear, taking the hose off him and turning off the water.

John stood looking at the 5th engineer, trying to control his temper.

"I'll bloody kill the bastard. He'd better be off this ship before we sail from here, or I'll feed him to the sharks."

"Keep your cool John, he'll be in front of the skipper after the chief has had his say, you watch. He's not worth it, so let him be." Blackmore said gently, holding John long enough to prevent him lunging out and strike the 5th.

It took several moments for John to regain his usual composure and to find that Day was on the scene trying to deduce just what had happened for the Deck officers to complain about the mess.

"We can think ourselves lucky that you've prevented a large oil spillage, John. But then again, consider yourself lucky you didn't drown the 5th." Day remarked quietly, before he turned to the 5th and told the man to report to his cabin in ten minutes, fully changed and properly dressed.

"It appears that as you were the instructing officer John, I need you also to attend my cabin. I have to make a full report to the captain as to what happened. He has to make an oil spillage report to the Harbourmaster before we sail."

"As it happens chief, I have my instructions and details still on me. I can accompany you right now if you wish.

Only this mess has to be cleared up and the ship put back into order again. Perhaps if you'd ask Blackmore to do the honours for me instead." John sighed.

A Beach Party

"Yes John, you go, I'll see to it." Blackmore agreed, and left to get his men to work.

"In that case, lead on chief!" John replied, following Day to his cabin.

"I'm quite satisfied with your instructions and the figures tally with what I had ordered, 3rd. The thing is that the 5th here is quite adamant on the amount of FFO. If that is the case then its either he didn't understand what you said to him, or he can't read a flow meter correctly. I have a third theory which may be the answer to it all." Day announced, before he turned to the 5th engineer.

"Now in regard to your claim against what the 3rd had instructed you, I've listened to the two stokers who were on fire watch duties. They both state that they heard the 3rd emphasise the amounts needed and which valves you were to operate. They also heard the 3rd instructing you that if you had any problems you were to contact the engine room immediately. Did you carry out those instructions 5th?"

"No chief! I was told to take on 200 tons of fuel, measured in Imperial gallons, so that what I was making sure we got." The 5th replied vehemently.

"The tonnage is not the real problem 5th!" Day sighed, then went over to a locker and pulled out a flow meter and held it out in front of him.

"Okay then 5th. Here is a standard flow meter, explain to me exactly how it works, or at least in principle as to how you would deduce the amount needed. To give you a clue, the gauge is set for the fresh water system." Day said smoothly, handing it over to the 5th.

The 5th took the brass object, looked at it carefully then explained how the meter works and what the operator was to look for on the dials. Once he had finished, he handed it back to Day.

"You have the fundamentals on the workings of the gauge okay, but I want you to show me, by making a line on the gauge as to where you think the 200 tons of FFO measured in gallons would register on it. Then when you've done that make a line on the gauge where the 1 ton of diesel would register." Day replied as he handed back the gauge and a crayon for the 5th to use.

The 5th muttered a few calculations to himself then marked clearly on the glass of the gauge his reckoning, before handing it back to Day.

John listened closely to the 5th's mumbled reckoning and witnessed the marking of the gauge.

Day looked at the gauge then turned it to show John, and then turned back to the 5th.

"5th, what is the standard measurement of weight register per gallon per ton of water?" Day asked

"Everybody knows that a bucket containing 1 gallon of water weighs 10 lbs, therefore to give a rough guide you get 240gallons of water per ton. Hence my 48,000 gallons of FFO." The 5th said defiantly.

"Then it's just as I suspected 5th, you stupid cretin. The marks you made on this gauge, in your own hand, which tells everybody that you forgot your conversion register. You used the register for litres instead of the register in gallons." Day shouted, showing the 5th his own markings, then added.

"Therefore, not only did you double the amount of FFO taken on board, but you've also jeopardised the whole weight distribution of the ship."

"To confirm your theory chief, I wish to ask the 5th a question." John asked, and got a nod from Day in response to his request.

"If water is 240 gallons per ton, how much is FFO, and again how much is diesel?"

"All the same weight per ratio 3rd." the 5th said defiantly.

John sighed as he looked at the amazement on Day's face.

"It is part of your basic skills training to know that FFO is only 110 Imperial gallons per ton, whereas diesel is 250 gallons per ton. Again you should know that a litre of water measures a

A Beach Party

pint and three quarters to give you the volume of fluid metric to imperial. That is the reason why the FFO was spurting out of the standpipe. But what happened to the spillage of diesel?" John asked sharply.

"I started to take on the diesel whilst the FFO was loading, but when I saw the FFO spurting out of the standpipe I left what I was doing to shut off the FFO line. I must have forgotten to shut off the nozzle for the diesel and it had overflowed by the time I got back to correct my mistake." the 5th stated in a more humble tone of voice.

In disgust, Day threw the gauge at the 5th, who just managed to catch it before it fell.

"You will no longer be in charge of even an oily rag from now on. You are, as of now, busted to ordinary stoker rank. Now get out of here before you get several lace holes of our boots up your arse." Day shouted at the man, who cringed at the verbal onslaught.

"But you can't do that, I know my rights." the 5th stammered, as John grabbed hold of him and literally threw him out of Day's cabin.

"The captain will be issuing your orders to leave the ship before we sail from here, and it's only what you deserve." John remarked, and kicked the young 5th up his arse, which sent him tumbling towards the deck.

Day retrieved the gauge again and looked at it, shaking his head in wonderment.

"We have a big clearing up operation down in the engine room but an even bigger one which is not apparent right now John, but it could be a total disaster whilst we're at sea. We can either off-load some of the FFO, or jettison some of the cargo we've got." Day said in a much calmer voice.

"If it's what I think you're thinking Happy, then not to worry as it's only an extra hundred tons or so that we had room for anyway. According to my reckoning and based on our voyage transit from our outward point, we don't cross the equator nor enter the Southern Hemisphere. And, as you know and will appreciate, the extra load does not become critical until we're at least 10 to 15 degrees further south of the equator." John assured him.

"Yes John, you've guessed my thoughts right, but based on what knowledge, given that you've not seen any of the captains charts?"

"As you know, Radio Officer Larter and I are close friends. Well, as it happens, he always keeps a large sea chart of our voyage movements. He explains that it was necessary to keep track of these things to help him with his radio 'propagation'. Without that he would not be able to work out which radio station he was best able to contact, and also for use in emergencies if he's got to send out our position whilst in danger. It is clearly marked that we don't cross the equatorial line." John explained quietly.

Day looked at John and smiled.

"Is there no end to your talent John? I will accept your explanation on that. The only thing for me now is to go and see the captain, to explain the oil spillage, the over-spending on the oil taken on, and the fact that I've still got a duff officer on board."

"We can't cry over spilt oil, that's for sure. If the captain knows that he's got an overweight of oil then it only means that he'll be able to speed up to full power to burn it off. It might even save him the bother to re-fuel when we reach our destination port. Besides, our famous passengers, the King and Queen of the 'FAT ARSE' tribe would be thankful for a speedier voyage and we'd probably enjoy those extra few days ashore basking in their gratitude. And of course enjoy a decent speed bonus on top, for a change. That is my honest opinion to it all Happy."

Day looked at John for a moment before he spoke.

"Okay then John, we'll call an end to this affair. It would not be fair to have your papers marked for this incident as you were

A Beach Party

only doing Blackmore a favour. That was why I made allowances for your outburst of, shall we say, anger. Your instructions and evidence clears you from it all, so think no more of it. I'll go and see the captain and see what he says. In the meantime get that junior engineer put on extra engine room duties such as bilge cleaning and the like until I get to give him his, shall we say, his official punishment."

"Fair enough Happy, and glad to be of service. Perhaps now that the tannoy has announced the lifting of the smoking ban, we can all have a cigarette now." John smiled, and left the cabin fumbling for his smokes.

"Ask the 2nd engineer to come to my cabin, John!" Day called out, but got no reply.

Instead, John was down at the other end of the corridor and stooped down at the huddled and sobbing figure of the junior engineer, telling him to pull himself together.

"I never wanted to come on this voyage. I never even wanted to be an engineer either." the 5th said miserably, wiping away his tears.

"It's all your fault 3rd, you never reminded me about the different weight scales. Just wait until I tell my father about you, he'll have you sacked before you reach the UK again. Now go away and leave me alone, and you can stuff your engine room right up your arse too." he said defiantly, as John helped him to his feet.

"We all have our crosses to bear 5th. So be a man and carry your own, and face up to your own consequences. But whatever you do, make sure you're down that engine room before the chief is and especially before the captain gets to know of all this." John whispered ominously, before leaving him.

'Not one, not two, but three bloody duff engineers! And all on the same ruddy ship? And here's me thinking that only the Inverlaggan was jinxed. What a bloody way to run a shipping company.' John said quietly to himself, making his way back to his cabin.

Chapter X
The Phatts

The ship sailed from the crowded waters of the Panama Canal harbour and into the vast and deep ocean of the Pacific[*].

Her destination was a small elliptical group of tropical islands some 4,000 miles away, that would take her a good 10 days cruising to reach, before turning round and swimming her way back again. For the educated crewmen on board, these islands can be found on Longitude 178 degrees West, Latitude 1 degree North. For the rest of the uninitiated on board, it is just a large X marked right in the middle of a blue chart, and several inches away from any other markings indicating other islands.

As each inch on the chart represented 500 miles of water, the passengers held a daily lottery as to how far the ship travelled each day. This and other such trivia were introduced to keep them occupied on what would be for some, a very monotonous and boring cruise. But for others it would be the cruise of a lifetime even though it was on a cargo ship and not on one of the fabulous cruise liners that float majestically around the globe.

The *Inverlogie* however, had special passengers on board who were returning to their own people, and becoming happier each day as the ship neared their islands in the sun.

The crew had immediately dubbed them the 'Fat Arse' tribe due to their size and that their backsides were even larger than those of a Hottentot. But the fact that large was beautiful to these people meant 'ordinary' eastern bodies were looked upon as ugly and deformed. The bigger you were the more beautiful and wealthier you became. So it was no surprise that their King and Queen were the biggest and wealthiest of them all, even though in their eyes, they were very small compared with their

---

[*] The Pacific Ocean, which means 'The Peaceful Ocean', was so named by Magellan in 1527, after sailing through a gap known after him, the Magellan Straits, on the southern tip of S. America.

A Beach Party

forefathers. To have seen just one of them would both beggar belief and have been a sight for sore eyes.

As their body sizes were in gargantuan proportions, and so was their friendly nature and seemingly more open and almost naïve way of life. They always had a smile and a greeting to any of the crew who happened to pass by when they were on deck. Because of this sunny disposition that matched the warm tropical days, the crew were only too pleased to see that King Phattoleii, his Queen Phatt and all the rest of the Phatties were kept happy, as if to protect them from the bad world outside their own little idyllic world*.

For John it meant that he had to ensure that the special, extra large inflatable swimming pool that had been installed for these people, was full at all times. For when certain bodies got in, most of the water went out, over the side.

"I might as well leave the pump running, 3rd mate. Just shut it off and stow the hose when they've all gone in for supper. From now on, just get a man to re-rig it each morning and have it topped up before our guests arrive after breakfast." John said to the 3rd mate who was dressed in a crisp white tropical uniform.

"Judging by some of those delectable beauties that Phatt and Phatty deem as unnatural, they like to take their dip au naturel, so there'll never be a shortage of volunteers for that job, me included." The 3rd mate grinned.

John smiled at the thought of the squabbles created among the men to do just one job when it was always a hassle to get them to do some of the others on deck.

"Well, make sure your men are not caught spying on them, or Phatt's bodyguards will make mincemeat of them. They are all off limits to the likes of you and me, so tell your men to beware. On that score, even though their pool is just for their use and on the boat deck, you'd best provide a screen such as an awning over the entire deck, thus keeping the passengers cool and shaded.

---

* Pronounced as Fatty-o-lay-ee.

But more importantly, it will stop the crew getting a sad case of the 'Drools'. Apparently, the classic symptoms to look out for are 'organ stop' eye balls, and there's no known cure for sunburnt tongues." John replied, and left to conduct his early evening rounds.

John made his routine verbal report to Tomlinson who was almost listening to him, whilst he worked on his sea chart. Which was why John had to repeat himself on several occasions.

"Captain, with respect, I'll come back later when you're less busy." John offered, remembering his protocol.

Tomlinson stopped what he was doing, looked up from his chart and frowned.

"No that's quite alright 3rd. I heard what you said but try not to repeat yourself too much else the men in white coats will be taking you away. To make life simpler for us both, and just for the duration of this cruise, you can dispense with these reports. From what I can remember, your maxim goes, see me only when there's something wrong, not when all is well."

John smiled at Tomlinson's attitude, quoting one of John's own maxims.

"Aye aye captain." John replied officiously, and then quietened his voice to add.

"Glad to be with you Joe. I'll just file my daily reports with Happy in case you need them. See you later perhaps in the saloon."

Tomlinson simply gave John a friendly smile, and nodded his head in response.

"And so say all of us, John. On your way off the bridge, ask Larter to come and see me."

"On my way." John replied, leaving the bridge.

"Bruce, the skipper needs your body on the bridge." John called when he entered the radio shack.

"Ohh get him! Now there's an offer you can't refuse duckie!" Evans said, puckering up his lips.

A Beach Party

"Well fancy that, my luck must have changed, and here's me in my old sarong, and need my make up on. Do you think he'll find me a fast piece if I turn up looking like this John?" Larter teased, and got himself ready to go.

John chuckled at his choice of words, as he suddenly remembered the steward off the *Inverlaggan*.

"Well, you'll never get another offer like that again Bruce. I'll wait here until you get back." He replied, as Larter left with a hand on his hip and doing an exaggerated mincing walk out of the office, brushing his hair back and blowing a kiss back to them before he disappeared out of sight. This short comical interlude was a classic example of the spontaneous camaraderie between fellow shipmates.

"You certainly know how to choose your words, John." Evans said after he had finished laughing.

"Well, if you can't have a laugh now and then you'd only end up in a loony bin." John agreed.

"Seriously though, I've come to see if you'd send an SLT for me Dave. One of the letters I got from the mailbag was from my mother who tells me that my father is bad and in need of special treatment, and I need to contact her to find out what it is. I would also like to send one to my girlfriend in Holland. Can do?" John explained[*].

"Okay then John, it's not a problem so let's sort you out. Just write down the address and what you want to say to her." Evans said evenly, handing John a pencil and a signal pad.

John sat down in an empty chair and wrote out what he wanted to say before handing it back to Evans.

Evans looked through the message first to calculate the word count for the costing, before advising John to reduce the number of words.

---

[*] An SLT is a Ship's Letter Telegram that is sent in morse code to a shore based Radio receiving station, for processing and forwarding to it's addressee from there, via the local postal delivery service.

"You're allowed up to 10 words for the address and a further 10 words for the message. I won't bore you with intricate details, but basically the rate being set is at 3d a word. Any extra words over and above that would be 6d a word. But due to its destination, your girlfriend's SLT will cost you almost double."

"I don't care Dave. They're the telegrams I want to send. How much do I owe you?" John sighed, handing the signal pad back again.

Evans muttered a few calculations and stated that it would be twenty eight shillings (equivalent to £1.40p), but it would not be sent for a while due to being behind UK local time."

"That's fine by me Dave, just put it on my tally and let me know when you get the reply to the one from home." John said, and then duly signed the transaction form.

Both men were enjoying a cigarette when Larter came back into the office.

"So how was your date Bruce?" John asked cheerfully but saw concern written on Larter's face.

Larter dumped his signal pad down onto one of the desks and went over to the sea chart.

After a little while of tracing his finger over it and writing down a few calculations he turned to the other two and said.

"We're only a couple of days out and already we have to make a detour. We're making to go around the back of these islands here, and wait until the coast is clear before we get back on track again."

Evans looked at the islands Larter pointed to and made his own summations.

"But that's a good day's steaming north of our course. Why Bruce?"

"Something to do with a big tropical storm caused by the El Niño effect and we're right in its path. So we're on a race to get behind those islands before we get hit for six. John, what is our full power speed?"

It was John's turn to make a few swift calculations before replying.

A Beach Party

"We're already doing almost 18 knots, but I reckon on full power with a speed of 22 knots, plus a further 5 knots if the wind and tide are behind us."

"Hmmm! As long as we're behind the islands by 0500 Zulu time then we stand a chance. We'll soon know from the new radar scanner we've got on board." Larter said, stroking his chin then drew a series of pencil marks down the whole length of the chart.

"That gentlemen, represents the waves coming our way, which at the moment are peaking at 30 feet high. According to one of the scientists on board, by the time they reach us, they could be a good 50 feet high. He also says that it's not only the height of the wave to worry about, but also its width, or thickness and something to do with being over five times its height. If that is so, then this is promising to be a bigger blower that will outshine anything else we've been in before." Larter concluded.

"And here's me thinking that we were in for a luxury cruise across the calmest part of the ocean Neptune could provide for us." Evans moaned.

"Something like this happened to the *Invelaggan* shortly after it sailed from Liverpool.. But maybe in this part of the world Davey Jones' locker is getting quite empty just like old mother Hubbard's, and he wants a few more sacrificial sailors to top it up for him." John quipped, as they broke up the little meeting.

"John's given me an SLT to send. As there's no more pending, we might as well send it off now." Evans said, and went to tune up the transmitter.

"Yes, the captain has given me a lengthy signal to send, so we'll establish contact now in case we don't get the chance later on. Especially if we're required to answer any 'Maydays'." Larter agreed, as John left the radio shack to get on with his own preparations.

The passengers were enjoying a warm and peaceful evening in the saloon, whilst the ship's company were busy lashing things down and preparing for the bad weather that was coming their way.

John was on board as the 'Trials Officer', which meant that whilst on board he was neither fish nor fowl. He was almost 'non crew' even though he helped out, but also a 'non passenger'. This left him lots of leeway to conduct his own affairs, just so long as his top priority, the trials, were seen to first.

He found that he had nothing specific to do at the time, so decided to sit back and let the rest of the men on board worry about all and sundry about him. He decided to take it easy in the company of a few of the scientists who were going to do a special survey of King Phatt's islands, with the king himself taking a keen interest into what they were discussing.

The scientists had a large-scale map of the group of islands that also had a page for each island in the group, and a model of the atoll.

Each map showed the topographic details of each island, of its vegetation, soil structure, the various depths of water reported around them and many other botanical details that would prepare them for when they arrived. Most of these maps were dated pre WW1, and had lots of areas mentioned that were not charted. This was their mission, plus the fact that they had to make a new survey of the main attraction of King Phatt's home, an active yet benign volcano, referred to by the scientists as a 'Smoking Geezer' (geyser).

"Excuse me gentlemen, I am 3rd engineer Grey, the refrigeration trials officer on board." John said civilly, introducing himself to the group of men

"If the two main islands are deemed 'hot places' how would the islanders be able to keep all this cargo we've got on board, in the conditions I've got it now?" John asked, perusing over the maps and information of the main islands:

> 'The Darnier Plateau, (Discovered by Capt JL Darnier RN 1798). There are 2 crescent shaped islands around 450 feet high and joined at the narrowest end by a sandbar. Each side of this horseshoe atoll has a wedge shaped island of around 300 feet high, and seems to be part of what appears to be the

A Beach Party

remains of the outer rim of some gigantic volcano. There are another 2 similar wedge shaped type of islands of around 300 feet high and each about half a mile long on the opposite side, consisting of the original rock formation. There also appears to be several small low lying coral islands at shoaling point and which could become permanent coral islands in the future. Therefore, in total there would be a minimum of 15 islands, which forms an elliptical bracelet formation and was given the name of 'The Taraniti Archipelago'.

The plateau itself has been discovered to be two hundred miles long and about fifty in width, going from East of Northeast to West of Southwest. It has various depths of sea of between 5 and 20 fathoms. There are 2 lagoon within the ring of islands, but only one suitable for shipping. The larger of the two is 3 nautical miles long by 1 wide, whereas the smaller one is only one sea- mile long by about half mile wide in between the 2 halves of the island, which has the depth of 1 fathom. On the other side of the twin islands where the water is around 20 fathoms there appears to be a barrier reef some 3 furlongs long, that would become an established island in due course.

The Atoll is situated between 175 and 178W and between 1 to 2N, and is suspected to be a chimney for the main outlet of volcanic activity from the recently named Mulani Island, some 300 nautical miles due East South East of them. (Admiralty chart P70621/5 (1900) refers).

The larger lagoon is a natural basin and comparable in nature to the much larger one found at the Truk Archeplago, with a depth range of between 2 and 8 fathoms. This lagoon has implied warnings, which presents a serious danger to any approaching shipping. All vessels must proceed with extreme caution and are advised to enter only through the narrow channel found due northeast of the 'Ilani' island. (Admiralty chart P70621/5-8-5b (1920) refers.

This Archepelago has been declared as of utmost importance with that of the GALAPAGOS Islands, as charted by Mr C. Darwin whilst he was on board HMS Beagle c 1850's.

Average annual air temperature is around 35 degrees, rainfall of 150 inches. Subject to brief tropical storms. (Admiralty Instructions D/9732150 (1927) refers)'.

One of the scientists stood up and returned the courtesy by introducing themselves to him.

"Glad you asked that Grey, because whilst both semicircular shaped islands belong to the same active volcano, only the one on the right (Maoi) contains the heat. The other one (I'ti) has a different rock formation, which contains mostly solid rock. To put it another way, Maoi has porous rock which oozes hot water and other minerals, but I'ti has impervious rock and therefore is stone cold." Bowman stated

"A choice between the cooker and the fridge? To live slap bang in the middle, now that would be handy." John marvelled

"Since the original survey, there have been a total of 10 more coral islands which have grown around the plateau and can be likened to the Tuvalu islands only much bigger. As a matter of fact, the last time we were here some five years ago, the causeway between the two islands was completed and built on top of the natural sand bar that originally connected the two.

In fact, we helped the King and his tribe to complete a road and tunnel under it that would put the London Underground to shame. But the top hat was when we discovered a large natural cave in the middle of it, so we had it converted into storm shelters. You should see it, it's absolutely breathtaking."

"So you're coming back to take another look at the place to see what's changed?"

"Not exactly Grey. We have a specially made survey vessel on its way there for us to carry out various experiments and further explorations of these fascinating islands. This is an exceptionally rare island group, which poses more questions than we can give answers to. Hence the special echo sounder trials this ship has been doing for us in the meantime." Collier advised.

"I thought there was something more to just sailing a ship out to the furthest point on the map and see how the cargo stands up to variable climatic conditions. Maybe my cargo temperature trials also have some bearing on your experiments too?"

A Beach Party

Before the scientist had a chance to speak, King Phatt came over and peered into John's face.

"You chief ice man? You make my food nice and fresh?" he asked in pidgin English.

John looked up and merely nodded, in case he said something that might have offended this mountain of lard in front of him.

King Phatt gave a beaming smile, then reached down and embraced John, lifting him right up out of his chair in the process.

John gasped for air as Phatt hugged him for a moment, before he put John gently down again.

"This ship has my ice maker to keep my food from rotting. You will bring it ashore with you and show me how it is worked." Phatt demanded in a booming voice, but with a large smile still on his face.

John managed to recover his breath before answering.

"It will be my pleasure your majesty. In fact as far as I'm concerned, you can have the whole ship."

Phatt kept smiling and nodded in agreement, holding out his enormous hand.

"We will shake upon this agreement." he boomed and almost shook John's arm out of its socket.

The scientists stood up and clapped politely both as a diplomatic gesture and an excuse for John to extricate himself from this man mountain, which he promptly did by sitting down again.

"We will find lots of new things for you, your majesty. Our Queen wishes it that we will bring you happiness and prosperity." They avowed, as Phatt gloried in the tributes and praises that were heaped upon him.

"Thank you all. Now I go to bed a happy man. Maybe tomorrow we can face that terrible storm coming our way." Phatt boomed, clapping his hands as a sort of command, which was the signal for all his entourage to leave with him.

Soon the compartment seemed totally empty and quiet, yet there were several other passengers still sitting demurely and enjoying the ambience of the saloon.

"Phew that was a close one, Grey! You are now in his good books, so you'd better keep it that way. But what is this storm he is on about?" Collier asked.

"Something to do with the El Niño, but we've been diverted to hide behind some islands to the north of us." John volunteered.

Collier looked at his fellow scientists for a moment before replying.

"It appears that our King Phatt is more in tune with the elements than all our so-called sophisticated equipment we have brought with us. Let's hope we make good speed to recover our time, as we've got several serious tests and experiments to conduct in less than ten days when we board our own survey vessel."

"Maybe if you asked his majesty to accompany you on these surveys, he'd fill you in with most of what you want to know." John replied, then stood up and went to get himself a well earned drink.

Chapter XI
Shields

"3rd, wake up! You're required to report to the bridge." the steward announced, shaking John roughly by his exposed shoulder.

John woke up and immediately climbed out of his bunk and started to get himself dressed.

"What time is it? What's the panic? You're my new steward aren't you?" he asked in rapid order.

"Yes my name is Handy Henderson."

"Well, erm Handy. Any chance of a cuppa before going?"

"It's 3.45am. There's a storm brewing up and coming our way, so we're about to take shelter in the lee of some islands and you're needed for duty. Yes I've brought you a cuppa, in that order 3rd." Henderson chuckled, because he was told always to expect at least three questions from John every time he was woken up, and the cuppa always being his last one.

"Good, then let's have it." John asked, taking the cup of tea and drank it straight down without stopping.

"Cheers, I enjoyed that even though it probably went down without touching the sides." John grinned, pulling on his foul-weather gear. The motion of the ship hampered everything he and even anybody else on board tried to do, for the ship started to feel the effects of the oncoming storm.

"Don't bother tidying up, better get turned in if you can. See you at breakfast." John advised then left his cabin.

"Reporting as ordered captain." John announced, when he came up to Tomlinson.

"Well done 3rd. I need you to start from for'ard and work your way aft until you meet up with Blackmore, as he's working from aft to fore. His and your task is to ensure all watertight doors and hatches are secured. If you need assistance whilst on deck, you will have the assistance of the 2nd mate. Judging by the radar we have about 30 minutes to prepare for those ruddy great waves coming our way. The island we're behind might not be high enough to shield us, so be prepared for a deluge. Report to me when completed, but from wherever you are. Don't whatever you do attempt to come on deck until I give the all clear." Tomlinson informed .

"Aye aye captain. I've already gone through one of these incidents before on the *Inverlaggan*, and know what to expect " John responded, turning on his heel and scrambling down the gangway ladder onto the foc'sle.

The entire crew was working hard and furiously, as did John, who worked swiftly but methodically through the bowels of the ship, shutting down all bulkhead doors and hatches to give the ship a chance of survival. He got some of the sailors to double wrap the cargo hold covers, and even managed to shut down most of the upper deck vent shafts that posed a water ingress threat to the ship. In the meantime, the passengers were already assembled in the saloon with the stewards giving cups of tea or coffee to those who desired it.

John met up with Blackmore briefly, before he made his report by phone to the bridge.

"Is that you Andy? Tell the captain all watertight bulkheads and hatchways secured. And good luck Andy." John said quickly. "Yes John." Sinclair said and John to hear Sinclair shout out the report to the captain.

"Report acknowledged John. Get yourself up to the bridge if you can, but via the crew's access." Sinclair replied. But his voice was drowned as the ship's siren blasted off, which was the signal to clear the decks, get below and hold on tight.

John slammed the receiver back onto its cradle.

"Blackie, the waves are about to hit us. Get yourself down to the motor room as you'll probably be needed more there than with me. I'll take care of your outside duties, just be careful and I'll see you soon. Now get going!" John said urgently.

A Beach Party

Blackmore nodded his head and disappeared down the engine room hatchway leaving John to secure it again.

John raced through a special corridor that took him to an access ladder, which led directly up to the bridge, and managed to get onto the bridge as the waves smashed, with an almost ear-shattering slap as it met the island the ship was hiding behind.

The waves that met the island seemed to be stopped even though some of the water got washed over the top or around it. Whereas the rest of the waves rushed past the island in gigantic lumps of water that were as high as the ship's bridge. But within moments the island shook violently, and started to crumble away at the edges and fall down towards each side of the ship, as the succession of waves thumped into it.

'This must be the wave effect the scientists were referring to, as the rest of them have just passed us by, thank goodness." John muttered almost to himself.

"Whatever it is, this is the first time I've witnessed such a sight, John. Let's hope we live to tell it." Sinclair responded, gripping the spokes of the steering wheel.

"The 'Mad Monk' met the same conditions on the *Inverlaggan* and kept the ship directly behind the highest part of the island we were sheltering behind. That time it was caused by a wave surge due to the winds. Perhaps this is the same. So be alert my friend." John whispered.*

"Bosun. Keep us directly behind that hump in the middle of the island. The waves will pass either side of us and carry any large lumps of island with it." Tomlinson called, pointing to the highest part of the island and continuing to scan the rest of the island with his binoculars.

Sinclair wrestled with the steering wheel until he had the ship lined up with the hump, before he was satisfied that the ship was shielded and safe from the vortex the waves were causing as they passed the island.

---

* See *Fresh Water*.

"That was the easy bit John. Now all we've got to do is ride out the storm." Sinclair said loudly over the noise of the howling wind and rattling of the rain dashing against the bridge windows.

"How long do these type of storms last then." John asked as he held onto an upright structure.

"Anything between two to three days. Providing the ship can last this type of storm, that is." Sinclair replied, pointing to the inclinometer.

The brass pointer swung on the inclinometer from one critical mark on the port side then swiftly over to the marker on the starboard side.

"We're meeting the weather head on instead of beam on, but we're sheltered by that island. Think what it would be like otherwise, John. We'd all be Submariners by now." Sinclair observed, holding on tight so as not to be thrown around like a rag doll.

Tomlinson climbed down off his high chair and went over to the chart table for a while before he came back and settled back into his seat again.

"We've got a hole in the radar which means that the storm's eye is nearly upon us. That will give us about an hour to get some food down us, and check up on the storm damage to the ship.

Bosun! Get the first mate onto the bridge. 3rd, before you go for breakfast, make a test on each cargo hold in case they need ventilating. If they do, you've only got that time before shutting it down again for the second half of the storm." Tomlinson ordered swiftly.

"Aye aye captain. Do you want me back onto the bridge again afterwards?"

"No 3rd. I'll send for you as and when."

John nodded and waved to Sinclair before he left to check on the several thousand tons of King Phatt's groceries.

John had his breakfast in the company of Day and Blackmore, and managed a brief conflab before they went on their separate ways.

A Beach Party

"I've done a quick monitor of the cargo holds Happy. We've got a slight defrost in one corner of No 4 hold. Suggest we've got a malfunction with one of the coolant motors."

"Yes John, I've traced it to one of the extractor fans, and have one of the boys onto it even as we speak." Blackmore replied.

"Make sure your Co2 absorption units are functioning normally John, or there'll be a build up of gas to cause the same effect." Day instructed, and John nodded in appreciation at what was said.

"Oh well you two. I'm off to sort out the delicate matter of a flooded bilge. Keep safe." Day concluded, leaving his two junior officers.

"That cretin of a 5th has been put through the mill by the chief, and the skipper has stopped his pay until we reach our outward destination. Lucky he wasn't put off at Panama though, else he'd have to find his own way home again." Blackmore said glumly.

"Only what he deserves. He tried to make out that it was my fault, but the chief and the captain saw through his lies. Maybe it was that, that made them very harsh on him, the lying that is.

Otherwise, it would have been a much lesser charge of stupidity instead of gross incompetence." John replied, finishing off his breakfast cigarette.

"Oh well Blackie, I'm off to do a quick deck rounds before this bloody storm hits us again. Just as well it's only wind and rain this time, for the tidal surge that came before it was horrendous.

It almost flattened the island we're hiding behind. I'll tell you about it some other time, as I really must go."

"Sounds good stuff John, can't wait. Yes, see you sometime." Blackmore replied before both men left the warmth of the dining room.

"John, would you please do a couple of hours in the engine room, as the second has gashed his arm and needs the doc to sort him out." Day asked, when he re-appeared into the dining room.

"I'm just on my way to do the upper deck rounds Happy, so give me about an hour would you."

"Fair enough John, but as soon as you've finished come straight down. See you then." Day conceded before he disappeared again.

'Some busman's holiday I'm getting. I must remind myself to get a ship that's got the proper amount of engineers on board.' John muttered and went out onto the draughty weather deck and started to make his rounds.

A Beach Party

Chapter XII
Stan

Yet again the *Inverlogie* proved to her makers that she was a good ship, as she had weathered yet more fierce onslaughts that nature kept throwing at her. For 2 days she held out against the fierce attentions of the El Niño, as it sent its first calling card of the year to the shores that man inhabits.

Then she was able to move out from behind her little protector, the much-battered island that was now a former shadow of itself, and resume her voyage as her masters intended.

"Bosun, get us out of here on a course of 250. Tell the engine room to make speed for 20knots. Inform the passengers that they may now access the upper deck if they choose. And get me the 2nd mate." Tomlinson ordered, crossing swiftly over to the chart table.

John arrived onto the bridge at the same time as the 2nd mate, who was about to deliver his upper deck rounds report.

"Ah 2nd! We have a problem with cargo hold 4. Check that the cargo-hatch covering has not been compromised. If so, then get it repaired. I also want your men to get the hoses and yard brushes out, and have them scrub the upper deck and paintwork as clean as possible. We're not going steam around looking like a filthy tramp steamer, so speak to 3rd engineer Grey if you need extra pumps. I need a report on the lifeboat stations, so have the 3rd mate report to me on your way aft."

"Aye aye captain. Do you want the awnings re-rigged on the boat deck again?" the 2nd mate asked politely.

"Yes of course we bloody well do. If King Phatt sees that he's really on a crabby cargo ship, with no shade for him to take his afternoon dip, then we can all look out. Standard procedure if you please 2nd."

The 2nd mate merely nodded his head and left the bridge in a hurry.

"We've got a slight leak in our cable locker. I've managed to get a temporary plug into the hole, but need some time to weld a proper skin over the damage. I need about 1 hour to complete it but you'll have to sail in a different direction to keep the pressure off the hull for me." John reported.

Tomlinson looked at John for a moment, and nodded.

"If you say so 3rd then so shall it be. 1 hour you said?" Tomlinson replied in a more civilised manner than he had to the 2nd mate.

"I've already got a sheet of metal and a welder standing by to tack it on, even as we speak captain. Mind you it would have to be an external job, like those navy divers did on the SFD2." John replied with a nod of his head.

"Ah yes, I remember. But didn't they have special welding equipment to do it?"

John smiled and produced a metal object to show Tomlinson.

"This is what the navy wallah gave me before he left us. It is a simple and outstanding device he had invented, and is exactly what we need to perform the work whilst in wet or underwater conditions. I have taken the liberty of making a couple of exact copies in case we need more than just the one. His patents have not been affected as I've already sent him my drawings and alterations to it, although he has as yet not replied to my correspondence."

"Glad to hear it 3rd. Let me know when you want me to alter course, only I don't want to loose any more time than necessary." "I don't think somehow King Phatt would quibble over one more lousy hour. It just means that we can steam at full power that little bit longer. Don't forget, we're still overweight with the extra fuel."

Tomlinson grinned and nodded his approval, before he lowered his voice so that only John could hear.

"Just like old times John. Do what you have to, no matter how long it takes."

"Thanks Joe! See you shortly." John responded in an equal tone as he left the bridge, but met Day on his way to see Tomlinson.

A Beach Party

"Happy, I need an immediate supply of an extra bottle of oxygen for a rush patch job. Can you get it to me on the foc'sle within 15 minutes?" John asked, nodding his recognition of Day. Day looked non-plussed for a moment before he agreed.

"If it's an external weld John, make sure you've got the right welding rods. The ones you want are blue with a yellow band around the rod. If you get the green ones, then make sure of a double weld, as they're only for tacking jobs and not a full scale seam weld."

"Blue with a yellow band. Double weld on the green." John responded automatically and fixed his instructions into his mind, then added.

"Right, I'm on my way. By the way, the captain has agreed on the repair." John said with a grin, pointing upwards towards the ladder leading to the bridge.

"Why thank you John, I would never have guessed!" Day chuckled, as they parted company.

Tomlinson turned the ship so that the swell and tide were coming from astern, thus giving John and his gang of welders more expanse of hull to be able to do their task. They had to wait until the swell passed from under the ship for them to weld the lower part of the patch onto the hull.

"It's like working on a lift that can't decide whether to go to the top floor or stay down in the basement. And we've got to double weld every inch." A stoker moaned, whilst working frantically to complete his little piece of metal before another wave bobbed him out of reach.

"Sorry about that stokes, only we're fresh out of rivets to do the job properly." John said, sympathising with the man, then joked.

"Still, think of it this way. The next time you're asked to help the sailors to paint the ship, all you've got to do is just stand there with your brush, the waves would do the rest."

The very thought of what John had said, amused the rest of the team, lifting their spirits up and giving them a new bravado instead of fearing where the next wave might take them. Up or down.

Within half an hour the team had finished their work and John conducted his internal inspection to see if the welded patch was in fact watertight.

"Well done men, its all dry as a bone. Get yourselves back on board and stow your gear before you take the afternoon off." John announced happily to his team.

"The afternoon off 3rd, is that a promise?" one of the stokers questioned in disbelief.

"That's a promise." John replied, then went and reported to Tomlinson.

"And I said that the men could have the afternoon off." John concluded.

"Seeing that I'm now getting back on track again, that'll be fine by me 3rd. No doubt the chief will endorse your decision, just as long as it doesn't interfere with your mechanical routines. What do you say, engines?" Tomlinson asked, as Day was about to leave the bridge.

"That's fine by me captain. It's about time we got into a relaxed watchkeeping pattern again. Our 3rd will be required to contribute toward that though." Day responded with a big grin.

"But of course chief, anything to keep the peace, you know me." John retorted with an equally large grin.

"That settles it gentlemen, now let me get on with some real work. Before you go engines, I need you to provide me with a new set of fuel figures. Kindly provide them by lunch time if you would." Tomlinson said, concluding the little impromptu meeting.

As the ship sailed merrily along during seemingly endless succession of days, she left a large black ribbon of smoke trailing behind her funnel, and a silver wake to mark her passage. The subject of their recent escape from the El Niño storm and the damaged islands, was getting a bit stale to discuss. This was a natural phenomenon with long distance passengers, and boredom was setting in. They had nothing better to do than just sit around on deck chairs and drinking themselves almost into oblivion on the freely available beverages that were constantly passed around by the stewards.

For those who had no imagination and merely accepted their daily lot, this was one thing, but for others who had things to do or discover, that was a different matter as they found things that kept themselves busy.

It was during this time where John found himself immersed into the mechanics of making his 'STAN' (Steering Aid to Navigation) more efficient and more 'operator' friendly than he had previously planned.

"Right then Andy. I've put in a new pipe to make the response to the telemotor rams much quicker and more efficient. Let me know when you're on a steady course, that has less than 1 degree of alteration either side of the datum line." John said quietly, keeping the quiet efficiency of the bridge intact.

Sinclair nodded and got just what John had requested.

"Now John."

John flicked the control arm of the rams into position, then pulled a lever to start the telemotor system working.

Both men looked at the ship's repeater dial that told the helmsman what course the ship was on and the amount of rudder that was used on each turn of the wheel.

The indictor arrow moved slightly to port, which was followed by a faint noise as the control ram moved the wheel a little to bring the ship back onto its bearing again. Within moments the movements were going on the opposite side before the arrow got reversed and back to the bearing again.

"Seems okay Andy. I haven't taken into consideration the natural movement of the ship going through this swell. Does the ship always move off course on every wave?"

"That's because we've got a 'stern' sea, but in fact it's coming from our starboard side aft. If we had an oncoming swell or tide or running exactly in front of it, then there would be even less of a movement than what you see now." Sinclair responded, gazing at the mechanical wizardry that was now doing the job for him.

"Well, as long as the ship is on a steady course, with a plus or minus of say a two degree alteration on either side, then this is working correctly, as it will maintain your base course. All you've got to do when you need to change course, is to pull the operation lever before you pull away the con-rod, then when you're on course, simply re-engage them again and in the same order. Bear in mind its STAN that's keeping the course from its settings and not under the influence of the repeater.

If the natural sway of the ship makes the rudder move more than three degrees either side of the base course, then you disengage and start again. However, if the swing is more than five degrees, which is probably due to heavy weather or higher than normal waves or in fact you're altering course slightly, then disengage it altogether and operate manually." John advised at length.

Both men stood looking at this machine for a while. Sinclair observed the ships head and course, with John looking and checking the movements of the machinery.

"Well Andy, it's time for our bosses to see what we've been doing to their ship. Let's surprise them by asking the chief onto the bridge, then when he arrives, you go and fetch the captain. He'll be very surprised when it's you he's speaking to when you should in fact be at the helm." John chuckled.

Sinclair grinned at the ruse, and agreed by phoning up the engine room and asking for Day to come to the bridge.

"Hello John, what's the problem?" Day asked, when he strolled onto the bridge.

John seemed not to hear him and pretended to work on the steering wheel.

Within moments there was a loud shout coming from Tomlinson's bridge cabin, and Sinclair came hurrying back into the bridge with Tomlinson in hot pursuit.

"Get back on the..." Tomlinson started to shout, but stopped when he saw John and Day standing next to the wheel. He

A Beach Party

suspected something was afoot so looked enquiringly, first at John then at Day.

"What's the matter with my ship now 3rd?" Tomlinson asked with uncertainty.

Sinclair went and stood next to John, who gave him a nod before both men stepped aside to reveal that the wheel was moving gently on its own, and the ships compass repeater showing a steady course.

Tomlinson and Day moved quickly over to the wheel and examined the two pieces of metal protruding from it, before both looked amazed at the same steady course the ship was keeping.

"Okay then John, tell me it's all done with mirrors!" Day whispered, with his eyes glued to the machinery.

"I know, you've got men down in the emergency steerage position working their balls off just for you to show off." Tomlinson ventured, as he too was mesmerised with the steady course.

"Actually it's STAN, that's doing it. Part of him is here, the rest is down in the steering gear compartment." John said quietly, pointing to the pieces of metal.

"Who is STAN when he's around or need I ask such a stupid question?" Day asked.

"I have given its official name which stands for 'Steering Aid to Navigation'. Basically Happy, it's a small telemotor pump that operates a 2-way piston, which repositions the steering wheel, when it gets to certain correction limits. It can be altered to take a deviation of wheel movement up to five degrees either side of the base course. The toleration can be adjusted downwards to almost half a degree, but no more than the upward limit of five. It can be disengaged when altering course, then re-engaged again when onto the new course. In truth, it'll be better than the average helmsman. In other words you'd have this machine at your disposal, which is almost as good as Sinclair, here. Bear in mind, it's only for long voyages that use straight lines across the chart. Harbour navigation would still need a real helmsman like Sinclair." John advised humbly.

"See, he's trying to take over the ship on his own captain." Sinclair joked, standing by the helm and watching it keep course just as if he was doing it.

Tomlinson and Day looked on for a while longer before they asked to see how a change of course would be done.

Sinclair smiled at John, and did exactly what John had shown him.

"Say I want to change course on to 280. I alter to port as normal, then when on course, simply engage the con-rod then the motor lever." Sinclair said, and did just that.

He left the ship go a few moments on that new course before he reversed the procedure and got the ship back onto its base course again.

"Simple as that!" he concluded.

"Okay then Einstein, lets see the mechanics of this wonderful invention of yours." Day said with grudging approval.

John led Tomlinson and Day down to the steering ram compartment and showed them the box of tricks he had introduced.

"As I've said Happy. It's just a simple telemotor pump and a 'D' valve that flip-flops the tiller, with the tracking gear engaged to follow suit. I had tested an earlier model on the *Inverlaggan*, but found that I needed a double 'D' valve to cope with the tolerance levels, which at the time were too harsh for just the one pump to keep up. And before you say anything about the *Inverlaggan*, no it wasn't engaged at the time we hit the mine that sunk us." John said as an afterthought.

"We wouldn't dream of it John, just as we wouldn't have dreamed up this new invention of yours.

As far as I'm concerned, we need to test it to its limits to see if it stands up to normal operational requirements. I'm game if you are chief!" Tomlinson said, observing that the steering gear hardly moved.

"Yes, indeed I am. But John would have to show me his drawings and workings as to how he came to such an invention.

A Beach Party

We can give it a good going over for him before he gets it submitted, and certainly before any of the ships board of governors get wind of it." Day said earnestly, before he turned to John.

"You have certainly proved me right when I made my recommendations about you whilst we were on the *Brooklea*. We two, are not part of the skulduggery and thieving of our ship owners, so we'll keep an eye on you in case they try anything on you like they did on the *Brooklea,* and the *Inverlaggan.*"

"Thank you both for your support gentlemen, although I can't understand your own involvement outside of the ship owners. Fortunately for me I have met and sailed with you both and trust you with my work.

Therefore, I will certainly offer you my drawings and contemplation's as to how I came to my conclusions, as I saw them. I only hope that after this voyage, it can be accepted as a step forward in the lives of a mariner." John replied earnestly, looking intently into the eyes of his two seniors.

"Welcome aboard the Free Enterprise Mutual Trust movement, John. You can take it from us that we'll ensure your just rewards, as we have enjoyed our own efforts through the same movement. To give you a clue as to just who is one of the major players in the scheme of things, and to help you conjure up a name. He is a mutual acquaintance to all three of us. No names or kitbags, but he is a certain dockyard superintendent. But for now, we'll get back onto the bridge in case of prying eyes." Tomlinson said with pride, and patted John on his shoulder.

"In that case I consider myself honoured. However, the bosun is a close friend of mine, who would probably embrace this 'movement' as he too comes up with lots of practical ideas in his own world of sailors." John said with pride.

"Ah yes. You, he and Larter, are the strangest crew combination we've ever met. Well, let's hope we of the movement get all three of you in the one recruitment." Day smiled, as he too patted John's shoulder, yet without patronising him.

John looked at the two officers and grinned.

"I think we'd better get out of here else we'd be accused of mutiny if a certain skipper or chief happened by just now." John said, leading his two senior officers back up onto the bridge.

"Gangway for senior officers." Day and Tomlinson said in unison and followed in single file behind John.

'Things will be getting quite interesting if Fergus McPhee has his way. Good old Fergus!' John thought.

A Beach Party

Chapter XIII
The Usual

It was early in the morning when the half-asleep helmsman alerted the captain on seeing what he described as a firework display, making the captain rush to the bridge to see exactly what it was.

Tomlinson arrived onto the bridge to find a couple of the scientists there with their binoculars looking at the source of the wonderment.

"Morning captain. That is the Mulani pyramid you see ahead of us. It appears that it's in a temperamental mood today." Johanson who was one of the scientists greeted, offering Tomlinson his binoculars.

Tomlinson looked through the binoculars for a while, then scanned around the horizon before handing them back to the man.

"Thank goodness for that. It means we're on track and on course. If it's 550 feet high and just over the horizon for it to be seen like this by the naked eye, then we're about 40 nautical miles away." Tomlinson muttered, as he went over to his sea chart and proceeded to calculate his exact position on the chart.

"Mr Johanson, can you give me a clue as to how far out from the pyramid I can expect any sort of fallout. Only my course takes me almost within five sea miles to port." Tomlinson asked politely.

"I cannot tell for certain until we're much closer captain. This particular volcano is a highly dangerous one in the same ilk as that of Krakatoa and Vesuvius that was, or Tristan da Cunha and Etna that is. But from what we can see from its present performance, I'd say it's still sleeping, or just having the year off. However, I'd be more inclined to give it a wide berth and give it at least double that distance." Johanson said quietly, still looking through his binoculars.

Tomlinson returned to his chart then ordered a course change that would loop him around the danger area and back onto his base course again.

"New course set captain, STAN engaged." the helmsman reported, and stood back to keep a watch on this new machine.

John came up onto the boat deck to sit in his favourite spot behind the funnel, and have a quiet, early morning pre-breakfast cigarette.

"Morning John! Come to see the fireworks have you?" Evans asked cheerfully.

"Morning Dave. What fireworks are they then?" John asked with surprise.

Evans pointed to the horizon, then handed John a pair of binoculars.

"Here, take a look at that then." He said

John stood up and looked out to sea at the glowing light and sparks coming from the now visible volcano.

"Flippin' heck. Who towed that out here?" John whistled, and quickly scanned the horizon and back to the show of nature.

"It's only a large blip on our radar screen at the moment. But at least we know we're in the right part of the ocean and only about two days off our next port of call." Evans opined, as John handed back the glasses to him.

"I just can't wait, Dave. Especially when we're about to be lectured on what to expect from the place. The scientists already have a plasticine model made up of what the place looks like."

"Yeah, I saw it too. It looks like a paradise island but with a smoke chimney stuck up its backside. Still, a week there lazing on the coral sands with a few of those delectable maidens attending our every wish, would be worth a kings ransom." Evans chuckled.

"Don't even think about it Dave, despite what you see and hear on board. Best see what it's really like when you get ashore, that's my motto. That way you'll never be disappointed."

A Beach Party

"Well, one can only wish and hope, even to dream of such places."

"Never mind Dave, it's time now for something more tangible to enjoy. I'm starving, so what's for breakfast?"

"The usual. Fruit juice or cereal, beans on toast or a boiled egg, toast, and marmalade or jam." Evans said glumly.

"What no bacon, even braised kidney on fried bread, or shit on a raft as the stokers would have it? Whatever happened to yellow peril with poached egg?" John asked, wickedly.

"Crumbs, you must be on a different liner to the rest of us John." Evans snorted.

"Only joking Dave. Anyway, must go now and have my buttered rolls and tea before I get my deck rounds done. I'll be up to see you both later. See you." John said cheerfully and went below for his breakfast.

"Morning Blackie! Going on or off?" John greeted, as he sat down next to Blackmore.

"Morning John. Have come off early, and am away to bed after I do my deck rounds." Blackmore replied tiredly.

"I did the last part of the first watch for the 2nd, and am not required now until the afternoon watch. I'll do the deck rounds after breakfast, so you can get turned in right away. I'll give you a knock around lunchtime to see if you're still with us."

"Cheers John! Will be glad to get into harbour for a few days rest. Our trip back should be a doddle after this bloody one, that's for sure."

"Well, let's hope so. But I have a funny feeling in my water that our return trip will be a much longer one. Anyway Blackie, we'll cross that bridge when we come to it. See you later." John smiled, leaving the dining room to conduct his rounds.

"Morning 3rd! Glad we're giving that box of tricks a wide berth." the 4th mate greeted when John arrived onto the bridge.

"Morning 4th. Yes, it certainly would mess up our paintwork if we went too close to it. Just as well we're an oil burner to make our steam and not relying on the coke its chucking out." John joked, taking another look at the glowing island that seemed only a few miles away, yet was in fact just over the horizon, some 30 miles away.

"You can even smell the stink from here too, it's like rotten eggs."

"Oh so that's what it is. Thank goodness for that, as I was beginning to think my overalls needed a good bath as well as I do."

The 4th mate, sighed, and shook his head.

"I always thought you engineers were a queer lot. Anyway 3rd! I'm the duty officer on the bridge, have you come to give your deck rounds report?"

"No, just checking on STAN, and the bosun."

"The bosun has just gone off watch, but who the bloody hell is STAN?"

Now it was John's turn to sigh.

"If you, as the duty officer on the bridge does not know who or what STAN is by now, then it is not my place to tell you. Suggest you speak to the captain when he next comes onto the bridge." John replied in disgust, and left the bridge to go into the radio shack.

'I can put up with the 'don't know but I'll find out' type, but I'll be blowed to help those who are too lazy to find out about things they should know in the first place, no matter what rank they hold. Happy called it incompetence.' John muttered, and made his way into the wireless office.

"Morning Bruce, how are things this end?" John asked breezily, as the change of scenery was just the tonic to cheer him up from his last place of call.

"Morning John. We've picked up a distress call from the other side of that volcano. Judging by its position, it's only about ten miles off it and we're about two hours steaming from it. Dave has gone to see the captain about it, so stand by." Larter volunteered, opening his cigarette case and offering John one.

A Beach Party

Shortly after they finished their cigarette, Evans came bounding into the shack stating that they would be responding to the distress.

"Better get some fire fighting equipment ready then, Bruce. What type of ship is she?"

"She's a 10,000 ton Panamanian registered cargo ship out of Valpariso bound for Osaka. She's been struck by some of the fall out from the volcano, and has caught fire on deck. It's loaded with hardwood timber so that's no surprise, but she has 15 passengers and 35 crew on board." Evans replied.

"If we get extra passengers then what a sight the Phatties will make if they have to play at sardines." John mused, which brought a smile from the others.

Larter sat in his chair and proceeded to tap out the response signal on his Morse key, as Evans got on with the rest of the work.

"Well, must leave you two and get myself prepared." John replied and left the radio shack to go back to the bridge.

On entering the bridge, he heard Tomlinson shouting at the 4th mate, who he guessed was the outcome to the question he suggested the 4th to ask Tomlinson.

"3rd engineer Grey. Glad to see an officer with some common sense. For God's sake, take this bloody 4th mate with you and prepare the decks for fire fighting. We're about to render assistance to a burning ship the other side of that bloody bonfire." Tomlinson said with exasperation.

"Yes captain. I know the situation, and will get as many pumps available as possible. But please remember our cargo, and the delicate balance we must strike."

Tomlinson looked at John and pondered on the problem for a moment before answering.

"Yes, right! We'll have to stand off to receive the survivors. However, if we can help them save the vessel then we'd need maximum pressure to play the hoses onto her. I would need at least 5 cables distance between us, therefore you'd have to use your maximum hose pressure."

"My porta-pumps can deliver that, but we'd need a good half of them for boundary cooling. The ships ballast pumps can pack the punch no problem if you feel the need to lay off even further, captain. We'll just have to play it by ear."

"I think you're right on that point. Anyway, sort it out so that we do not melt even one ice cube, or King Phatt and his gang will see that we don't get his franchise. Business before the practical in this case 3rd."

"Aye aye captain. On my way." John responded and left the bridge.

A man-made object such as a ship being slap-bang in the middle of Mother Nature's house, is prone to all sorts of happenings, be it from man himself, a freak happening from Mother Nature, or even incurring her wrath in some way. Happily and on most occasions the ship will survive her chance misadventure with Mother Nature and arrive at her chosen destination. Sometimes the ship is lucky to find somebody nearby to help them, but for the rest, there would be no chance for her or her human cargo to survive.

On this occasion and by a fluke, another ship was occupying the same deserted area of ocean and already steaming full speed to aid the stricken vessel and all on board her. This is the unwritten code of all mariners no matter what nationality, in their endeavour to help all those in peril on the sea.

"Stand by starboard side, ready to receive survivors." Came the terse tannoy announcement, as John got his fire fighting crews ready to commence their allotted tasks.

"Commence boundary cooling. 4th mate, make sure the ships deck hydrants are on full, and have the men direct the water onto their bridge." John shouted, with his ship closing within seemingly touching distance with the big ball of flame that was the other ship, although they were almost 200 yards apart.

The sheets of flames from the burning wood on the stricken ship were nearly obscured by the thick black smoke coming out

A Beach Party

of its funnel. John saw that men were trying to jettison the deck cargo, but their efforts looked in vain. He could see the glowing sides of the ship, which suggested that the fire was now deep into the holds and that the ship would be doomed no matter what they tried to do to save it.

"3rd mate. Get the two port side pumps over to the starboard side and have the teams spray our decks. 4th mate! Get another 4-man team and get the spare hoses rigged up and flowing. Have the water directed towards the lifeboats, that ship is leaking fuel oil which is catching fire all around them. Put a syphon onto the end of the hose and use a drum of foam powder to spray over the burning patches the lifeboats have to come through." John shouted over the loud noise the fires were making.

The *Inverlogie* fought the blazing ship for 30 minutes, and managed to snatch as many people off the doomed ship as possible, before it sank beneath the waves.

The flames of the burning wood were quickly extinguished, as were the burning waves that carried the globules of fuel oil, before there was a loud but muffled explosion from the sinking ship, when the cold water hit the hot furnaces of the boiler room. A few large air bubbles burst onto the now empty space, which disgorged all sorts of flotsam that refused to go down with the ship. Soon all that was left was the slowly circling raft of debris that marked yet another ship's grave.

"All survivors are to be brought into the saloon." the terse metallic instruction from the tannoy managed to pierce John's thoughts, and he tore his eyes away from that empty spot.

"Right then men, secure from fire fighting. Stow all hoses and pumps before you go below." John shouted, beckoning the 4th mate over to see him.

"4th mate! You'd better get some of your men together and get those lifeboats shipped, preferably up onto the boat-deck. Failing that, put them on the after cargo deck. Then get the ship cleaned up and looking like a ship instead of an old coal barge.

Do that and you'll be back into the captains good books again, even for just a few more hours." John advised.

"Just what I thought 3rd. I'll get the after derricks to hoist them into position." the 4th mate agreed, and left to get the task done.

John went to his cabin and taking a hot shower, dressed into clean tropical uniform again before presenting himself to the ships community again.

"How many did we get Handy?" John asked politely, meeting Henderson coming along the cabin space aisle.

"Don't know 3rd. But I'm afraid that we're about ten cabins short. I've been given instructions to help you and the other officers to double up. The 2nd engineer will be sharing with the chief, you've got Acting 3rd Blackmore. The 4th engineer and the other two junior engineers will share. The first mate will be sharing with the 2nd, and so on. The crew are back to hammocks again, worst luck." he grumbled.

"Well at least we won't starve, what with all this food on board." John replied cheerfully.

"You must be joking. Those 'Up your Phattarsolas' tribe have almost scoffed everything from the ship's larder, and won't let us take some of their cargo to make up for it. Mind you, the skipper has told the King and his Phatties that due to the extra mouths to feed, he'll have to limit them to just three courses per meal instead of the usual 7 that they scoff at their mealtimes. Talk about pigs at the trough, these are even worse than that. Still, the chef is quite chuffed about that, as those Phatties are a pain in the neck to please. The good thing is that it's only a couple more days and we'll get shot of them. God knows what we're going to do for food when we're on our way back again, though."

"I suppose we could stuff and roast a couple of them then pickle them to tide us over, Handy. Then again, all of us who's got a rod with them can have a few days off to catch plenty of succulent fish. From what I understand from one of the scientists,

A Beach Party

there are plenty of coconuts and bananas. So we definitely won't starve." John said with a grin.

"Well if their bananas are as big as that lot then I suppose one banana between ten of us would suffice. But then we'd end up looking like ruddy monkeys."

"Gibbon half the chance I suppose you're right there." John replied swiftly, which resulted in a stifled groan from the steward. "Must get on now. Oh I nearly forgot, the chief wants to see you."

"Thanks for the message. Do me a favour and put Blackmores' stuff at the other end of the cabin, and give him the seat locker bunk. See you later!" John concluded, making his way to see Day.

"Hello 2nd, haven't had a chance to speak to you since you hurt your arm. All okay now?"

"Hello 3rd. Yes it's coming along nicely, thanks. What brings you here?"

"I've got a message from the steward that the chief wants to see me. Any idea what the score is?" John asked civilly.

"Not quite sure, except that it will probably be something to do with your monitoring program. He's on watch until lunch time, best see him afterwards."

John looked at his watch and was surprised how quickly the time had seemed to vanish into nowhere.

"Flippin' heck 2nd. Is that the time? Last thing I knew was we were fighting a blazing ship, and taking some poor oil-soaked souls on board." John said in amazement.

"Wish I was back on the decks again 3rd, as you seem to get all the action and fresh air. It was just another watch for us, except for the unusual telegraph orders slap-bang in the middle of the ocean."

"I'd swap with you any day of the week 2nd, if only to get out of the way of those bickering deck officers. Anyway, must go now, and make my daily monitor check. When you see the chief, tell him I'll see him probably in the dining room during lunch." John replied, and excused himself from the cabin.

A Beach Party

Chapter XIV
Clever Stuff

The usual 'last night' of the final outward leg of the voyage was a pleasant one for the *Inverlogie,* as everybody was now getting land-happy again.

King Phatt and his tribe were chattering away like monkeys as they pointed out the different 'attractions' his coral island kingdom had to offer. The down-side were the glum faces of the survivors as they knew it would take a very long time for them to get to their real destination, a further 3,000 miles away to the north.

John was sitting in the saloon talking to one of the passengers who was a civil engineer, when Johanson came and joined them.

"So you've met our chief civil engineer McIntyre, then Grey. He's the one who installed the piping systems on the islands and we've come to see how he did it for our own island." the scientist greeted.

"Yes, he's told me about the underground plumbing system, and a pretty comprehensive system it is too. But what about your island, professor?"

"We Icelanders have several volcanoes, that we wish to harness in the same way. We would be able to provide a heating system for all our people and at the same time generate our own electricity without the continued reliance on expensive imported coal or oil to so. Unlike the inhabitants of the islands who mostly live in underground apartments, to let their vegetation have more room to grow in the open and rich fertile soil, our rock is too solid to excavate to do the same. Therefore we're forced to limit our efforts into under-soil piping only." Johanson explained.

"But if you have under-soil heating, then you'd be able to grow a better crop, as the earth would be that much more warmer for the plants to survive." John observed.

"Yes there is that as a spin off I suppose, but the main object is to get the heat to our islanders and the electricity as I've just said." Johanson said with a nod, and pulled his enormous pipe from his be whiskered face.

"Mr Bergerman over there designed the special turbines to cope with the superheated steam which produces their electricity supply. They still have several steam engines to pump the hot water around the islands, and even more to pump the fresh water in the opposite direction. The problem there, is that these engines are getting very ancient now and are wearing out too easily." McIntyre explained, as he showed John some pictures of the caverns that housed the steam engines and electricity turbines. "By the look of those caverns, that's a lot of tunnelling. I heard that there's a six layer of roadway running through the islands, and of course the living quarters. Where did all the rock go to?" John asked, astonished by the pictures he looked at.

"It's taken over 50 years to get things almost right for the islanders. The rock was used to re-inforce the bridge of coral between the two islands and the islands next to the atoll, and also to construct the harbour complex.

If you look at the model, there's a small barrier reef at one end, which is the open end of the two islands. When we've finished the last housing area and the reason why you're on board, we hope to build a solid landing platform for aircraft instead of using the lagoon for flying boats." McIntyre replied.

John thought for a moment to take in this information before he asked his next question.

"I can understand the trials of refrigeration on a ship, but what use would it be on land, even in a cave?"

"That Mr Grey, appears to be our objective from the statistics you have been providing us with." A voice boomed, as yet another scientist joined the discussion.

Johanson introduced the newcomer as Professor Chandler, who pulled up an empty chair.

"You see Grey, we have an abundance of heat in the rocks of the Maoi Island due to the volcano, but both are heated on the outside by the sun. But the principle of digging below 'sea level' where the land is supposed to be at a constant 10degrees C, does not apply. Therefore we need to find a reliable method of

A Beach Party

coolant such as this ship has produced, to be able to replicate it ashore. In that way, the inhabitants would be able to keep cool rather than sizzle away like slabs of pork. Johanson here has the opposite problem, as his island is naturally cold, and they want to be warmed up naturally with those volcanoes of theirs." Chandler informed in a loud voice.

"So it's a question of out of the oven and into the fridge." John said with a grin, so as not to trivialise the discussion, and was met with a chuckle from the others.

"But if a volcano only kicks out molten rock and give off gases now and then, how does this volcano only produce hot water. Where does it get its source from?" John asked quickly.

"See that area there, just at the side of the volcano slope? Well, there is a ring of coral next to it that contains the conflagration. Nobody but nobody, goes near that area as that particular place has the sinkholes for the volcano. On the incoming tide, the water flows over the ring of coral and runs straight down those holes, estimated at about 900 feet deep. Only when the water reaches it's high tide level mark, which covers the coral ring, do the holes finally become full. Then when the tide returns to its low water and the coral ring comes back into view again, the water start to sink slowly down into the hole. The volcano has two double vents. One gives off a permanent plume of super heated steam, whereas the second one gives off puffs of ash or gas. But three days later when you hear it hum which turns into a melodic but non-descript tune, that is when both double events of the volcano turn into a full-blown geyser of hot water. All of which gets blown across the tops of the surrounding islands by the tropical winds. This geyser will spurt a good 500 feet upwards and will last for about four hours.

As you can see from the model, at one end of Maoi there is a natural basin almost 300 feet high. It's formed by an extinct vent some 100feet long, 60 feet wide and approx 500 feet deep. Due to the prevailing air-currents, that is where a lot of the fresh water from the volcano ends up and where the Islanders get their fresh water from.

Sometimes, and especially after a tropical storm which coincides with the geyser, there will be too much water for the basin to hold it. So an overflow in the form of a waterfall spills over the lower lip of the basin and down into the shallow lagoon between the islands. Not often it happens, but pretty spectacular when it does." Chandler expounded.

"We suspect that the water goes through its own channel system and gets heated up by the Mulani volcano, before it travels back here again. We also suspect that the small Maoi volcano is just a safety valve for the much bigger Mulani, else if Mulani blows, then it will devastate most of the islands in this sector of the Western Pacific, as it did about 150 years ago." Johanson said grimly, with the other scientists nodding in agreement.

"The water travels from here to Mulani? But that's a good day's steaming from here. How does it regulate the flow from cold sea water in, to hot water out, or is there another underground channel?" John asked in amazement.

"Not only that, if the islands are deluged in hot fresh water how does the plant life survive the onslaught? How does it affect the lagoon if the water gets siphoned off by the sink hole?" John asked in quick succession.

Day was passing by the group and heard John's rapid-fire questions, and chuckled.

"Pardon me gentlemen, but you'll have to excuse my 3rd engineer. He's always asking questions, not in ones but normally in threes or fours." Day stated.

The scientists and the civil engineers looked at John then at Day, before McIntyre answered.

"A good engineer always asks questions. Else how would he know to do what is required of him? Grey here must do you proud chief."

Day smiled and nodded to John.

A Beach Party

"Well at least John here is in good company then. Let me have him back when you're finished with him." He said then left the table.

"The hot water we refer to is not the scalding water you'd normally associate with making a cup of tea or coffee, but is only a constant 60 degrees centigrade. By the time it gets air-cooled and falls back down onto the islands it is only tepid, and almost the same temperature as the tropical rains. The water being piped from the vent holes are sufficient to provide the heating for the underground dwellings, but as we've already stated, it's the superheated steam that turns the battery of turbines to provide the electricity.

Therefore in between geysers, it's the electricity that heats the water, thus keeping a constant supply of hot water until the next time. Very clever stuff, I might add." Chandler said slowly and precisely.

"Self created energy to make a giant kettle, now that could be very useful, especially on board ship." John said quietly, looking again at the photographs of the massive turbines, and the boilers for the water.

"Indeed Grey, but you'd need a mobile volcano to provide the heat to turn the turbines to make the electricity to boil the water to turn back into steam and start all over again." Johanson said, and smiled at John's comment.

"Well, I for one would like a good look round at this seemingly idyllic set up, if someone would offer me the courtesy of one." John said enthusiastically.

"All in good time Grey, we've got the small job of getting your icebox set up first." McIntyre laughed and nodded his agreement to John's request.

"Raise your glasses gentlemen. I give you a toast to a successful scientific expedition and for Grey here to be able to satisfy our hosts, King Phatt and his tribe." Chandler said cheerfully, holding his drink up for others to do the same.

"A successful expedition." Came the chant from the others, who raised their glasses and drank to the toast.

John felt out of his depth with these scientists as they started to discuss various aspects of the expedition, but took a particular interest in the photograph of the research vessel that was waiting for them.

After a little while, John excused himself stating that ship duties called, and was glad to leave the saloon in order for him to get himself organised for the next day's activity.

'Judging by all the attractions these islands offer, maybe I can get a trip out into the big lagoon and try my luck on some big fishing, before we sail off again.' John sighed, climbing wearily into his bunk for a well-earned rest.

Chapter XV
A Proper Fix

'**O**nly 5 in the morning and yet it seems as if I've been in my bunk forever.' John whispered to himself, rising up from his bunk and tiptoed around the cabin to gather his things together, in case he woke his fellow cabin mate.

He left the cabin and managed to see Henderson who was bustling around as usual.

"Any chance of a quick early morning cuppa Handy? I'm due to make an extra monitor of our cargo before I do the morning rounds." he asked quietly.

"Then you must have shit the bed 3rd, as I was just on my way with your tray. You can take your early breakfast in the utility cabin." Henderson replied, leading John to show him his cabin.
John took the tray off him and looked around the tiny space, to find that he must be 'in residence'.

"So this is your cabin? Not much bigger than a broom cupboard." he observed.

"That is exactly what it is 3rd. I've got four Philipino sailors in my own just down the corridor, although I can't understand what they were doing on that ship. Still, at least this place is all mine." he said bravely, as John started to eat his early breakfast.

"Is it like this for all the rest of the crew ?" John asked between hurried mouthfuls of rolls and sips of tea.

"Yes, the rest are in hammocks now. But they don't mind because we're due in port later on for the survivors to move out again. Pity really, because those Philipinos seem to be a good bunch of sailors, and we'd be happy to keep them on board, providing they work for their living, that is."

"Yes, I'll agree with you there." John replied, giving Henderson his empty plate and cup.

"Many thanks for that! Must be off now. Blackmore is due on watch at 6 o'clock, be kind as to make sure he's had a cuppa before he goes. See you later, and cheers!" John said then left the cabin.

"Morning 3rd mate! Fancy meeting up with you this early in the morning." John greeted, when he met the 3rd on the boat deck.

"Morning Grey! Just stowing all the swimming pool gear away as our guests won't need it again. Mind you, I've got the problem with their dreadnoughts." the 3rd said, pointing towards the specially re-inforced whalers.

John smiled and commiserated with the man.

"Maybe they'll want them lowered to row themselves ashore, perhaps in their native customs or something."

"Better than that, Grey. The first mate tells me that we've got to get the Med ladder ready. Something to do with the Phatties own launch coming to meet us. On reflection, I think I'd better double reeve the ladder to take their weight. Wouldn't do to dunk a King in the oggin in front of his own people." the 3rd chuckled at the thought, which John appreciated and laughed with him, sharing the same thought.

"No indeed. Anyway, I've already made my upper deck rounds and found all is well. I shall not make my report but you can relate that fact when you do yours. I've got a sick generator to see to, so see you later 3rd." John stated, and made his way over to the radio shack.

"Morning gentlemen. Tea for two is it?" John announced, stepping into the frosty atmosphere of the compartment.

"Morning John. Yes, make it two large ones, as we're ruddy freezing in here." Larter moaned, climbing out of his camp bed, still with his blanket around him.

Evans woke up with a snort and a yawn, and he too climbed out of his camp bed, still fully dressed.
John laughed at the sight of the two bleary-eyed radio officers, but felt a shiver down his back as his body had just felt the real effects of a properly air-conditioned room.

A Beach Party

"I'll put the kettle on, and maybe raise the temperature for you." he said as he tweaked the controls of the unit, then made them both a cuppa when the kettle had boiled, and offered them a cigarette each.

"Oh! Cheers John. Can't fault your timing. We're flippin perishing in this place." Evans said, swigging his tea and smoking his cigarette.

"Well gentlemen. You asked for a decent unit, and that's exactly what you got. Do you wish me to take it away?" John teased, watching his two friends still shivering inside their blankets. But kept quiet about the fact that he had a special duct rigged up to the shack that came directly from the main refrigeration plants.

"No, that's okay by us. Once we've got out onto the deck and had the sun on us, we'll be fine. Besides, it's good for our equipment." Larter said, and walked out of the shack and into the early morning sunlight.

"When is our docking time Dave?"

"We're due to contact the local harbour master in about 5 hours. So I reckon around 1200."

"Speaking of which Dave, better switch onto their radio frequency, and according to the notes, there should be a local commercial station that we can fix onto." Larter responded, and throwing off his blanket plonked his empty mug onto a shelf.

Soon a melodious tune came from one of the receivers that Evans was tuning into, as Larter operated the large DF box in the corner of the shack.

"Got him on Red 15." Larter stated as he checked his compass, then added.

"That's strange? That should be at least Green 5."

John listened to the two officers discussing the differing angles as what was supposed to be from the chart.

John thought of the ship's gyro and its compass and as to what would be the cause of a difference in angles.

"The skipper has dead reckoned our position, and as far as I'm concerned he's dead on. If your radio beacon is smack on and the direction that the commercial station is coming from, then I'd say we've got about a 40 mile gap, instead of my listed gap of about 5." Larter said with concern.

John understood tolerances within mechanical constraints, and likened it to the constraints of the radio waves and their directions.

"Will the magnetic effects of a volcano have anything to do with it?"

"Yes, John! Unless the captain used relative bearings from prominent points off the volcano and plotted it onto the chart, rather than relying on the ship's head, then I'd say we'll miss our arrival point by at least 40 miles. The proof in the pudding would be when we spot our islands and on the course we're heading, and of course the relative bearings as shown on the radar when we pick them up." Larter said slowly, concentrating on his direction finder.

John thought about this information for a moment, and excused himself as he went onto the bridge.

"Morning Andy! Enjoying a hands free cuppa this morning?" John greeted.

"Hello John. Yes, it makes a treat thanks. But what brings you onto the bridge at this time of the morning?" Sinclair asked politely.

"How long have we been on STAN? More specifically, what course are we steering and how did the captain set it?"

Sinclair looked at John for a moment, and realised that his questions were not idle ones, before he started to gather his information.

"According to the bridge log, the skipper took 4 relative bearings in the space of half an hour. Then calculated his course for the Atoll from the narrative that was kept to render assistance to that ship.

Again, that was taken from the true course that STAN was taking to that point, and was re-set when the skipper gave us the course we're now on."

A Beach Party

"So in other words, STAN has kept its mean course up to the point of going manual. Then on resuming the base course it was re set to steer on this present course. Is that right?"

"Yes John. Apart from eyeballing the Atoll and taking a bearing from it, we've got the radar to give us a proper fix. But why these questions, or is that a foolish one itself?" Sinclair enquired.

John asked Sinclair to show him on the chart, the present position of the ship.

Sinclair took the compass, and made a few calculations before making a neat pencil line on the chart.

"We're on this course, and here is our present position, give or take a few miles." Sinclair declared confidently.

"Hmm! The Mulani." John started to say when Tomlinson arrived onto the bridge from his night cabin.

"Morning 3rd, taking a few navigation lessons, are we?" Tomlinson greeted with a smile, coming to the chart table.

"Morning captain. Just checking up on STAN and the likelihood of magnetic interference from volcanic activities it might have on it, that's all."

Tomlinson looked at the chart and Sinclair's faint pencil line then at John.

"It appears that our bosun is good at his navigation plotting, but I feel there is something that you're not telling me. If I didn't know you as well as I do John, I'd say it's something to do with the ship."

"I've just come back from speaking to Larter, who has discovered, shall we say, a mismatch with the ship's course and the ships gyro, if that was at all possible. Having said that, I need to go below and check STAN in case he's had a chronic failure in trying to keep the ship on course." John explained.

Tomlinson went over to the repeater that the helmsman keeps his course with, then over to the ship's compensating binnacle that tells the real heading of the ship. He took a few moments to work out a few mathematical items before he spoke.

"It appears that STAN has kept our course as per track, but in fact the binnacle is showing that we should be at least 40 miles further west. That cluster of islands is only 30 miles wide, which means that we could miss it completely. As for this occurrence, I'd better have one of the scientists up here to explain what is going on."

"Sorry to be the one that brought the bad news Joe, but I had to check up on it of only to see if STAN was behaving as it should in these conditions." John said defensively.

"On the contrary, John. It proves your invention works perfectly even in adverse conditions. I might add that since taking into consideration of the fact that we're between two volcanoes, any magnetic activity would definitely affect our steering systems. I'll get a confirmation of this from the boffins."

John left the bridge swiftly and went below to check on his machinery, leaving Tomlinson working feverishly on his chart.

Larter arrived onto the bridge at the same time as Chandler, and between them, worked out the reason why the ship was not on the projected course as Tomlinson had plotted..

"Magnetic fields from Mulani must have affected the ship's compass before we got wise to it. But we'll soon know when Maoi becomes visible over the horizon, and when the radar can give us a proper fix." Chandler stated, coming over to the steering wheel.

"Your mechanical device for automatic steering has kept to the original base line course, despite the difference in course." Chandler observed, as John re-emerged back onto the bridge.

"I've checked the governors and limiters on the steering tackle. STAN is working normally without any undue stress. In other words, the settings I placed on its own little repeater is still showing what you're now seeing at the helm." John reported, breathlessly.

"It's okay 3rd. Tell us when you've got your breath back." Tomlinson said gently, seeing that John was holding onto Larter whilst he got his breath back.

Everybody waited until John was ready, for him to repeat what he had just said, but also explain in a much more detailed way as to how his STAN stood up to the conflicting signals the ship was giving it.

Chandler insisted that only Mulani would affect the ship's compass, for the ship to finally get back into its prejudged track again.

Tomlinson looked at the radar screen, which showed a blank picture showing that there was nothing within 20 nautical miles from the ship. He went out onto the bridge wing with his binoculars and swept the horizon from beam to beam but saw nothing.

"Tell me Mr Chandler. If we're now getting a reasonable reception from the local commercial station, and the Maoi volcano is a good 550 feet high, how is it we can't see it yet?" Tomlinson asked.

"You won't be able to see it for at least another two hours, and even then it will only be its plume of steam. It's all due to heat." Chandler started to explain but was cut short by Tomlinson.

"I understand only too well the heat haze and the mirage effects it has on ships, Mr Chandler. But a flippin volcano just over the horizon is another matter. But why can't we see even a trace of it?" Tomlinson replied irritably.

Chandler, now joined by Johanson, took a pair of binoculars from the chart table and looked out to sea for a while before he answered Tomlinson's question.

"It appears captain, that a down wind is carrying the discharge of moisture which is obscuring our vision. If you look behind us to port, you'll find a different optical effect. For you to get your ship in a direct line between Mulani and Maoi is a marvel, because of the unfavourable magnetic disturbances that would affect anybody's compass. A bit like the phenomena we've discovered off the coast of Florida and Bermuda. Suggest you keep on this mechanically contrived course until you get close enough to take a proper land fix. If you use relative bearings then all will be well but you can forget your ship's compass to provide your fixes." Johanson said quietly, taking the glasses from his eyes and handing them back to Sinclair.

Tomlinson thanked the scientists for their trouble but told them that he was about to make his morning star sights.

"That gentlemen, by guess and god, is the sure-fire way of telling me exactly where I am." He sighed, then took out his sextant, and went out onto the starboard bridge, telling Sinclair to write down his findings.[*]

The morning star fix took only a few moments, as did the calculations and the final placing onto the sea chart, before Tomlinson declared exactly where the ship really was. Right on the course he had set almost two days ago.

"It's just as well you're a good navigator captain, as many a ship have missed the Taraniti Archipelago by several hundred miles, or ending up some days later by floundering themselves on the extended barrier reef the other side of the Darnier plateau." Chandler said with a nod, and the scientists left the bridge with John following behind them.

---

[*] The captain's experience of taking sun / star sights with a sextant rather than rely on any navigational aids, such as the Decca or Loran arrays used in that era.

A Beach Party

Chapter XVI
Take a Seat

The sun rose out of the black ocean like a yellow ball, and took its place in the deep blue sky that was devoid of any cloud, save the long thin wispy trail of steam from the volcano made by the soft tropical breezes.

John was on the boat deck taking his after breakfast cigarette, and listening to the soft music coming from the faraway atoll that, like a pimple, was growing up out of the horizon.

He saw a large sea bird land onto the deck, it had a really long beak with a vicious-looking hook at the end of it, and very large webbed feet. The plumes of feathers of several different colours were stunningly iridescent, and they seemed to shimmer in the morning light. He kept very quiet so as not to spook this amazing bird, as he watched it waddle along it for a little while before it gave a large squawk and flew away up into the morning sky.

'I wouldn't mind getting a few of its feathers to make my lures. I wonder what type of fish I could catch with them.' he mused, finishing his cigarette and going below to his cabin.

"Morning Blackie. Going on watch are we?" John asked civilly, meeting Blackmore struggling with his greasy overalls.

"Just come off actually. Missed breakfast, so ask the steward to rustle me up a bite would you John."

"Certainly! By the way, it looks as if land is in sight, and we'll probably be along side for lunch." John volunteered.

"Oh well then John. I'll be able to grab a few hours kip before then, that's if you'd do the honours for me on deck when we arrive."

"No problem Blackie, wouldn't miss it for the world. I prefer being on deck during those times anyway. Ah! Here's the steward, he'll put you right." John replied, beckoning Henderson to come to the cabin.

Both men had a few minutes chat before John left Blackmore to get turned in, as he was now on his way onto the upper deck to enjoy the spectacle of the ever-growing atoll that the passengers were gazing out to from their own little places on the deck.

When John arrived on deck he was amazed, as indeed were the rest of the people on board, at the sight unfolding right in front of them

King Phatt and his entourage emerged from the saloon and onto the deck, all bedecked in their finest national costumes, much to the surprise and delight of the other passengers.

King Phatt and his Queen were dressed in golden robes with large iridescent feather plumes on their heads. From their ears, necks, hands and feet hung thick gold chains with ivory and coral trinkets dangling from them.

The so called 'ugly' females were totally naked save for the several golden chains adorning their bodies, not even a piece of cloth to save their modesty. Each one of them carried an ivory rod with a large multi-coloured feathered fan on the end.

They were followed closely by two large men of almost Sumo Wrestler build who carried a large white banner between them which portrayed a large red sun over a menacingly wicked bird clutching a garland in the shape of the islands in its talons.

John managed to liken the large sea bird he had seen to the one depicted on the magnificent banner, and marvelled at the richness of colour the maker of the banner had managed to capture to make such a startling likeness.

The girls were singing in harmony that would grace any decent chapel choir, as King Phatt and his Queen strutted around for all to see. Then from almost nowhere, six equally naked men, daubed in various gaudy colours of paint, pranced around shaking their large spears and swords in a threatening manner at anybody who dared to come too close to their monarch. All this was done in time to the beat of some sort of ukulele or guitar type of music and drums that a second group was playing as they too arrived on deck.

A Beach Party

'Sounds like the type of music we're getting from the local radio station.' John whispered, and spontaneously clapped his hands in unison with the rest of the passengers, when the music had stopped.

King Phatt pointed out to the atoll with his gold and jewel encrusted ivory stick, then uttered a spiel in his native tongue. When he had finished speaking, the music and songs took over for a few minutes until he spoke again in Pidgin English.

"We have made the long swim to see the great white Queen from the east, and we bless the lord for our safe return. We thank the great white Queen for her gifts and may she long reign in peace over her people. We have brought an iceman to help us fight the fiery demons and live our lives as befitting a noble race, and we offer thanks to our traditional gods of the Fire Mountain Mulani for his deliverance."

Once the men stopped prancing around they disappeared, only to return with two large ornately carved ivory chairs that were covered in precious metal and stones, with a large canopy over each of them made out of the same iridescent feathers as the fans. Once these chairs were placed onto the deck, and the two monarchs sat upon them, the flag bearers and the fan wavers gathered around them.

'The King and Queen of the Phatties were now in residence.' John guessed, as two carved wooden stools were placed under their feet, then the music started up again.

John stood at his chosen spot on the foc'sle to watch the ship skirt around the coral reef and islands that marked the outer boundary of the 'deep' lagoon.

The atoll looked breathtaking as the two emerald green islands rose starkly out of the sparkling blue lagoon.

He had his binoculars with him to see a flotilla of out-rigger type fishing boats being rowed swiftly alongside a very large wooden craft that to John looked like an ancient Greek Trireme.

The multi-coloured vessel moved majestically through the water as the two tiers of oars moved in unison to propel it along.

The carved figurehead on its prow was an exact replica of the motifs on the banners. Between the wind filling the snow-white sails that bore the same motif and the figurehead with its outstretched wings, it seemed as if the sea bird was alive and pulling the craft along with ease.

'Must be the national flag and the symbol of these island people' he guessed, as the craft glided to a stop in the only safe entrance to the lagoon.

The *Inverlogie* was almost stopped by the time she arrived at the entrance, but could not go any further until this replica of an ancient craft moved out of the way.

Virtually all those on board who were able to do so were on deck to watch all of this, and stood silently to witness the home coming ritual of the King and Queen of the Taranitian people, but recently re-dubbed by the crew as the Phatt-arsed tribe.

The magnificent wooden ship moved slowly and gracefully alongside the *Inverlogie,* as trumpets and drums were being played. King Phatt and his retinue slowly descended the steps of the Med ladder and stepped onto his own ship. Once all his retinue were on board, the King turned and waved his ornate baton, which was the signal for his ship to move away. In a cacophony of sound from the drums, horns and a melodious chanting from the attendants, the craft sped away with each impeccably timed strokes of its oars.

John felt the ship tremble slightly and seeing a puff of smoke coming from the funnel, guessed that the ship had been given permission to enter the lagoon, by following a small outrigger fishing boat which led the way to the harbour complex.

The ship seemed to squeeze its way through the narrow entrance of a very high outer wall, which formed the breakwater for the harbour. Tomlinson had turned the ship around so that it entered the snug harbour going astern. There were two smaller ships at the other end of the harbour with people lining the side to watch the much larger *Inverlogie* stop neatly alongside its allocated berth.

John noticed that all the walls, buildings, docksides and warehouses were slate grey and made of solid concrete or rock,

A Beach Party

but there was an abundance of colours everywhere as if to make up for its drabness. He also noticed large metal doors that were opened to reveal dark caverns in the towering rock formations.

He had to crane his neck to look up a steep cliff face to see what looked like a castle hewn out of the rock, and ancient cannons poking their muzzles out of the battlements.

The familiar nudge of the ship as she kissed the dock was the signal that she had finally arrived safely into port; from her own long swim that has taken her from her home to the other side of the world.

Just like the model in every detail. Including the palm lined avenue of the causeway between the two islands. It's going to be fun exploring this lot.' John mused, but his exploratory gaze was interrupted by the sound of rhythmic music and singing coming from the dockside.

There were several lines of topless girls only wearing grass skirts as they sang and danced to the music played by equally dressed men. Each person had many colourful garlands of flowers around their necks and was throwing flower petals up into the air for the wind to scatter, making their way to the ship's side before coming to a halt by the for'ard gangway.

To everybody's surprise, Tomlinson walked slowly down the gangway, dressed in his white tropical uniform but with a blue and gold trimmed ermine cloak draped over his shoulders and wearing the coronet of a lord. When he stepped ashore the music played into a crescendo before it stopping for a bevy of girls who came forward, each placing one of their garlands around his neck. Just when it seemed that he would suffocate from them all, two very large men appeared with a sedan type of chair, that Tomlinson climbed into before being carried away by the same dancing and singing crowd.

"Fergus told me that he was a lord, but it looks as if he's much more to these people." John whispered, still watching the welcoming ceremony of the local people making their way out of the dockyard.

"Still talking to yourself John? But you seem to be right there.

Let's hope he has a few of those beauties spare for us to borrow for a few days." Sinclair answered with a grin, as he arrived and stood next to John.

"This place is becoming a rich tourist attraction that would outshine most other places around the world. Apparently there're a few good hotels on the island, several beach bars, a casino and even a government run brothel, for the likes of us to amuse ourselves with. There're also a couple of jails with very large policemen in them, so don't go looking for trouble as those girls you've just seen are definitely jail bait, Andy."

"How do you know all that John?" Sinclair asked in amazement.

"Simple dear friend. Perhaps you don't know it, but apart from what I've been doing aboard, my primary duties on board this vessel were to ensure the safe passage of the cargo we're carrying. All of it is in refrigeration or kept in a reasonable condition for these islanders to consume until the next vessel arrives to top up their supplies. As such we have been a trial ship with refrigeration, radar, echo-sounding equipment and other such gadgets around the ship with our group of scientists and the two civil engineers we brought along.

These people have been here several times before and are the very ones that helped rebuild and modernise the infrastructure of King Phatt's kingdom some years ago now. They were the ones telling us about the place and what to expect. In fact, one of the engineers is from your part of the world, but he says that as he's been coming back to these islands time after time, he's deciding to stay here for the rest of his natural. Save on bus fares he reckons, but admits to the fact that King Phatt has promised him a reward and a place of his own. "

"If he can get his hands on a few of those beauties to keep for himself just to tide him over, then who'd blame him, lucky bastard."

"What would your maidens from Barbados say if they had heard what you've just said, Andy?"

A Beach Party

"S'pose you're right. Anyway, Barbados is nearer to home than this." Sinclair conceded glumly.

"Whatever, Andy. Anyway, once the customs people and the local medicine man has seen to you all, you'll be able to step ashore and taste the local delights at your will. According to Bruce, we'll be here for a good 7 days, maybe a little more for everybody to enjoy themselves. He's been given several brochures on the place for us to use, but from what I've been told, tell your men to steer well clear of the local bobbies and out of trouble. They might wear the same blue helmets our Bobbies wear, and speak our language up to a point, but although they wear long white skirts, they're all the size of a Sumo wrestler. Add to all that, they're also armed with razor sharp spears that would do a Zulu proud."

"Trouble? What me! I'm as quiet as a lamb and wouldn't hurt a flea, John."

John laughed at his friend's pretended innocence before he decided it was time to get himself organised

"3rd Engineer Grey is requested to attend the saloon." came the announcement from the tannoy system.

"You heard the man Andy, so time to get moving. I've got a meeting with the scientists before they go ashore. Give me about two hours, but get Bruce and I'll see you both on the gangway." John concluded then left.

"Hello Grey! Come and take a seat." Chandler invited, as John entered the saloon.

John smiled and sat in the seat offered and was given a drink from an attending steward, whom he thanked, before taking a sip from it.

"Now that we're all here, and before we leave the ship for our hotel, I wish to toast our arrival and I would like to take this opportunity to wish us all a successful expedition. Here's to the expedition!" Chandler stated, raising his glass for everybody to join him.

Chandler then went on to outline their objectives and joint efforts that would include their new research vessel, which was due to arrive shortly, then offered one more toast, before Johanson took over.

"To the *Maoi I'ti Princess!*" Chandler pronounced and everybody drank the last from their glasses before the ever-alert stewards quickly refilled them again.

"You're among the elite around here 3rd. Just as well the skipper is ashore with King Phatt." Henderson whispered in John's ear, handing John a fresh glass that seemed fuller than all the others given out.

"Cheers steward! This will definitely whet my appetite for the delectable food the chef has lined up for us." John whispered aside, but with sarcasm.

"We've got fresh fruit, veg and suckling pig for dinner today, thanks to our Phatt friends. I'll keep you a plate if you're not around." the steward whispered back, smiled and left.

"According to our engineers, the new food reception area is now ready for the refrigeration units to be installed. Mr Grey here will be assisting us in that endeavour." Johanson said, outlining the work to be carried out, and in such a short space of time.

To John there seemed to be a hidden agenda somewhere for everybody was eager to complete their various missions by a certain date. He couldn't put a finger on it nor could he get any answers from his direct questioning. In the end, he decided that whatever it was, he'd hope to conclude his own side of the work just so that he could have a few days off, and just do what only he wanted to do without anybody impinging on his own personal time.

John noticed Day had entered the saloon, dressed in civilian clothes, which meant that he was now officially off duty. He was joined by a couple of the other officers and just sat at the bar taking it easy whilst this meeting was taking place. He managed to catch Day's eye, and acknowledged Day with a nod of his head, who returned it with one of his own.

A Beach Party

"And so to the nitty-gritty. Mr Grey will be in charge of the cargo discharge and the installation of the insulation and refrigeration units that are on board. That should take us two days, with a further day to get the desired result Mr Grey has achieved on the ship. That gentlemen, is the real challenge, as the rest is just down to survey and research work." Johanson concluded, and looked over to John for comment.

John acknowledged the polite clap of appreciation as he stood up to make his own speech, which he likened to the one he made in Las Palmas seemingly a lifetime away.

"Thank you all for your support gentlemen. I fear that my end of the bargain as struck by his majesty King Phatt, will be the easiest to accomplish. This has been due to the not inconsiderable efforts as performed by the officers and men of the *Inverelogie*. For me to get the right results, I must insist however, that before I start, I must be taken around the entire underground system to be able to set my benchmarks by.

It would be no good to have a fridge right next to a furnace, if you get my meaning. Until I personally am satisfied with the unloading conditions, the cargo will remain on board. The sooner we get organised, the sooner the islanders will be able to enjoy the delights of their Kings' shopping list, so to speak. His majesty has already dubbed me his 'Iceman' so to keep the honour going, I give you the success of Operation Ice man." John said evenly, and raising his glass gave the toast.

John observed that everybody stood up and drank the toast, including all the other officers that were in the background. He noticed that Day was now in company with Tomlinson and saw the satisfaction on their faces, as they too offered their salutations in unison with everybody else.

The meeting seemed to finish abruptly as the scientists and other passengers started to gather their already packed suitcases and belongings, before making their way out of the saloon and down onto the gangway, where several porters were waiting to receive them.

John escorted them down to the gangway and waved them off as they were taken away by a gaily-coloured motor vehicle, which looked like a miniature train towing several equally colourful trailers with rows of seats to sit upon.

Once everybody was on board the conductor picked up a long pole and hooked it to an overhead cable strung between poles along the entire length of the road. There was a spark of electricity from the cable before the vehicle moved off with a buzzing noise, passing a similar one coming the other way.

"A cross between a small train and a standard Belfast trolley bus." John whispered in amusement, listening to the hum and crackling of the pantographs that connected the overhead electric wires and the drive vehicle.

A Beach Party

Chapter XVII
A Stuffed Pig

"It's like an underground city, with plenty of light and fresh air too. These caverns must have taken ages to hack out. Unless of course they used a tunnel maker, what do you say Happy?" John asked, as McIntyre conducted his tour of the underground workings from the back of one of the trolley trains.

"Very impressive stuff, but I've already noticed the variety of machinery and how some of them look as if they came from the proverbial ARK. See that one over there John? It is one of the old 2 stroke, direct blow steam engines, and by the look of it is used as a mid-flow pump."

"It's as if somebody didn't send them the same machinery for they are mixed and matched, so to speak. I for one would like to know where they keep the manuals for them, as they seem a nightmare to maintain."

"The trick there John is to remember that most of this hardware is run by steam. It's the electrics and suchlike will invoke a few nightmares.

The train stopped at a large steel door that seemed to have more rivets than expanses of steel.

"We are now 50 feet below water level gentlemen. This is the Turbine cathedral, which is the biggest of them all. The reinforced doors you see, are exact replicas of those watertight doors you have on the *Inverlogie*. They shut automatically by a special alarm system, which is activated by any leakage or ingress of water along this tunnel. Any personnel trapped within it, has a special exit lift shaft to take them up through the ceiling and onto the first tunnel level. All sealed in case of flooding, naturally." McIntyre explained.

The group of officers and scientists were taken around the massive cave, and shown the very large turbines that were humming loudly as they spun in their mountings, as they dwarfed the humans they in turn were dwarfed by the cave.

"Here are the pipes that have been injected into the steam vent. They each have a special flap valve which drops into place to prevent any water coming through when the vent changes from steam to water. We don't need any gauges or alarms as the vent-shaft itself acts as our alarm, due to it vibrating to give off a harmonica type of sound which tells us that water is about to come up instead of the steam. The other vents in the main volcano shaft act the same way and a bit like organ pipes. Thus when it is ready to blow the water out, it builds up to a four note harmonic sound which tells everybody on this side of the atoll to get under cover at whatever level they might be next to."

"Excuse me, but if the steam gets shut down therefore the turbines get switched off for the duration, what makes the electricity in the meanwhile?" Johanson asked politely, gazing around the equipment.

McIntyre pointed to another but much larger set of pipes coming from a different part of the vent wall.

"When the water spurts upwards, it spins a series of impellers that rotates these pipes which turns the second set of turbines, which when connected up to a large dynamo, produces the amount of electric needed for emergency usage only. The pipes turn just like propeller shafts on a ship, and in fact that's just what they are and where they came from."

"How thick is that vent wall? In fact how were you able to stick these props and all the other pipes into it without getting cut to ribbons by the steam, or scalded by the water?" Johanson persisted.

McIntyre stated that all information and other assistance would be given him in due course, but for him just to see everything in situ.

"I have just one question for you McIntyre. Considering the mix and match of machinery, and all this iron and steelwork we've seen, and with no apparent steelworks on the atoll, where did everything come from for you to assemble such a mechanical marvel as this?" John asked with keen interest in all he had seen.

A Beach Party

"Ship salvage, Mr Grey. These islanders are excellent recyclers of old ships, and have been doing so for the best part of 200 years. Especially the ones that founder on the coral reefs surrounding the lagoon. These people had stripped every piece of debris, and even whole ships down, like a plague of locusts they are when a ship goes aground. The steel doors you saw, are probably the remains of the sides of a ship. The pipework, ladders, capstans, engines, valves, tools, cabin furniture even personal belongings are brought ashore and kept in a special cave for 'After life' as the locals put it." Chandler answered.

John looked at Day with amazement at what they had heard.

"So that's it Happy. They want to strip our ship of its insulation and probably right down to its bare bones, so that they can have their refrigeration unit. But if that's the case, what's the hidden agenda from Belverly and co? I mean how can they explain away a very large freighter and the loss of the entire crew?" John whispered.

"Maybe the captain can answer that when we see him, John. I feel as if we're the next victims waiting in a slaughter house." Day responded.

As there were no further questions, McIntyre called the guided tour to a close and got everybody back onto the train to leave.

"For our return back to the dockyard, I have saved the best to last for you all. It is a natural wonder that is but one of many these islands have to offer the scientists of the world, such as our very own Speleologist, Professor Turner. He's absolutely the number one in the study of caves and tunnels." McIntyre announced, as the train buzzed along the wide tunnel that ran under the entire length of the causeway between the two main islands.

Soon the train stopped at a large flight of concrete stairs that ascended up to a large open doorway, akin to the one each tunnel entrance has. The fresh sea air and the sounds of people on top going about their business was an odd experience for them all, but it was the short and equally solid stairway to a shut steel doorway that was the real attraction.

"Here we are gentlemen. When it is necessary for everybody to get below, including any livestock that they might have with them, everybody goes in through these doors, like so." Turner announced, and turned a large wheel that started to open the heavy doors.

When the doors were fully opened there was an eerie light glowing from the otherwise black hole.

"It's all right gentlemen. Come inside and see for yourselves." he assured, waving everybody inside, then explained exactly what and how this breathtaking vista existed.

"It is an underground lake, complete with its own coral sand, and even with its own fresh air breezes. The phosphorescence makes the light you see, which comes from millions of little organisms called plankton. Almost as bright as the rising sun, wouldn't you think?

The water in fact is fresh, as are the fish that live in it, and has a maximum depth of 2 fathoms at the bottom end. The cave ceiling is over 80feet high, and covers virtually all the seabed area from the 'pink lagoon' above us. The rock is of the impervious type and belonging to the I'ti' island as opposed to the porous type on Maoi. We've been puzzling as to why there is a slight tide, albeit 6 inches or so. We suspect that the water is coming in from the fresh water basin, but where exactly it leaks in and out from is one of our projects on this visit. If one of our theories proves correct, then it won't take long to find out. In the meantime, this is where a lot of the islanders like to come and see their 'ancestral spirits and ancient gods' despite the Christian face of King Phatt and his family." he explained to the amazed group of men.

"This place is a paradise for you scientists, and a nightmare for us sailors. Especially those of us from the engineering world." John stated civilly, picking up a handful of sand to smell it then dipping his finger into the water, tasted it to find it was pleasant.

"This sand is fresh, as is the water. This place is like a desert oasis." he added.

A Beach Party

Collier nodded his head and asked them all to get back aboard the train for them to get back.

The train arrived in the small terminal cave next to the Harbour masters building complex, where everyone was obliged to get off and walk the short distance to the ship.

John noticed that the two smaller ships had left, but a bright-red painted ship was docked in their place.

He judged by the strange gantries and equipment that the ship was possibly the research vessel Chandler was on about. He decided to go on board instead of satisfying his curiosity, as he would probably end up on it during some time or another before he left these strange islands.

"Just in time for lunch John!" Larter greeted, as John arrived into the saloon.

"Hello Bruce! Good show, but I'm here for a thirst quencher before that. Any mail for me?"

"Yes, you've got the replies to your two telegrams, but they're in the office at the moment if you want me to fetch them for you. Obviously I know their contents John, and it's just as well we're good friends so I can mention one of them. I say this because of the nature of the message, and to prepare you for what you will read." Larter said with enough concern, for John to sit down with his newly acquired drink.

John looked at Larter for a moment then said quietly.

"It must be bad for you to say so Bruce, and I've a feeling it must be something to with my parents. Perhaps if you'd get them for me, I'll wait here before we go to dinner."

"On my way John. See you in about two minutes." Larter said and quickly left the saloon, bumping into Day on his way past.

"Your friend is in a big hurry John, what's wrong with him?" Day asked, rubbing his shoulder where he got bumped.

"On a mercy mission I guess Happy, you know what Sparkers are like. Anyway, what about that tour we did. Pretty horrendous don't you think?" John replied changing the subject.

"Yes it certainly was. Now we know the extent of the strip down John, just as well you containerised all the cargo, like you did on the *Inverlaggan*. I'll get some real info from Tomlinson later when I've had my lunch, as I'm starving."

"Well according to Walters, we've got stuffed pig for dinner. But I've got the feeling that we're going to be the bloody stuffed pigs around here."

"Yes indeed. Still it's probably not what it seems, and there's probably a good explanation even if mirrors by the boffins do it all. Speaking of which, get yourself free later on this afternoon, as we've been invited on board their ship. Something like the do in Barbados I shouldn't wonder, no excuses or absentees I understand."

"Well Happy, you know what happened there. I for one will definitely not be there to face another go at it. Anyway, I've got other things to take care of, so kindly offer my apologies for me." John said defiantly, to which Day responded with a shake of his head.

"Sorry to pull rank on you 3rd, but I need my officers to show willing and offer me some support you know. In the meantime, I hope to get our mystery solved by the captain before then."

"Putting it like that is tantamount to blackmail chief. But if you insist, then who am I to say otherwise. Anyway chief, how's about a nice cold beer whilst we're waiting for lunch to be served?" John smiled, and held his empty glass out for Day to take.

Day took the empty glass and grinned at John's cheeky response.

"At your service. One cube or two in your drink Mr Iceman?" he asked, tugging his forelock, before going to get a drink for them both.

Larter arrived back with the two telegrams and handed them over to John, who examined them to see which one he'd open first.

He read the one from Helena first and was cheerful about what she told him and what he could look forward to when he got home again.

A Beach Party

"That was the good news John! Now for the not so good!" Larter said softly, as Day arrived with the drinks.

"Give John a moment will you chief, he's got something to get his head around first." Larter advised, as Day put John's drink down in front of him before he too sat down.

John read through the telegram a couple of times, before he spoke.

"Bruce, Happy! How can I send a large amount of money home that I don't have? Only my mother needs several hundred pounds more, to send my father to a special medical treatment centre in Switzerland. So far she's already spent over two thousand pounds, which has wiped out all our savings, including my 'pension funds', leaving us almost penniless." He asked glumly.

"Simple John. Go and see the purser and ask him to remit the amount directly from your pay account in Belfast, instead of drawing it whilst on board. You're worth a good £500 since we left Barbados, and probably still got enough to settle your tally on board, now that we've arrived at our outward destination. If you need more, then you'll have to ask for an advance of pay to be taken from your account on the return leg." Day answered cheerfully, trying to make light of a grave situation.

"Hey! The man's right John, and that should help you to reply back. Anyway, let's have lunch now, and you can go and see him afterwards." Larter agreed, giving John a pat on the back.

John looked at his friend's faces and judged that they were right and not just trying to cheer him up.

"Well that's that sorted, and bang goes my excuse for attending that boffins do, Happy." John finally replied, with a grin on his face.

"Come on now 3rd! You're starting to push your luck on that score. Family bad luck is one thing, but this is a different kettle of fish. If I've got to go, so will the rest of you. Besides, we're all engineers and boffins together." Day said with a grin, tapping the three gold bars on his epaulette.

133

Chapter XVIII
Delivery Boy

"**G**ood afternoon gentlemen, its good of you to attend our little celebration." Chandler greeted, when Day; John and two other engineer officers arrived into the saloon of the research vessel.

After the introductions were made, two men carrying a large map and some paper rolls appeared, with Sinclair coming behind them, and proceeded to set up some sort of display with them. When it was over, the men sat at the back of the gathering as two scientists got up and positioned themselves by the display.

"I am Professor Mackenzie of the Hydrographic survey team, who's job it is to analyse the logs and tracings of the new echo sounders that were placed on the *Inverlogie* and the *Maoi I'ti Princess*. It therefore gives me great pleasure to announce a major geographical discovery. Here we have the large area map of Mulani. The unbroken line you see is the route of the *Inverlogie*, and the dotted one is the route taken by our own vessel." Mackenzie stated, and went through the rolls of paper explaining what the squiggly lines on them meant, before he delivered his explanation as to what the discovery was.

"The *Inverlogie* was given a special piece of sounding equipment to test, that measures the depth from the ships keel to the sea-bed, and is known as a deep-water echo-sounder. Basically it bounces a beam of sound downwards then measures the time it takes for the echo to return, thus indicating the depth of water. In fact it's based on the same principle as the new radar scanners. This ship was also equipped with the same equipment, and wherever both ships went, the echo- sounder marked its trace onto these rolls of paper. On the downside of it, both ships should have recorded different parts of the ocean as they traversed it, thus helping us to create a better picture of the ocean floor. Then again, on the upside of things however, and is where science makes it more interesting, is that both ships courses ran

A Beach Party

pretty well on a similar bearing up to the point marked on the chart, until they took opposite courses around Mulani, that is. From the rolls of both echo-sounder logs the traces registered a mean depth of the ocean floor. As you can see, pretty much of a muchness." Mackenzie said, pointing to the places on the paper where he wanted everybody to pay close attention to.

"There gentlemen, you see that the *Inverlogie* trace shows a deep area measuring some 1200 fathoms, along its course for 3 nautical miles up to the next X on the chart. The *Princess* who was some hours behind her shows exactly the same depth, but as I've said, measured it from the other side of Mulani, before both ships crossed onto their new courses. Therefore gentlemen, what I've discovered is a new trench in the Pacific seabed circling the Mulani volcano that was not recorded nor discovered earlier. There is my proof and as the discoverer, I have the traditional right to name it." Mackenzie said with excitement, with all the rest gazing at the evidence of what was a profound discovery.

Mackenzie picked up his drink to indicate that he was to name his discovery and make a toast to it.

"Gentlemen, I give you the Mackenzie Trench!" he said proudly.

"To the Mackenzie Trench!" was the polite reply as everybody toasted the man, before giving him a loud applause and a hearty cheer.

After a few speeches and vows to undertake various pathfinding surveys and researches of the Darnier plateau, it became apparent to John and the rest of the ships engineers that they were only there to make up the numbers.

"I don't know about you Happy, but I want some answers from this lot before our ship gets used as a spare parts store for this place. Any suggestions?" John whispered aside to Day.

"You and me both, John. I have something that springs to mind that maybe you'd appreciate, seeing as I lectured you on the subject in Belfast. So here goes." Day whispered back, before he cleared his throat noisily and posed a general question to the scientists.

"Whilst we of the *Inverlogie* are simple mechanical engineers by your standards, can somebody explain how, or the logic behind the principle of freezing a cubic area the size of two football pitches with only bare rock as its walls? Also, just how would it be possible to maintain the critical temperatures required by different products that share the same storage area?"

"It's quite simple Chief Day, it's all to do with temperatures." a scruffy man started to say in an arrogant and condescending way, but was cut short by John, who stepped right up close to the man.

"Look here pal! We're marine engineers, and I'm the one that conducted the trials on board, and maintained the critical levels required for the cargo to arrive here in safety. That was despite bumping into a burning ship let alone a ruddy great furnace you lot call Mulani. So cut the bloody crap by looking down your nose at us, and give us a proper and civil answer that those questions demand." John snarled.

John's outburst silenced the place instantly, which led to a pregnant pause before Chandler stood up and told the man to sit down and shut up.

"Kindly accept our apologies for any indiscretion by Moore here. Your questions do need careful consideration but all we can say is that until we actually install the equipment then the products, there's not a lot we can offer you. Your trials have been completed, now it's all down to Mr Moore and his team to sort it all out. We plan for you to have your equipment taken off the ship tomorrow morning and to receive the ships cargo."

"That's all fine stuff Chandler, but just how do you intend keeping the cargo safe until then?" Day asked politely, which drew anxious looks between Moore and Chandler, and yet another awkward pause.

"We've already got the place in 'CHILL' mode as a temporary measure, but we need the rapid speed of which the cargo gets

A Beach Party

unloaded and stored is the criteria and the most critical stage of the operation." Moore said truculently.

John looked at Day and the other two engineers and spoke quite bluntly to the scientists.

"We've heard enough. If you want a swift discharge of cargo then that's what you'll get. I don't know about you chief Day, but I feel a distinct 'Barbados moment' coming on. Let's get out of here." John snarled and stormed his way through the scientists and made his way off the ship, followed closely by the other engineers, with Sinclair tagging along as 'Tail end Charlie'.

"I swear to God, I would have swung for that Moore, Happy. Let's get back on board to a more sensible bunch of men, even though they are the crew."

John was on the for'ard cargo deck, taking charge of the discharge of cargo from the ship.

"Blackie, that's the last acu and fridge trials unit gone ashore, let's hope they know how to re- assemble and run it. Get the ships' own units ramped up and in full flow, as I don't want to lose any cargo on the stupidity of those so-called boffins we met yesterday. 3rd Mate, get a team of men and start dismantling the cargo holds, starting with the after holds 5 through to 8. The local dockyard matey will be using his crane to off load the cargo, so when you've finished, I want you to have your team to assist him by using the after derricks, and pile it up onto the jetty for the dock workers to clear away. You will appreciate that as this is virtually a furnace of a place, discharging the cargo must be done quickly to prevent defrosting or spoilage. 5th Engineer, you will sit somewhere prominent and write down all the cargo types that are being off loaded, from for'ard as well don't forget. When the last cargo net has been landed, you'll get yourself into the stores cave and see how the cargo has been handled. By that I mean, if it's under air conditioning or just left lying around. I shall be along to check up on you, so unless you want several more lace holes up your arse then do the job properly." John explained, before asking for any questions or observations to be made by the men. As none was offered, John started them off, then went for'ard to the bridge to see Tomlinson.

"Morning Joe! I've come to let you know that we're all set to off load our cargo from aft. That will go first as it's 'live' and will be the first to try out the island's new ice cave." John stated evenly, when he entered Tomlinson's cabin.

"Hello John! Yes, that's fine, but I'm a bit worried about the for'ard cargo and its discharge. From what our boffins have told me, they're not ready to receive it, yet you've already stripped the equipment and sent it ashore. Why's that?" Tomlinson enquired, reading through a thick book with the title 'FINAL DISCHARGE'.

"Once the boffins told me to strip down the trials equipment for them to re-assemble in the ice caves, the onus came off me and onto them. I warned them that if they denuded the cargo holds of that equipment, the ships own units would not cope with the extra demands. I also told them that before the transfer would take place, they had to have a specially cooled holding area until such times as the caverns had reached the optimum temperatures.

As that would take several days and they were in a hurry, I was shouted down by their own man in charge of the operations, whose only strategy is in the speed of transfer from ship to cavern.

He opted for the 'live' after cargo to be taken first, which and according to him, would give him a bit more time in preparing for the 'dead' cargo from for'ard. But then I'm only a mere 3rd marine engineer, so what do I know." John replied nonchalantly, which was noticed by Tomlinson.

"You seem to forget John, we've got a company duty to uphold, let alone the goodwill of the King and his government. What does Chief Day say about all this?"

"He's in full agreement with me. He states that they need separate holding areas or caverns with the suitable refrigerants

A Beach Party

and temperature controls, just like the ship had, otherwise there will be a high cargo wastage, and in the end only fit for dumping overboard. Also given that this place is smack on the equator and with a huge fire on the arse end of the islands, it would be foolhardy to even attempt such a transfer."

"Well this is just a trial run John, and the company has already accepted the probability of a 95% cargo loss, or dunnage as its known by. Anyway, they've already got the underwriters standing by to cover it. I have noticed a small clause in the rules governing my actions, or interpretations of them that is, which means that once we've discharged our full cargo we no longer exist as a fridge ship. I have the authority to collect what suitable cargo there is between here and Australia or Malaya, before we return to Belfast with it."

"Now he tells me that I've been wasting my time on a mere 5% success. All those days working all those hours for just that? Why didn't you tell me before we sailed Joe, it would have saved us all the bother of coming out here in the first place." John said, beginning to feel angry at the position they were in.

"As I've just said John. We had to give this trial a good go, without any pre-knowledge of what the ship owners were up to. If the ship gets stripped right down so that it's only a general goods freighter then so be it. It's their ship John, but at least we've proved we've done our job to the utmost as we've been paid to. We can hold our heads up on that score, even if the ship gets trashed by that so called boffin Moore."

"But that is a total waste of a good ship Joe. This part of the world must be crying out for our type of vessel, especially if we could bring tropical fruits back to the UK, or even a whole shipload of Aussie or Kiwi mutton. There must be somebody in the meat trade that would pay top money for this type of ship, Joe."

"I'm fully aware of the opportunities John, but at the moment we're at the mercy of the boffins. If they take all our insulation and equipment just to bolster theirs, then we're stumped."

"I haven't had the time to get ashore to enjoy this island, but from what I've read from the brochures, there's plenty of natural minerals we could bring aboard, and say, ship to Australia. You could organise a dickey refit to re-install our insulation material so that we can return the way we came, a fridge ship full of much needed fruit, or whatever. I mean, let's face it Joe, we were on a hiding to nothing from the word go anyway, so what's to lose?"

Tomlinson looked at his book then at John, before he finally spoke.

"If we're to offer the boffins all of our insulation material just so that they can fulfil their own ends, then it would certainly let us off the hook as far as the King and his government is concerned. Mind you, we'd have to be re-imbursed with a high value cargo in return, that would be valuable or of great use to another country. I have a few ideas on that score myself, but it's still in design stage until I let the rest of you know. As I've already been in the King's court and conducted business with his government today, I suppose they'll find my proposals harmless and probably laugh amongst themselves at being able to outwit an 'Eastern' sea captain."

"In that case Joe, they'll have the lot and I'll get the cargo dumped ashore just as they wanted it.

It will take me a day or so to re-organise the cargo holds again, mind you. Not being a deck officer, I reckon that we'd be talking about three days before you get a cargo together, and maybe a further day to load up before we sail. We don't have to refuel as you know, just some fresh provisions to get us to wherever you wish to take us, Malaya or Aussie land."

"That just about sums it up John. In the meantime, I'll get the first mate to have his men working overtime to get the cargo off my ship and have it ready for re-loading in three days. Unless the chief has anything further for you to do, as far as I'm concerned you can take a well earned rest ashore."

"That's fair enough Joe, and thanks. Must be getting back to my tasks now or the crew might get restless." John stated, as he went to leave the cabin.

A Beach Party

"By the way and just before you go John. I heard about your Father and hope he makes a full recovery, but if you need an extra couple of hundred for his treatment just see the purser, and I'll underwrite it for you." Tomlinson said in a softer tone of voice.

John looked at Tomlinson's face and knew he meant it, and accepted it gracefully.

"Thank you Joe, I'll do just that. That will take a load off my mind for a while anyway."

"Glad to be of service John. Now get that ruddy cargo off my ship if you would, and let them worry if it rots on the jetty. See you sometime." Tomlinson concluded with a cheerful smile then dismissed him with the customary wave of his hand

"3rd mate, commence the off loading from aft now using the derricks, then inform your 2nd mate to start off loading the cargo from for'ard at the same time. We have to do it in tandem or the ship will take on a dangerous list, so just pile it neatly on the jetty for the dockworkers to shift.

Once the holds have been cleared and cleaned by the men, they can wrap in. Tell them it's job and finish for a day or two at least, that will get them working like Trojans." John ordered, beckoning the 5th engineer over.

"5th, you be on your toes now. You've got both main holds being discharged, but to help you and you'd better listen up carefully. All the for'ard holds will be offloading 'dead' cargo, which are all the deep frozen stuff, tinned products and the like. The after holds have all the 'live' stuff such as tea, coffee, sugar, etc. Make sure you log each batch coming off, such as 20 tons of tea, 200tons of powdered milk etc. The 5th mate will have the cargo manifesto and will be with you to help out. Have you got that, or do I explain it in more detail?"

"I understand you 3rd, and I've got my thermometer ready too." the 5th replied, holding it up for John to see.

"Well at least that's a start 5th. Once the cargo has been cleared from the ship, you take your list to the chief, then report back to me. I'll be with the acting 3rd engineer in the motor room, when you see me. Now get going." John concluded, and waved the man away, to watch the offloading activities.

The *Inverlogie* was disgorging its cargo at a hectic rate, so much so that the dockworkers found themselves inundated with so much cargo that they were not able to keep up with the removal of it.

The little trams were almost like a conveyor belt as they shuttled back and fore from the deep caverns to the dock, but even they could not cope.

Before long, two of the scientists came scurrying along and shouted for the crew to stop their unloading, but they did not want to listen, as they were on a promise. Job and finish for a couple of days.

John was enjoying a leisurely cigarette whilst watching from a vantage point on the poop deck, when Moore spotted him and made his way onto the ship to talk to him.

"This is your fault Grey! Tell your men to stop loading, as we're getting overloaded and can't stow the cargo quickly enough. Our system has been overloaded and cannot cope with the different temperatures needed. Unless you stop and keep what's left in your own fridges then there will be a massive loss of cargo." Moore screamed.

John had grown up a quiet and unassuming young man, but the ways of life at sea put paid to that when he first came across his erstwhile chief engineer, Cresswell. Since then he had had to grow fast in the dog-eat-dog world called 'a life on board ship'.

John pretended not to hear him and carried on smoking, when he felt Moore striking his arm. He turned around and thumped Moore right on the chin, knocking him cold for a few moments. Another and much bigger man, looking like the side of a mountain, stooped down and tended Moore before he stood up and spoke.

A Beach Party

"I am Mr Lewis, the Kings' storeman. All incoming goods to the island are checked and stored under my jurisdiction. We've been working hard for months now in readiness to get this shipload of provisions here, and in one day you're going to ruin the lot, by offloading it too quickly. Tell your men to stop loading and get it all back on board again until we're ready." Lewis shouted angrily.

John looked down at Moore who was starting to get back onto his feet then at Lewis.

"Mr Lewis is it? Well let me tell you this. Moore here is the scientist, who's in charge of the offloading, so speak into his shell-like earholes. If you're the Kings grocer, then think on me like this, I'm only the delivery boy, full stop." John replied calmly, feeling his anger evaporating in the blazing sun.

Lewis turned to Moore and asked if it were true, and received the confirmation to what John had told him.

"He's speaking the truth Lewis, but then it was his own idea, and to quote his own words, 'Speed in offloading is the secret. The sooner it's offloaded and into the caverns the quicker we get the temperature stabilised again." John added.

"When I said that I meant, in an orderly fashion so that we could freeze each load as it arrived, with your cargo holds keeping the cargo at a steady temperature until we were ready." Moore wailed, said, rubbing his sore chin.

"Look here Moore, you stripped the ship of any capability to do that when you ordered it all to be re- assembled in the caverns. If it wasn't for my chief, you would have taken the ships own fridge units away too. You've even made certain that most of the ship's insulation around the cargo holds was stripped off and installed into your so-called citadel of ice. You've had a good day and a half to install all this in preparation of receiving the cargo yet somehow you've managed to cock it up good time. And just to make it crystal clear about all this, once the ship was stripped of that capability, the cargo was at the mercy of the elements with no back up system to maintain even a cool breeze over it. You, Moore are what they call in the movies, 'the effing ASS HOLE." John replied with relish.

Lewis turned to Moore and grabbed him by his lapels.

"Is this true Moore? You stripped the ship of everything and left the cargo unprotected, and now it's still not protected because of the rapid offloading that you and your men can't handle?"

"But Grey is the one at fault. He shouldn't have offloaded so quickly." Moore whined, before looking appealingly to John.

John saw the look of pleading then stated firmly.

"This should teach you a good lesson on not to look down your nose at a mere Marine Engineer. I warned you the other night but decided to let your arrogance and ignorance show you up. Now you know why we ships' engineers left your stupid backslapping party the other day."

Lewis threw Moore onto the ground like a rag doll, and turned to John.

"It appears that I owe you an apology Grey, and I'll see the King about this. Moore might as well pack his bags now and catch the next flying boat or even a fishing boat out of here if the King gets hold of him. Especially if any of his groceries get ruined because of Moore's stupidity as he hates that more than anything else."

Moore finally stood up and croaked.

"I'll see the chief scientist about all this. I didn't come here to be insulted. I'll have you know, that I'm top in my field of deep freezing and temperature controls."

"You appear to know nothing compared with Grey, here. Now get yourself back into the caverns and sort it out. Grey here is only carrying out your instructions to get it offloaded, and thanks to you, he has been given no other alternative do so. So shift your carcass and have this lot stowed by sundown, if you don't want to be made a human sacrifice to our god Mulani." Lewis threatened, kicking Moore several times for Moore to leave in haste, then turned back to John.

A Beach Party

"If I get more men to help shift the landed cargo, how long would it take to complete it?" Lewis asked in a more civilised manner.

John called the 3rd mate over and asked him the same question, in front of Lewis.

"When the trials equipment was in the process of being unshipped and taken away, I've had your deck cargo of timber, corrugated sheets of aluminium, and all the other builders materials offloaded. We have also offloaded your dry provisions such as tea, coffee, powdered milk, your cordage, bolts of silks, cottons, drums of latex rubber, medical equipment and all other items that did not need refrigeration. What you're seeing at the moment is tins of foodstuffs coming from the after deck, and now, all the meat carcasses, such as beef, sheep, pig, chicken and venison for the King. In all some 12,000 tons of cargo as your delivery." the 3rd mate recited before he showed Lewis his cargo manifesto.

Lewis looked down the rows of ticks and the items that were mentioned before he answered.

"It appears to be well organised and well discharged 3rd mate. I shall want a copy of these lists to match up with my own, but for the moment I request that you stop the frozen stuff for an hour or so until Moore comes back to me."

"We can't do that Lewis, as the holds are just as hot as the dock-side now, despite me having cold water hosed over the decks to keep the temperature down. Your only chance is to get it all into the caverns, for at least it will have a 10C temperature instead of a 35C+ at the moment.

You are advised that any foodstuffs that have been defrosted by about 20 percent should be consumed within 12 hours. It simply means that for a while, the islanders will eat 'high off the hog' as the expression goes. This is my opinion as the delivery boy who is also a qualified marine engineer officer and who was responsible for looking after it, all the way out from the United Kingdom some 15,000 miles away."

"Thank you for your candid opinion Grey, and one that I shall act upon. Maybe we'll be able to get off lightly with only a 5 percent loss, unlike the last time, which was almost 85percent, and the main reason why our King decided to go for this 'ice citadel' here as he called it. The UK government is paying for it by the Overseas Aid Grant system, so if we lose this lot, then the UK government would have to send another shipload to make up for it. Now that's being candid back to you, Grey, but don't mention it to that fool Moore, or he'll be absolute hell to live with." Lewis admitted, with a big smile.

"Just make sure the king knows the true score on this as we officers and our crewmen, are looking for a decent few peaceful days ashore." the 3rd mate insisted, and left to carry out his duties again.

Lewis nodded and left with the parting word.

"Glad to have met you Grey, at least you're an honest man that I can deal with, not like some of these so called boffins who try to fleece us blind with their promises of good times ahead but it always costs you. See you tomorrow when I've had the chance to check everything my end."

A Beach Party

Chapter XIX
Underground

"**M**orning 3rd! Here's an early morning glass of juice, it'll set you up for the day." Henderson said cheerfully, when he entered John's cabin.

"What? Glass? What time is it Handy?" John asked, sitting bolt upright in his bunk.

"It's 6 o'clock and nearly time for early breakfast. I've put your fresh tropicals out, and your civvies will be ready for you later on in the morning. Chief Day asked me to tell you that he wants to see you around 0900 in his cabin."

John rubbed his eyes wearily, and moaned about being woken up this early in the morning.

"Now that the ship has been emptied of cargo and passengers, we've gone into tropical routine. Breakfast at 0630, start work at 0715, mid morning cuppa at 1030, then wrap up for the day at 1230, lunch at 1300 then simply bugger off, subject to duty of course." Henderson said rattling off the daily itinerary.

"Sound good to me. Plenty of shore time by the sounds of it. Have you been ashore yet? What's the place like?"

"I went ashore with the chefs and had a whale of a time in a local hotel on the other side of the island. The Blue Coral Hotel, if I remember it rightly. We spent less than ten bob each, but we ate, drank and fornicated all day for that, and even had the change to come back on the all night tram system."

"Lucky old you, but let's hope your mackintoshes were up to standard or you'll all be visiting the Rose Cottage before tomorrow is out."•

"We were told that it was the only place that had guaranteed 'clean' women. Mind you though, all of them were supposed to be guaranteed virgins." Henderson replied then hesitated.

• An expression used to describe the special clinic that treats/ cures V.D. (Venereal Diseases).

"Come to think about that, the one I went with must have been the best part of 50. So how can she be a virgin with all those stretch marks around her belly?" he asked, scratching his head in puzzlement.

John laughed at the steward's apparent naivety, and threw his leather sandal at him.

"You must have been three sheets to the wind. The world is full of second time around virgins, if only to get a drunken sailor to part with his wad. Still, if ten bob was a good bargain, then I suppose you'll be ashore casting your nuts elsewhere today, looking for another 50 year old guaranteed virgin." John said with a chuckle, and got himself washed and dressed for the day. Chief Henry Obediah Day.

"Morning Happy! Understand you wish to see me for some unknown reason?" John greeted cheerfully, knocking the door and entered Day's cabin.

"Morning John. Yes, take a seat. Want a coffee or something?" Day asked pleasantly, which John politely declined.

"I've gone over your final figures and those which the 5th engineer made for the cargo discharge, and have discussed them with Tomlinson. We're of the same opinion that the final spoilage of 10% was due to the inappropriate handling of the cargo once it got ashore. I'm telling you this because our King Phatt was most annoyed with it, especially when it was promised that all would be well. Your friend Moore, by the way, is to be sent home in disgrace on the next available transport.

A certain Mr Lewis, whom I understand you've already met, has reported that if it wasn't for your suggestion, the figure would have been much higher, to the tune of around 50 %. Therefore, given the unforeseen problems with the trials shore-side and your side of the experiment, it has been deemed as an unqualified success. Belverley has been informed by telegram of this, and is pleased with the outcome, even though he didn't give us much of a chance in the first place, as you already know. I'm telling you this John, because I've been authorised by Belverley to offer you

A Beach Party

the temporary post of acting 2nd engineer. But this also means two things." Day stated, offering John a cigarette and lit one up for himself.

"The ship is now almost worthless as a fridge-ship due to the loss of most of the insulation in the holds. It will be your task to try and make some sort of Heath Robinson affair to counteract this difficulty, so the ship may carry at least some sort of cargo back under frosted conditions.

The second reason is because, as the trials have been completed and your function on board ceases, you will be required to sign new articles with the purser to remain on board as crew.

Because we're down two engineer officers, and we've got to slot you in somewhere without stepping on egos or toes, so to speak, Belverley has agreed on your temporary rank of acting 2nd. In truth, you will become the full time outside engineer over Blackmore, but with that added job to do in the meantime. So what do you say to that John?" Day explained.

John thought for a moment, whilst finishing off his cigarette.

"I've no problem with that Happy. But I do need to turn this so-called temporary rank into a proper one, if I'm to enhance my career prospects."

"Glad you said that John, because that's just what we had in mind. I'll get some of the guff together for you to peruse through sometime during this stay in port. You will be required to offer assistance in the engine room from time to time, naturally." Day said amiably.

"So if I can help get some sort of frosted cargo back to Blighty, complete a few dickey tests on board, I shall get my papers on arrival back in Belfast?"

"Something like that, John. And by the way, when I referred to we, I meant the captain and me."

John looked first at Day then out through the cabin window for a few moments before returning his answer.

"It's nice to have friends in high places Happy, glad you're one of them." John replied with a smile then offered his hand to shake Day's, who shook it briskly.

"This backslapping is getting almost on par with those bloody scientists John. Sufficient to say that as long as you do your duty and in the manner which we're accustomed of getting from you, then you've no worries. As far as I'm concerned, you're now off duty until Thursday morning, have a good time ashore. But don't forget to come back then and sign your new articles as 'Acting 2nd Engineer' or he won't be able to credit you with your food and bar bills etc." Day concluded

John nodded in acceptance of him being dismissed, and left the cabin with mixed feelings about the whole conversation.

John was finally going over the gangway for his first 'tourist visit' ashore since arriving some three days ago, when he met Larter coming his way on board.

"Hello Bruce! What's it like ashore?" John greeted affably.

"Hello John! If you wait about half an hour then I'll show you the sights. Only Dave and I've just come back from the local radio station on the other end of this island. Bloody good gear they've got, let alone the quiet and almost secular way of life compared with the rest of the islanders. Hang on here for me, won't be long." Larter replied, and disappeared into the ship's superstructure.

John waited on the gangway and passed the time of day with some of the crew who were just to go ashore. He was given lots of advice on where to go and what not to say or do, and the kind of drinks you'd avoid and how much you needed for a 'short time'. He listened to the lewd conversations and advice but kept his own ideas and thoughts of a run ashore very much to himself. After all, he was an officer and a so-called 'gentleman'.

"Right then John, lets catch the next tram going across the causeway, I'll take you on a conducted tour around the islands. It should take us about two hours going up through just three levels on both sides, before we arrive back here for tea. After that, we've got to register in a local hotel until Thursday, when we've got to come back and re-sign our articles again. So let's go John,

A Beach Party

and boy are you in for an eye opener as far as these so-called 'friendly' people are concerned." Larter greeted, re-appearing with a bulging holdall in one hand and a briefcase in the other.

"It looks as if you're intending to stay much longer Bruce, judging by your holdall." John responded with a smile.

Larter glowered at the ribbing, and ushered John over the gangway to meet the oncoming tram that stopped right in front of them, to be met by a conductor who stepped off the last carriage and approached them.

"Morning conductor. How much for two round trips?" Larter asked politely but in pidgin English.

"All the way around both islands?" the man asked, then pulled out a large well-thumbed booklet that was his timetable and ready reckoner.

"That will be one half crown each if you please. But you'll have to change at the end of each island terminals. In the event of an emergency, for the flood barriers to be shut during our lower level route, then you'll have to disembark and take one of the several lifts up to the next level. Just listen for my whistle and the siren for all clear."

Larter handed the man the money and thanked him for his information, before they sat down in the rickety carriages.

The tram buzzed its way through tunnels under the dockyard walls before they emerged out into the bright sunlight and the wide palm-tree lined avenue that was the causeway. Entering into one very stifling tunnel with heat and lack of proper ventilation, they came to yet another tunnel that was thankfully very bright and breezy.

As they went along the tunnels, people were walking along them, stopping to enter doorways that were carved into the rock, and even passing simply open spaces with big holes in the rock for the air and sunshine to come through.

"It's just like the London Underground, Bruce. I presume that those doorways are the entrants to those peoples' homes. If so then presumably they've got big holes carved out of the rock as windows, as I've seen along the side of the mountain.

From the ship, they look like windowless holes, but each hole seems to have a pair of shutters that look like storm doors. Mind you, it seems that only the first three layers have these window shutters. But why does this island have a scarcity of homes 'above ground' even more than that of I'ti, Bruce?"

"From what's been explained to me, it's because the two atoll islands are very fertile and need as much ground space as possible for the islanders to grow their crops. Only a few of what the islanders call 'food tenders' such as lesser tribes who make up the farmers and fishermen, live on Maoi and is the factory and office space, if you like. Whereas King and his tribe of walking lard mountains, live above ground on it and the 'Iti' island. The other coral islands that you saw have a separate tribe on each one, and growing specific crops for the benefit of the rest. But they rely mostly on the atoll to provide them with things that are luxury items to them but everyday things to us. Each tribal chief is part of their government, where they make democratic decisions that would put our own self-aggrandising, money grabbing, two faced, move your nose down the trough, MP's to shame. King Phatt's tribal system is the secret of their success, and that's why there's been total harmony within the Archipelago." Larter explained, pointing to the various points of interest as the tram went upwards in the layer system of the roadway.

The tram went along various tunnels and openings in the rock sometimes like a roller coaster. John was accustomed to rapid height movements such as on board a ship during a storm, but he decided that some of the tram movements would be decidedly dodgy especially for those unaccustomed to it.

"We must be changing height layers Bruce. Presumably we're about to return to the dockyard and go through the I'ti island complex then?" John shouted over the noise of the tram.

"Yes John. Our next stop is the Harbour Masters' building where we change overhead tracks. It's got a higher voltage and has more 'traffic' buzzing along compared with Maoi. You'll see what I mean in a minute."

A Beach Party

"From my own conducted tour of the underground workings, the other day, I noticed several lifts. Is that what the conductor was on about earlier?"

"There are lifts everywhere there is shaft opening or tunnel entrance. Each one, especially the tunnel entrances have their own steel doors that is manned 24 hours a day, just like the signal boxes on the railways. Something to do with tropical storms that can start up within minutes and create waves over 20feet high, let alone the occasional tidal wave that is usually 35 foot high." Larter said nonchalantly, continuing to point out the attractions they passed.

"The ocean side of I'ti' is the White coral side, with its own little coves that the fishermen live and use. On the ocean side of Maoi is the Black beach side, because of the ashes and debris fall-out from the volcano, that's where you find most of the farmers. On the harbour side of the causeway is the Blue coral of the so-called deep lagoon. In between the atoll where the shallow lagoon is, is called the Pink Lagoon simply because all the coral is pink. That is the recreation area for all the islanders. I was told that if you were in difficulty all you had to do is say the colour of the beach, and the nearest landing jetty that each beach has, then somebody would come and help you. When we get to top of the island where the radio and Met station is, you'll be able to see for yourself. I'll say no more now John so you can enjoy the rest of the tour in peace."

"No that's quite all right Bruce, I enjoy a decent tour around something absolutely fascinating. Anyway, isn't it time for a cigarette and maybe a beer or three to cool us down?"

"You'll have to wait until we get to the end of one layer and out into the open for a cigarette John. And as far as a drink is concerned, you'll have to wait until we get to a licensed premises such as a hotel, restaurant, or beach bar, or even some 'white man's house' to enjoy an alcoholic one. Fizzy or fruity drinks only are served otherwise, by decree from our favourite Phattie. Swearing, littering, or any other unsociable behaviour will incur the brutal force of some 'Bobby's truncheon on your skull, or shoved up your arse, so beware.

Oh and while I'm at it, no tapping up the local girls unless invited, and no fornication unless you're 'married' for the night. In short John, be on your best behaviour whilst out in public, and make sure whatever you do, is behind closed doors and with a willing partner, even though she is a reputed 50 year old virgin."

"Phew Bruce. Sounds like a concentration camp around here. How do the locals manage to keep such strict codes of conduct then? And here's me thinking that only a 'left footer' Catholic had to obey such palaver, especially on a Sunday when they're besides themselves muttering the Hail Mary's all day."

Larter laughed at John's attempted parallels of the Western world and the cultures of the East.

"I suppose that will do for the while John, but at least you've grasped what I meant by behaving yourself more on this island than how you would on say, Barbados, let alone snooty Bermuda."

"Can't wait Bruce. Anyway, I'm hoping to get a bit of sea angling in whilst I'm here, and according to one of the local dockyard workers, the fish around these waters are as many as the stars in the sky. He also said that I could expect to catch some really big ones off any cove or beach."

"Fishing is not exactly my idea of relaxing John, but good luck to you anyway. The things he didn't tell you was that there are certain fish you must not catch or try to eat, as they're deadly poisonous. If you go out onto the lagoon in a boat, then you've got to go with one of the local fishermen. As it's their way of life, you'll be forfeiting one fish per each fish caught for yourself, as it's deemed to be their very own local tax. Then of course if you catch some other certain types of fish, and the names escape me offhand, but when you do you've got to hand it over to one of the local tribal chiefs, or even directly to King Phatt himself. Something to do with and on the same lines as our own monarch, prize game, only fit for Kings and Queens. Whilst I'm at it, if 'His

A Beach Party

Maj' gets to find out you've kept something for yourself even as a souvenir, he'll send his bailiffs around and confiscate the lot. They are very jealous of everybody, and would take from those who needs it the most, of only to emphasise his authority as King, so be very careful ."

"Hmm, thanks for the warning. If that's the hassle just for a few hours leisurely fishing, then I just might restrict myself to just a few hours in the early morning off the ship side." John replied glumly.

"That is why I stick to something that everybody does, swimming and snorkelling. Maybe you'd care to join me, Andy and a few of the others this afternoon once we've registered into a smashing hotel that I came across yesterday." Larter responded, as the tram finally stopped at the end of the track, which was out in the open air and on the top end of the I'ti island.

"Here we are John. This is the local radio station where our music was sent out from, and the Met station which is manned by local scientists." Larter added, as they jumped out of the tram.

"We've got a 30 minute wait here before the next tram arrives John, so we might as well have a look round." Larter enthused.

"Lead on Gungadin!" John said happily, stretching his cramped legs and following Larter into yet another pair of steel doors that led into yet another cavern entrance, with a large ornate invitation sign above the entrance. 'Welcome to the KITE FLYERS CLUB.'

The short visit to the place was very interesting for John who posed so many questions, the people concerned were glad when the moment came when Larter announced that they had to leave again. They bade farewell and caught the downward tram for another roller-coaster ride before arriving back into the dockyard via the tunnel through the protective wall, which was the flood barrier for the tidal basin of the harbour.

John noted that the harbour caisson had been placed to keep the water in the harbour basin, whereas the water on the other side was notably much lower, indicating that the tide was out.

"If the lagoon is almost tide free on the other side of the islands, and if the so called deep lagoon is almost cut off due to the barrier reefs, how come there is such a drop, Bruce?"

"The barrier reef is riddled with holes that let's the tide in or out, but it's only the big rollers that get stopped by the reefs. The harbour is at best 6 fathoms deep on a high tide, but only just over 2 fathoms at low tide, that's why we had to wait until the full tide to give us free water under our keel.

As we've got a 3-fathom draught, we had to have the caisson shut to protect us from 'beaching'. At least that's what Andy explained. The captain already knew of the tidal system, which means that he had been here before, even though he pretends to be a 'first timer'. That's a different story for him to tell, sufficient to say that it's time we had some food down our necks before we hit the booze big time later on." Larter informed, rushing towards the dining room, with John at his heels.

"Yet another good idea Bruce, as I'm ruddy starving, especially after those several rounds of drinks those MET boys treated us to."

"Right then John, lets get ashore now for a well earned rest. Andy should already be ashore waiting for us in the Pink Lagoon Hotel." Larter suggested, as they left the ship again and waited for the next tram to come along.

John looked around the place and noted the cleanliness of the place and the lovely smell of the local flowers that grew in colourful abundance in seemingly any empty space where you could put a pot or large container.

The tram was heralded by its loud buzz in the now empty dockyard, and stopped by the ship's gangway for John and Larter to embark.

"Two singles to the Pink Lagoon Hotel if you please." Larter said affably to the conductor.

"That will be one shilling each." the conductor replied, then taking two small pieces of cardboard from a wad of them and clipped them with his ticket clipper.

A Beach Party

"One shilling? But we're only going about one mile along the first layer." Larter protested, but in vain.

"Sorry boss, but it's still one shilling each." the conductor grinned, showing his full set of gleaming white teeth.

"Thank you conductor." John said quickly to save any further arguments, which pacified the guard who left them and carried on down the tram.

"You're too gullible John that's your trouble. You're supposed to haggle each price with these people, or they'd charge astronomical prices. The thing here John, is if they state a price and you don't state a lower one right away, then that's the price you're stuck with. No wonder he was smiling when he left." Larter moaned.

"Maybe it was the only price the conductor had remembered, Bruce. Otherwise it was yet another half crown each like the last time, which you didn't haggle about." John said with a smile.

Larter managed a grin as he shrugged his shoulders at John's simple logic.

"Wait until you see the hotel John. The prices there are sky high compared with most of the others, on account that it's a so-called Hilton hotel. But at least you get your money's worth."

"Sky high as Bermuda prices, or cloud high as in Barbados prices Bruce?" John teased.

"You wait and see!" Larter answered and changed the subject whilst he offered John a cigarette.

"Glad we've got decent fags on board John, as the ones ashore are what the locals always smoke, and taste like camel shit. Yes John, I've already tasted camel shit just in case you ask. And no John, I didn't get it direct from the camels either." Larter said quickly as if to ward off yet another bit of ribbing from John.

"Would I ask you such questions Bruce? Me, who's one of your favourite fans?" John asked innocently.

Larter ruffled John's hair and chuckled at John's mock horror and offence.

"You've come a long way since Andy offered you one of his 'ticklers' way back in Belfast, John. So you've obviously tasted the Yanks and the Frogs brand of fags for you to remain British. These are Gallaghers Greens, but I've also got several hundred packets of du Mauriers as a change, whereas Andy likes the Capstan full strength, or Players Weights, that he gets in tins of 50's. You mostly smoke Senior Service non-tipped when you can't get the State Express or whatever."

"You've obviously given serious thought on our smoking habits Bruce, maybe there's some obscure reasoning for it. But whereas you keep losing your lighter, we always use matches. So here's your lighter that you left behind in the Kite club, and in the meantime have a light, or these fags will outlast the both of us." John said, flashing up a match, for them both to smoke their cigarettes.

"Sign here if you would gentlemen. Here are the keys to your rooms. Leave your luggage for the porter to take up for you. Each room has hot and cold water and you have a room service if you need anything during the night. Just use the hotel room phone system or ask the floor waiter.

The bar is open 12 hours a day but shut during meals. Evening meal is at 7pm prompt, so just sit at the table reserved for your room number. You will be required to settle your bill before you leave the hotel." The hotel receptionist stated in a tired but polite manner.

"Thank you. I'm expecting guests this evening who might require overnight accommodation. What do you advise?" Larter asked as he gave his baggage to the waiting porter.

"We have several rooms available at the moment, but should there be an overnight stop for the Clipper Service passengers, then your guests would have to share with you. That would then be doubled and added to your account." Came the bored reply.

"Fair enough, landlord, now where's the bar." Larter said impatiently, leading John through the reception area and into an ornate room full of gaily-attired people.

A Beach Party

There was a combo playing soft music from a small stage area, whilst people took their drinks and chatted quietly amongst themselves.

Larter spied two empty chairs with a table nearby for him to drag over and suggested that they make themselves comfortable, as a waiter arrived to take their drinks order.

A few drinks later, a loud gong was heard that indicated it was time for the evening meal, and everybody filing quietly out of the saloon and into a mirror lined room with neatly laid tables for the guests to use.

"Here John, here's our table. Wait here until I get back, I won't be a moment." Larter stated and John sat down to read the menu booklet.

Larter arrived back as promised and was given the menu card.

"The lobster salad looks good Bruce, and the mango and guava starters seem a good idea. How about a nice chilled bottle of bubbly to go with it? Although, I'm puzzled as to how they managed it without ice cubes."

Larter chuckled and shook his head.

"Now now John, you know the natives here don't like nosey people. Give your brain the night off, and enjoy yourself."

"It must be all that fish we've been eating lately, it certainly gets the old grey cells working."

"Pity you didn't tell those MET boys, John. They were glad we left when we did. Still, that's one more cross you've got to carry. Anyway, here comes our grub, delicious it looks too." Larter said with a smile when he received his food.

Their repast was taken leisurely and after drinking the last of their bubbly, Larter suggested they adjourn to the lounge again in case some of the lads arrived.

"I've reserved our table and seats from where we were before, that's where I went to John. Put a few of these snobs out it has, see the looks of disgust they're giving us." Larter said as he pulled two cigars out of a cigar case and offered John one.

"Here flash one of these up, then watch the men." Larter whispered, and proceeded to prepare his ready for smoking.

"You're in a devilish mood tonight Bruce." John replied, starting to puff away at his over-large cigar, and savouring its flavour.

The sudden mushrooms of smoke from their cigars filtered around the room that had most of the male guests looking with envy at the two friends, as they had to contend with what the hotel had to offer.

Soon, they were joined by Sinclair, then shortly after by Day and Tomlinson.

"There you are. I've had a phone message saying that two of my senior officers were setting fire to the place and polluting the air with their rich aroma of tobacco. We guessed just who they were and here you are. Shame on you to upset our fellow travellers! You should know better than that, especially officers from my ship." Tomlinson greeted with a stern voice, but gave a sly wink to let them know it was a put up job to please the whingers in the room.

"Sorry captain, won't happen again. Care for a cigar?" Larter asked with a glum face.

"Why thank you I think I will. It smells Havanish!" Tomlinson bragged, taking his cigar and starting to smoke it, again much to the disgust of other guests who were listening, but pretending not to notice.

"We've had word from his Majesty that we're to stay an extra day. Something to do with the incoming Clipper service from Suva Suva. Anyway, it will give us a little more time to get ourselves shipshape again." Tomlinson informed them, and took his drink from the waiter.

"Speaking of which Happy, they've got their fridge problem solved. Judging by the ice cubes in our drinks, that is." John remarked.

"Yes, John, I've noticed that too, which also means that you're redundant until Thursday. So how's about that then, you lucky toff!" Day replied with a grin, and whose remark gave way to mild banter from the other friends.

A Beach Party

The little party finally broke up with apologies from Day and Tomlinson as they had to head back to the ship.

"It comes to something when even the captain can't stay ashore, what do you say to that 3rd engineer Grey." Tomlinson asked teasingly, leaving the three friends and walking out of the hotel in company of Day.

"Andy, you can bunk down with us if you're staying." John offered, but was declined by Sinclair.

"I'm meeting up with some of the scientists shortly as they've promised me a trip on their research vessel, so I'll see you sometime tomorrow. If you don't see the ship in harbour by nightfall tomorrow, send out a search party. Their equipment is out of this world, but their bosun cant..."

"Yes, we know. Can't sail a wee wooden boat in a bath-tub." Larter stated, finishing Sinclair's sentence for him.

"That's it, you've got it lads. Well, see you then." Sinclair replied with a grin, as he too left.

"And now there is two, Bruce. Best get turned in ready for a hectic day ashore tomorrow. Remember, those Met lads promised us a trip in their spotter plane. Should be a good view of the place from the sky."

"Indeed, John. The bar's shut now, so we might as well get turned in. Breakfast is at 0700, so we'll have plenty of time to get organised before we 'MET' up with them." Larter quipped and followed John as the last person out of the lounge.

Chapter XX
Floating Islands

"Strap yourself in gents, because the sea is a bit lumpy this morning. We'll take off from the Pink Lagoon and circle the islands before we do our daily search." The navigator announced, with the pilot steering the small seaplane in readiness for take off.

The converted Lysander rushed along the lagoon as if to bash itself onto the barrier reef in front of them, before it lifted itself up gently and soared several feet above the workmen below them. Once the roar of the plane settled down to a gentle drone, the navigator spoke to the two friends without shouting.

"That reef is getting too high for us to take off from the lagoon, now. I remember it was only seen at low tide, now it's almost ready for the first non flying boat to land safely on it."

"Presumably the giant flying boats will keep coming and use the deep lagoon?" John asked

"Yes, once the runway has been completed on the atoll reef, and the aircraft pilots find it suitable and safe, then it will be the end of the flying boat clipper services. Pity because it's a wonderful sight to watch such lumbering aircraft take off and land with ease. But as we're the local Air Sea Rescue we must do our bit to keep the 'airwaves' safe."

"Never mind, you'll still have your little sea plane." Larter commiserated.

"Hah! Even that's been taken from us. We're getting a flipping whirlybird instead, that's why you saw the flat area marked out below the main office window." the navigator snorted with disgust.

The plane banked into a slow turn and circled around the twin island a couple of times, before the pilot announced they were heading due east towards Mulani.

"We have a flight time limitation of three hours and can only search an area 100miles square, due to lack of fuel. But you'll be surprised the amount of ships that we find wandering around due to their loss of direction. The volcano affects their gyro compass,

A Beach Party

until such times as the ships' captain can 'fix' his bearings properly before moving on.

Sometimes, we come across them just in time to warn them of the shallow areas around the plateau which grow shallower each year due to the corals getting bigger and higher." the pilot stated, handing John and Larter a pair of binoculars each.

"Here, take them and help us look for any fishing boat that may have got into difficulty. The ships are a much bigger target so they'd be easy to spot by the naked eye." he suggested.

John and Larter looked out of the window they were sitting next to, and began to scan the vast open ocean.

"We might get a glimpse of Mulani in a moment once I climb up to the next flight level. If it's performing today, then you should see the fireworks and smoke dead ahead. It'll be barely visible with your glasses mind you, as it's a good 350 miles away from us." Sandy, the radio operator said, whilst operating his radio, which Larter was taking a keen interest in.

"Looks like one of those transceivers we used to use in the war. Good sets too, so how do you keep it maintained?" Larter asked politely.

"I keep it serviced as best as I can, now that most of the spares for it are no longer available. As long as it does its job on here then that's all that matters. You saw the new transmitters and receivers yesterday, so who needs to cart this thing around all the time." Sandy grunted, straining to listen for any mayday calls.

"Sailboat approx bearing of red 15 or whatever you use on this." John announced.

"That bearing is fine by us. Yes I see him. Seems all in order." the navigator said after a moment

"Going down to have a look at him anyway." the pilot stated, and veered the aircraft around to descend almost to sea level before he approached the vessel.

"They're waving to us, but somebody is pointing to somewhere behind them." John said slowly, looking towards the area at which the person was pointing to.

"I see. There's a ship on the horizon with a rather nasty glow on it. I make it red 10." John said hurriedly, as the navigator looked to the suggested direction.

"She's too far out for us. Can you pick up her signal sparks?" the pilot said, turning his aircraft back onto his scheduled course again.

"Not a peep from anything skipper. 500kcs is the standard frequency I'm on but still nothing." Sandy stated.

"Try another frequency that some foreign ships use instead." Larter suggested, giving Sandy the frequency.

"Yes, he's there. Says he's a timber carrier from New Guinea and has caught a deck fire from the volcano fall out, and has lost its compass bearing as well." Sandy said with excitement and thanked Larter for his help.

"All we can do is report it to the harbour master, and have one of the rescue tugs come out. Contact the ship and tell him who we are and that we've seen him. Give him our radio beacon bearing to steer with, and advise him that a rescue vessel should reach them on that bearing in about three hours. Mind you, these Aussie tugboats are mercenaries, and don't give a damn what the ship's skipper tells them." the pilot said with a sigh, before he turned his aircraft around and commenced to search in another direction.

"Thanks to those fishermen down there, we spotted that ship. Let's hope they get rescued before they sink. But what'll happen to the ship if it does reach the atoll. Salvaged and recycled or what?" John asked.

"Usually, it gets towed to the outer barrier reef and stripped down to sea level. All re-usable material is then kept for any emergencies. The ship's carcass gets towed to a suitable spot in the reef then sunk in position to help the growth of coral. The overall object is to have the entire deep lagoon sealed off with a coral reef, thus providing extra islands for the natives to live on.

That is the official story and what is happening for real. The true story is that the ocean going tugs are under King Phatt's payroll. They get the tow duties, whereas Phatt gets the salvage.

A Beach Party

Providing that the survivors are taken off the atoll by ship or by the flying service, then all is above board. Mind you, virtually all the ships end up as scrap, in which case King Phatt ends up as the number one beneficiary. None of the tugboat crew dares to spill the beans in case they end up as coral reef shark bait. Besides, each member of the tugboats gets a phenomenal pay out, be it in females and plenty of shore facilities, or payment in lumps of gold that the volcano squirts from time to time." the pilot explained

"Something like the atoll reef, then. But where would all the extra rock and material needed to raise the reef right out of the water come from?" John persisted.

"The islanders have a specially made craft that dredges the area around the plateau and the atoll. Which gets dumped onto and built up into safe foundation layers. Due to the frequent tropical storms, some of it gets washed away, so they 'd have to go and retrieve it again. Mind you, they're so good at it, most of the barrier reef islands are a good 60 feet above sea level now, and covered in vegetation as you've seen. If that man Darnier, I think it was, was able to come back and see the place he'd have a shock at seeing so many new islands cropping up out of the sea. He quoted about 10 islands with coral reefs in between. In fact since his days there're 15 proper islands with some almost joined together as the coral links up with the next one in the chain. Having said that, it's a common occurrence around this part of the Pacific for great lumps of rocks as big as icebergs, to bob up from nowhere, and stay around for a while before sinking again. The islanders have a few legendary tales about that, as three such islands have remained within the bracelet, and have now been welded to the sea bed by the coral." The pilot concluded, and turned the aircraft around to make their way back to the atoll.

The craft landed smoothly back into the Pink Lagoon and taxied to its little landing jetty in it's own little cove.

"This is your captain speaking. Welcome to Maoi I'ti Atoll. Hope you enjoyed your flight. All passengers are to go to the arrival lounge where drinks will be served. All luggage will be offloaded and be available shortly." the pilot said in a polite but formal voice.

"Thanks pilot, we did enjoy our flight. Maybe we'll buy you a drink this time." Larter said gratefully as the men climbed out of the plane and stepped onto the wooden jetty.

"That's all right Larter. If that ship gets rescued and towed back here only for scrap, then the islanders will be celebrating the night away. Must dash now, as I've got some met info for the boys to mull over." The pilot said with a grin and left.

"All right sparks?" Larter asked the radio operator.

"Yes thanks. Maybe you could write down a couple more frequencies for me, although I've got a few new ones already lined up for the land aircraft that will start using them."

"You've got your radio beacon set up and the new radar is lined up. As it's only one aircraft per few days, and even then it's only in transit across the Pacific, you shouldn't have any worries. The time to worry is when several aircraft come at you all at once with nowhere to land." Larter stated knowingly.

"Besides, judging from what we've seen, that runway can only take the one aircraft at a time and even then only on a good day. Especially as there's no hangar or repair facility to stow the aircraft anyway." John added.

The navigator looked at the two friends and said.

"I've had that same nagging thought too, but the boffins and the civil engineers have shouted me down. They say that all the aircraft need do is take on fuel and provisions then take off again. Like racing cars' pit stop. The runway is long and wide enough for any size of aircraft, excluding the giant B52 bombers the Yanks have. Mind you though, Grey, since your suggestion of having rafts of fuel pods going out towards Mulani, we'd be able to extend our flight path further just as we're doing for the big jets."

"Thank you for taking my suggestion up and all might be well, but unless there is a regular tanker run to keep the aviation fuel in the first place, then it would be sheer folly to attempt to come here without that guarantee." John pointed out.

A Beach Party

"Speaking of which, there's supposed to be one carrying aircraft fuel due up from Brisbane, which hasn't arrived yet." the navigator replied.

"We've already got our fuel on board, but what happens to the ships that call in transit? I've noticed the fuel bunkers on the weather side of I'ti, do they have a special tanker to top that up too?"

"Yes, one does come every three months or so, but we salvage fuel from the scrapped ships as well. The islanders do well out of it. The King is trying to gear the place up for those large cruise liners, and perhaps set up a tourist trade. He's got a keen eye for trade that man has." the navigator ended, stating that he had to go and log the flight details but would see them after in the bar.

"Let's catch the next tram and go back to our hotel Bruce. I could do with a cool shower now after that heat in the aircraft." John suggested, which Larter agreed to, as they too left the landing jetty and walked into the tunnel for the next tram shuttle

.

CHAPTER XXI
Au Naturel

John was relaxing in the lounge, enjoying an after dinner drink with Larter and Sinclair. The place was quiet and cool as they talked amongst themselves, but the peace and tranquillity of it was shattered by a throng of people coming in, talking excitedly and generally settling themselves down to be served by the ever present waiters.

"Where have they come from all of a sudden? The next ship due in is tomorrow?" Sinclair asked with astonishment.

"Must be the TWA flying boat clipper on its way north somewhere. They park it at the other end of the beach from the harbour, that's why we didn't hear it coming in." Larter suggested.

There were some noisy children running around whose parents called after them to come back and behave themselves.

"What accent have they got Bruce?" John asked after a while.

"Sounds like Yank to me. A couple of Chinese among them too. Either way, they'll only be here for a few of hours, you watch."

"What a nice life to have. Just up and away to some place on the map without a care in the world. Must be in the wrong profession." John sighed; and spotted two pretty stewardesses arrive into the lounge and sit next to a uniformed man.

"He's probably the chief steward, lucky toff." Larter whispered, whilst eyeing up the girls.

"You're wasting your time there old friend. They're probably knocking off the pilot and his side kick." Sinclair said softly in an attempt to prevent Larter's apparent intentions.

"S'pose you're right Andy. Anyway, there's a nice beach bar on the Pink Lagoon side of the causeway I've been told has, shall we say, entertainment. So who's coming for a nice afternoon swim?"

"Sounds good to me, but we must be back for the evening meal." John said enthusiastically, as they got up and made their way out of the hotel.

A Beach Party

"What about swim trunks Bruce?" Sinclair asked, climbing aboard the shuttle tram.

"Don't worry about mere details, Andy. The bar has its own secluded little cove where au naturel is the order of the day. That's what I meant by entertainment."

"In that case, we'd better brush our teeth with coconut milk then." John responded, which made the other two to laugh at the idea.

The tram took several minutes to arrive and for them to make their way through a curtain made from palm fronds, and come across a large notice board, welcoming visitors to the beach.

They saw the bar at the other end of the beach and followed the trodden path to it, passing several groups of very naked people taking their ease.

When they arrived, Larter spotted the aircraft radio operator and waved to him, who came over to speak to them.

"Afternoon gents! This bar is well stocked, but you won't get served until you strip off and put your clobber in one of those baskets that are stacked behind the bar. You will collect a rubber ring with a number on it, which is the basket number your clobber will be kept in. You can have as much drink as you want, but no drunkenness or rowdy behaviour. The food and drink are very cheap, but you'll be expected to settle up before you get your clothes back. If you feel that you can't brave the challenge like the rest of us, then the barman will issue a loincloth to spare your blushes. Don't forget to get a decent size towel to lie on, or stay in the water if you don't want to raise the flag, so to speak."

"Thanks sparks. We'll take it from here." Larter responded, visibly drooling over a bevy of beauties that were playing beach ball.

"C'mon lads, last one back to the bar buys the wets." Sinclair said eagerly, and rushed ahead of the others.

Within moments, they were having a cold beer under the shade of the palm-thatched roof of the bar standing there in all their glory.

"Well Bruce, Andy! What're you waiting for? The sea is that way, if your eyes can direct you to it. Mind you don't pick any milky coconuts on the way." John joked, holding onto his loincloth.

For those who had been exposed to public nakedness such as the islanders, it was just an everyday thing, with nobody paying any attention to details. But John was still in the undecided category, and needed a little more time to get used to this strange feeling of nakedness in front of others, even though they were quite naked too.

The laughter and giggles from the girls in the water was the spur for Larter, who gulped down his drink, streaked down to the water's edge and joined in the fun. Shortly followed by Sinclair, leaving John to sit at the bar to enjoy a smoke.

The barman who was one of the local islanders came over and spoke to John as if to relieve his boredom.

"What part of the island work area do you come from?" he asked politely with a good standard of English.

"We're officers off the SS *Inverlogie*." John replied civilly.

Their conversation lasted a little while, interspersed with customers requesting drinks.

John asked if he could use one of the empty hammocks for a while, after he had a little swim, which the barman agreed to and took the note of John's basket number.

He watched his two friends cavorting with the girls and decided that he would have a quiet swim and a nice little rest to sleep off his drinks.

He swam around in the warm water of the lagoon for a while before coming back onto the beach and climbing into a hammock to rest. He settled down and relaxed whilst listening to the soft music coming from a loudspeaker that was attached to the tree above him.

'*A public address system all over the island to listen to the music, that is handy.*' John mused before he fell asleep under the shade of the palm tree.

John woke up with a start, feeling a chill wind blowing on him. Instead of the soft music he heard the raucous tone of an alarm sounding from the overhead tannoy.

A Beach Party

He looked down to the beach and found it deserted but what surprised him was that most of the water in the lagoon was vanishing quickly out beyond the reef, leaving a rock strewn landscape instead of a warm lagoon.

"John! John! Where are you John?" He heard from behind the now shut and locked bar.

"What the hell's happening Andy?" John responded to the voice.

"For God sake John, grab your things and get off the beach. We've got about ten minutes before a bloody great wave comes our way." Larter replied, who raced around from the back of the building and threw John's clothes at him.

"What wave is that Bruce?" John asked in puzzlement, rubbing his sleepy eyes.

"That bloody great thing out there. For Christ sake hurry up John and let's get to higher ground, or at least behind that storm barrier over there on the causeway." Larter said anxiously.

John took one look at the oncoming wall of water and spotted a lift that went up the side of the sheer rock face.

"Look, there's one of those emergency lifts. It'll take us up to the next two levels and to one of the shelters." John said quickly, managing to finish getting dressed.

They raced to the lift and made it take them up to the next level that was still open.

Two men who were shouting at them to hurry met them, and shut the cavern off in case the wave came into and flooded the tunnel.

John saw the wave splash over the newly constructed runway on the reef, and for it to come racing towards him before the steel doors clanged shut, just in the nick of time.

Within seconds, there was a loud rumbling and swishing noise that rattled the steel doors as if the water was trying to enter the tunnel. It took several seconds before the ear shattering noise died down and a few minutes before the two men re-opened the doors again.

The friends stood and looked out from their vantage point, which overlooked the lagoon, and saw the aftermath of what the tidal wave had caused.

"Bloody hell, look at the reef! Imagine an aircraft being on there at the time. They'll have to build it a lot higher than that if they want to keep it, or at least have the outer wall double its existing height" John said in amazement, as the friends looked at the battered and torn reef.

"Look at the causeway. It's been swept almost clean of trees. Our little beach hut and cove has been wiped out. The beach has been widened much more now that the sand has been piled up against what's left of that concrete wall. We wouldn't have stood a chance behind there." Larter observed.

"It appears that the islands have been given a hair cut all along the bottom half of the rocks. Look, not a scrap of greenery up to level of this cavern." Sinclair also observed.

John turned to one of the two local men and asked about that tidal wave and what would happen next to the islands.

The man answered him using mostly sign language that reinforced his poor English, but was enough for John to decipher what was said. He thanked the man before relating what he said.

"It was a 25 foot Tsunami that happens from time to time, the last one being three years ago. This one was only a baby one from the last one, which was over 50 feet. The islanders will just clean up and repair any damage. He said that big wall over on the I'ti side of the causeway was the shield for the harbour to protect the ships there. The wall along the causeway stops most of the wave as the debris gets collected on the silver beach side and into the deep lagoon. They just go and gather it all up again." John explained.

"We'll have to get back to the ship to see if she's okay. If the tram's are working then we'll be quicker on that." Sinclair suggested.

John stated that the trams were working normally except for the open causeway route. They'd simply use the underground one instead. Within minutes a tram did come along for them to jump onto it and make their way to the dockyard.

A Beach Party

The tram came out through the massive steel doors of the cavern that led to the docks, and stopped right by the gangway of the *Inverlogie*, for the friends to get off.

"She seems okay, and so does that research vessel on the outer wall." Sinclair announced when he had completed his swift surveyed around the harbour.

They raced across the gangway to be met by the 5th mate.

"Everything okay on board 5th mate?" Sinclair asked anxiously, but was met with a blank look from the young man.

"Why? What is the panic bosun?" he asked nonchalantly.

"How long have you been on the gangway 5th? Larter asked quickly.

"Since about 1600. Why, am I supposed to have done something?"

"Bloody hell man. You've been on watch all afternoon and you've seen nor heard anything?" Sinclair asked incredulously.

"Yes. I did hear something. First there was a loud siren then some water slopping over that wall over there. Why?" the 5th asked in total innocence.

John looked at the 5th mate then at his friends.

"It appears that we can all relax now gentlemen. I mean, a bloody great 25foot tidal wave coming at you at the rate of several hundred knots and you don't feel a thing, let alone notice anything. Just as well that wall was there or we'd be swimming home. I suggest that you enlighten this officer on ship safety, bosun, for all our sakes." John said sarcastically, pushing past the still non-plussed 5th mate, with Larter following behind.

"Hello Blackie, been on board long?" John greeted, on entering the motor room.

"Hello John. No, Just came on board as soon as I could. The ship is snug-as-a-bug, and all is okay as far as I'm concerned." Blackmore answered, before several of the stokers entered the compartment.

"Hello 3rd! And you, er 3rd! We came as soon as we could. We got holed up in the underground cavern of the causeway, and had to wait until the all clear to come up on top again." one stoker explained.

"That's all right men. All is in order, so you can carry on ashore again if you wish. But be back on board by 0900 tomorrow." Blackmore instructed, as the men cheered the news of the extra hours ashore, then also left in jubilant mood.

"It seems you've cracked it and got the men on your side now Blackie, well done." John said with a grin.

"Yes, I took your advice and gave them things to do. They're shaping into a good crew now, which means that our return voyage should be a peaceful one. Anyway John, I'm going back ashore now. See you sometime tomorrow."

"Why not, Blackie. I'm staying on board for a while, so see you then." John replied as both men made their way up and out onto the main deck.

'A ship is the home for her crew. That is why they would do their utmost to look after her and keep her out of harm's way.' John mused, walking around the ship slumbering peacefully at her berth.

A Beach Party

CHAPTER XXII
The Big Turn On

"**M**orning Happy, enjoy your spot of shore time? I came on board yesterday and caught up with a few items that I was mulling over whilst ashore."

"Hello John. Yes I did, apart from that little scare yesterday. Are you remaining on board now, or are you just visiting?"

"I've just signed my articles with the purser as you've instructed, and settled into my new cabin, thanks.

Glad to catch up with you, as I've got some semblance of a plan to roll past you, if you've got the time, that is."

"Yes, I've got plenty of time before I get the ship on 12 hours steaming notice. What have you got for me?"

John placed a large sheaf of paper in front of Day, and went through this plan, stopping to answer the odd questions that Day had put to him.

After about an hour, when John had outlined the entire plan and proposed, Day called for a quick break.

"We'll have a look at the hold, and see what else that can be done, John. But on the face of it, it should be feasible. Got to check with Tomlinson on the latter part though. He might not agree to his ship being altered in such a drastic way, but he can only say no." Day said, and left the cabin with John to go down into the cargo holds.

"You see Happy, there's enough insulation carcass left for me to convert just the one hold, and the reason why I chose No4 hold was because it was the nearest to the ship's freezer. According to the 3rd mate, we're getting about 200 tons of coconuts, pineapples, and bananas from the island farms. We'll also be loading barrels of Potash Nitrate into holds 1 and 2. And according to Larter, we're to take the cargo to Australia via the Fijian islands."

"You're certainly well informed John, I'll give you that. But how are you going to separate the different fruits to control their different temperature needs?"

"We've got several sheets of plywood left over, that I used to partition some of the last cargo. So I figured, that if we get the husks off the coconuts and stuff it between two plywood sheets, to make a kind of sandwich, then nail them together to form partition panels that should retain the chill. We have several open containers loaded with ice cubes for the fan to blow over them. That will give the initial chill factor, then when the ship's fridge kicks in, it will create a film of ice on the partitions. All the fridge has to do is maintain a constant temperature. Just so long as the chef doesn't leave the door wide open when he's in there. Speaking of which, there'll be a special apron for the fruit cargo to go though.

The reason being is that the apron will cut down the heat exposure when the cargo is being loaded on board. When it's all loaded up, an insulated cap will be nailed on the top to seal the partitions to prevent loss of temperature."

"The chef? Remind me again why he'll be there John."

"His fridge will be part of the hold, as opposed to a separate and independent unit. As I've shown you, we're stripping down the fridge and re-assembling it in the hold to create one large fridge. His supplies will be kept in a separate compartment and away from the fruit cargo."

"Of course! Simple yet ingenious, that's why your plan could work. Lets go and see Tomlinson to hear what he has to say, then get the cargo organised." Day said, stroking his chin in thought.

They made their way up to the captain's bridge cabin, but finding that Tomlinson wasn't there, they went down to his day cabin, and were more fortunate.

"Morning Chief, morning 3rd! What can I do for you?" Tomlinson greeted when the two engineers entered his cabin.

"Morning captain. Temporary 2nd engineer Grey has proposed a plan and a swift schedule of work on the ship that we both feel you need to be informed of, and for you to make the final decision on " Day said politely, with John standing next to him.

A Beach Party

"Ah yes, 2nd engineer Grey! Knowing you John, you've come up with something both Happy and I would be hard pressed not to accept. So what have you got for me?" Tomlinson grinned, and invited them to sit down.

John went through his plan just as he had told Day, before he delivered the all-important part, which Tomlinson had to agree with

"So let's get this straight, by tomorrow you'll have my ship ready to take on a cargo of perishables. Your partitioning idea is still a great idea John, but how, or is that a fool question to ask you?" Tomlinson asked civilly, perusing over John's sheaf of paper work.

John told him exactly what was required, how it worked, and an approx length of time to get it all working.

Tomlinson looked at Day with surprise, before he turned back to John.

"You certainly know how to deliver the killer punch, John. This is a relatively new ship, and needless to say our men in HQ would be howling mad if they knew what you're about to do to it."

"If you want my opinion Joe, it is a proper and feasible project, and I don't see why it can't work. Just say the word, and I'll get a team of men onto it and have your ship ready for loading, say by tomorrow morning. John will need to have it up and running overnight and ready for your load of fruit." Day opined.

Tomlinson thought for a few moments before he gave his blessing.

"At least I can get some refrigerated cargo capacity back again. Mind you it must hold until we get to Australia." Tomlinson stated, nodding his head in approval.

"That's just great Joe! You've got it! We can also pick up a few tons from Fiji on our way too, as hold No 4 would be empty as far as there. If not, then we can always have the ship repair unit in Brisbane sort us out for the return trip back to Blighty." John said with glee.

Tomlinson gave another puzzled look to Day the asked.

"How the hell do you know all that John, and here's me only just reading my prepared manifesto for the ship, as you came in?"

"You forget about his pal Larter, Joe. I found out the same way as you no doubt. Something tells me that we're in the wrong job." Day chuckled, and saw that Tomlinson had recognised that John and Larter were close friends.

"I think you're right there Happy. What are we going to do with this engineer of yours?"

"If all goes well then we'll get a bonus out of it, and John his papers for 2nd engineer."

"Amen to that Happy. Anyway, let's get this up and running, but let me know as soon as you're ready for me to take a look. I'll see the harbour master to get a gang of men onto stripping the husks off the coconuts. It's called copra, and can be a valuable cargo in its own right, except for all the fleas that it seems to attract. Which, and incidentally John, you're going to have to sort out before the fruit arrives."

"That's not a problem Joe, as the chill factor will kill them off anyway. But I'll see if some canvas can be tacked over the sections to form the flea barrier anyway." John replied, undaunted.

"See what I mean Joe?" Day laughed, holding out his arms palms outward and shrugging his shoulders.

"C'mon Acting 2nd, lets get the show on the road." Day concluded, leaving Tomlinson totally bemused by all what had transpired in his cabin.

"Put the switching array over in the corner Blackie. I need two more stokers to help me remove the fridge motor where I want it mounted on a low table. Then get a qualified stoker to tack-weld the copper piping around the outer walls of the hold, and also the fridge motor onto its mounting. We'll reverse the extractor fans so they blow instead of suck when the vats of ice are in position. We'll need to rig up a lighting system for the chef, but otherwise, have a blue lamp installed in each compartment.

A Beach Party

The less heat generated in here the better, is the paramount objective, Blackie, so have each fan's motor boxed off and lagged." John instructed, and directed the operations in the hold.

John worked non-stop, and had the stokers installing the plumbing and any during welding, whilst the sailors created the partition boards and lagged them before he felt happy to load the iceboxes with several bags of ice cubes.

When it was ready for the big switch on, Blackmore the 3rd mate and the two gangs of crewmen stood with bated breath, as John switched on the reverse fans. Soon a cloud of cold mist started to swirl around the hold, getting thicker and thicker.

"3rd Mate, kindly phone the captain's cabin and the chief engineers and ask them to come down to the hold. I'll wait until they're here before I throw the main fridge motor switch." John asked.

Tomlinson and Day arrived shortly and stood beside the other two officers observing the cold foggy conditions of the hold.

"Are you ready for the big one gentlemen?" John asked, then switched on the main fridge motor that began to freeze the mist, which started to coat the insulation and the partition walls with ice.

"There you are gentlemen. One refrigerated hold ready for use." John announced proudly, leaving the other officers gawp at the result of the whole night's work.

The officers clapped as the tired crewmen cheered heartily.

Tomlinson turned to John, Blackmore and the weary men, with Day looking on.

"Well done you two, we're now back into the fruit cargo business again. As for you men! To show appreciation for all that you've done, and the long hours you've put in to achieve this magnificent piece of work, each of you will be issued a day's pay from the purser, free and gratis. I don't want to see any of you on board now until 0700 tomorrow. So get off my ship and have a good time ashore, with our blessings." Tomlinson announced, which was received with a rousing cheer from the men, who left the hold in a mini stampede to get ashore.

"I'll be going ashore to see the harbourmaster later on to confirm our loading schedule, then for a meeting with the council of chiefs, which will take me most of the day. Our chief will be getting the ship onto a 12hour steaming notice as of 1900 this evening. So as far as we're concerned, neither of you will be required until at least 1700. Thank you again, for the long and hard work you've put in. See you both at the cocktail party." Tomlinson said, shaking John's then Blackmore's hand.

"I like it when a plan comes together Happy. Don't forget to shut and lock the main bulkhead door on your way out, gentlemen. See you later Joe. Oh, and by the way, give the key only to the chief chef. C'mon Blackie, we know when we're not wanted around here." John said with a big smile, and left with Blackmore following closely behind

CHAPTER XXIII
Nice and Crisp

John woke up during the morning feeling quite hot and bothered, as is normal in a tropical area of the world, and decided to have a leisurely shower before he took a stroll ashore to get some local island souvenirs as 'rabbits' to take back home with him.

"Morning 2nd! Care for a cool glass of pineapple juice?" Henderson greeted when John arrived back into his cabin from his cool shower.

"Yes please! I'm out of duty frees, any chance of fixing me up with a spare packet of 'tipped'?" John asked, taking the cold glass of liquid and drinking deeply from it.

"Yes 2nd! I've got a carton of Craven A, if you're interested. Mind you, the bond is due to be reopened soon so I can get your favourites."

"In that case, just lend me two packets for now."

"I'll swap you if you get me a tin of tickler instead. Same price and all that."

"You've got a deal!" John stated, looking in his locker for a clean shift of uniform.

"By the looks of it, I'm also fresh out of tropicals. Where's my clean shift?" John asked mildly.

"Sorry 2nd, forgot to tell you. The laundry was shut yesterday due to a power failure, and won't be able to provide your clean stuff much before lunchtime. If you're going ashore then I'll get something decent for you, otherwise you'll have to wear what you can until then."

"Well I was hoping to leap ashore for a couple of hours before attending the pre-voyage briefing. I've got a couple of whites somewhere in my locker, but they need pressing. If you'd do them for me, I'll make it an extra tin for you, how about it?" John asked.

"An extra tickler tin? You've got a deal 2nd." Henderson said quickly, grabbing the items and rushing away to get them prepared for John in case he changed his mind.

'Might as well relax for a while and read Helena's letter again. Hope Mam got the extra cash for Dad's op. Bruce should be getting an SLT reply very soon for me.' John whispered to himself.

He climbed up onto his bunk and laid there naked, with his thoughts of Helena and the moments they shared together, which spirited him away into a deep sleep.

"Here you are 2nd. Nice and crisp for you." Henderson said jovially, when he breezed into John's cabin.

"What? Crisp?" John asked disjointedly, for he had been woken up roughly from his very rude dreams of Helena.

"Here you are, just as you ordered. If you're going ashore and not here for lunch, I'll get a roll and a cuppa organised for you."

"Thanks Handy, much appreciated. I have to be back on board in time for the captain's briefing." John stated.

"We're probably sailing early in the morning. Something to do with the unusual tide changes in these parts. Bosun Sinclair asked me to tell you that he's going ashore in half an hour, so to meet him on the gangway."

"Thanks for the info. Here're my stamps for the DF's, so you can get them for me. Don't forget to trade 2 of them for your tickler." John replied swiftly, and sluiced his face in cold water from the cabin sink, before donning his clean clothing.

"Cheers' 2nd." Henderson responded, leaving the cabin for John to get dressed.

"Hello Andy! I'm here because I got your message. I'm still a bit tired from last night's efforts, so take it easy ashore."

"Yes John! We heard all about it from the lads, I'm going ashore to meet some of them and hopefully get a few last 'rabbits' before we knuckle down to the business of getting out of this place."

"Bruce is ashore with the lads from the Met, so maybe we'll bump into them in the 'Hilton'. Here's a tram, let's catch it." John said and racing over the gangway to stop the shuttle tram.

During the short trip to the so-called 'Off Islanders' duty-free shops, both friends had a chance to swap stories as to what

A Beach Party

happened yesterday.

"According to one of the scientists on the research vessel, that tidal wave was a standard height for normal fracture zone earthquakes. That is to say, the underwater earthquake shoves a length of land upwards, or even downwards, which gets to displace the water along its fracture. That's what causes the tidal waves. The higher the push up or down and the length of it, will depend on the height and length of the tidal wave." Sinclair explained.

"Heaven help it if the depth of the crack reaches the same depth of that new trench Mackenzie discovered the other day. We'd be in big trouble otherwise, Andy."

"No John, the wave is like an iceberg. Once the wave reaches a shallow area, only the top half of the wave survives. But as it was explained to me, it's not the height of the wave, but the thickness of it. The Krakatoa tidal wave was 120 foot high, but it was also nearly 200 yards thick. If an island of the same height gets in its way, you'd have thought the wave would be stopped at that point. In fact, the wave would only slosh over it and as the weight of water behind it takes effect, that island would be doomed, and get flattened, depending on the structure and the solidity of the island that is. He also said that a wave splash onto the island could reach almost the same height of the wave, which explained the vegetation loss on the islands that were way above the mean tide height."

"Bloody hell Andy! Do you mean to tell me that these civil engineers are trying to build a coral reef runway only high enough to combat the tidal wave height, and not it's splash height?" John asked swiftly, as his analytical brain started to switch into overdrive.

"Don't know about that John, but from what we saw, they certainly need to build that runway much higher than that. No way would an aircraft survive it unless it was just about to get airborne, or have some solid shelter to take cover."

"It looks as if the so-called boffins called it wrong again." John said softly, swiftly remembering Moore and his efforts.

The tram arrived at their stop where they got off and walking a few yards along the causeway met up with some of the crew sitting down at tables, near a makeshift beach hut and bar.

"Hello Bosun and you 2nd!" they chanted merrily, raising their drinking glasses towards them.

"What're you 'orrible lot up to! Who's the rum bosun? Make it two large tots." Sinclair greeted cheerfully and grabbed two empty glasses from the table.

"Coming right up!" was the reply, and took the two glasses away only to replace them with full ones, overflowing with rum.

"Cheers Lads!" John shouted and raised his container to them before downing his rum in one go.

The crew held their breath and watched John down his drink, then held his glass up side down to indicate that it was all gone.

"Hurrah the 2nd!" they cheered, as yet another full glass arrived to take its place.

Sinclair repeated the feat and had his cheer before they were allowed to sit by the men.

"I was hoping for a quiet couple of hours Andy, as I've got a lot of paperwork to sort out before the captain's pre-voyage meeting." John whispered in Sinclair's ear.

"Not to worry John, I'll make our excuses and leave. We've got to keep sober for the meeting with the scientists later, and before the skippers briefing." Sinclair answered back.

"I don't know about the scientists, but I've work to do Andy."

Sinclair simply nodded to John's reply and announced to the crew that they had work to do, but for them to carry on with the good work of cementing relationships with the locals before they went again.

Sinclair's little speech was greeted with catcalls and ribald remarks as he and John left the men.

John and Sinclair met up with Larter in the hotel, who was talking to Chandler, McIntyre and a few of the other scientists and the crew off the Lysander.

A Beach Party

Larter made the brief introduction between the scientists and his two friends, before everybody settled down to a more sedate gathering than was previously experienced earlier.

"How goes the loading of the fruit cargo Grey?" Moore asked in a sarcastic manner, which John ignored completely.

"I asked you a question 3rd engineer Grey!" Moore demanded belligerently, standing up from his seat and almost knocking half of the drinks off the table in the process.

John merely looked at Moore, then posed a question to McIntyre, who started to answer but was rudely interrupted by Moore.

"Now look here you jumped up oil rag. I've asked you a question. How are you going to take on board even one fresh pineapple as cargo, let alone some 10,000 tons of fresh fruit and ship it some 4,000 miles away without any refrigeration? Moore asked with a slurred voice.

John turned to Moore, and posed a question of his own as his answer.

"How are you managing to swig that ice-cubed drink when your own system failed on the first hour of operation?"

"What? Never mind that, I asked you a question, and I want an answer!" Moore blustered.

The other scientists were getting quite angry with Moore and shouted to him to sit down, but he persisted in his questioning.

Sinclair walked round to Moore, took his drink off him and set it down gently onto a nearby table, then turned swiftly and catching Moore unawares, gave him an upper cut punch that knocked him cold. Sinclair caught the falling body, and carried him to an empty armchair before dumping him onto it like a sack of coal.

"Maybe when your friend sobers' up and shows us some sort of decorum, we'll get somewhere." Sinclair said flatly then rejoined his group.

Chandler stood up and apologised to John and his two friends, for Moore's conduct, explaining that he was due to leave on the clipper but it had to make an emergency take-off in case it got damaged by the tidal wave. He also explained that a few of the passengers had been stranded ashore and would be boarding the *Inverlogie* as the first ship out of the islands because the *Princess* was only a research vessel and full of laboratory equipment.

"That explains the second delay for sailing, Bruce." John whispered.

"That's not all. King Phatt wants Tomlinson to take several tons of gold to Australia to pay for his latest ideas. Ideas that have only been discussed just before you arrived." Larter whispered back.

John was surprised with this news but decided to remain aloof and an outsider to these plans under discussion.

"Well whatever it is Bruce, I've got to be going soon, to get some work done before we sail."

"Glad you mentioned that John, I've got a couple of radio contacts to make before that too. Let's make our apologies and leave, before sleeping beauty over there wakes up and creates an even bigger political scandal."

Larter made the apologies to the scientists for their departure stating that work on board had to be done prior to sailing. Chandler gracefully accepted the apologies and thanked Sinclair for his crude but effective intervention of Moore.

"There's something up there with those scientists that I can't put my finger to. The island is giving me the creeps, as if it's waiting for an encore from that bloody tidal wave the other day." Sinclair said after they climbed off the tram and made their way onto the ship.

"That was Tuesday! Bloody hell, it seems like it was last week. But then I've been working overnight, so I've not caught up yet." John said with a frown.

"Well whatever it is, the captain will sort it out during his briefing. See you both later, I'm off to set watch now, and listen out for the Lysander's new voice frequency. That sparks had me slaving away with him just to get it started." Larter concluded and waved to his friends as he left.

"Yes Bruce, see you later. I've got to go too Andy, as I've got to reset STAN and get it up and ready for you tomorrow,

A Beach Party

so let me know when you've got the courses for me. See you then." John replied and left Sinclair on the upper deck.

"Good evening gentlemen. Since we've arrived a lot has passed under the proverbial bridge. Now that we're leaving we're finding ourselves with a set of passengers that had not been envisaged on the outward voyage. On top of that, we've got a re-routed voyage, that will take us to Fiji and Australia, instead of our pre-planned voyage to Singapore." Tomlinson stated, wading through his ream of papers. He explained what to expect and the dangers of this part of the world in regard to high waves and the instant tropical storms that could whip up in minutes. He issued orders and gave the officers a while to pose any questions before he concluded his pre-voyage meeting.

"We sail on the high tide with the research vessel at 0730 in the morning. Until then gentlemen, suggest you have a quiet evening on board with the passengers, just to make them more at home so to speak. For those others of you who can't keep their shorts on, make sure you've got your overcoats with you and that you're back on board by 0600." Tomlinson stated with a knowing grin, which was greeted with a polite hurrah from his officers.

"2nd engineer Grey, a word if you please." Tomlinson called, as John was about to leave the saloon.

"See you later Bruce!" John whispered, leaving Larter and going over to Tomlinson.

"Yes captain, what can I do for you?" John asked politely.

"Evening John! I understand that all the fruit cargo has been loaded and you've kept a monitor on them. Due to the increase of numbers on board, we've got to take some of the deep frozen supplies from the island depository; otherwise we'll starve. It'll only be about 30 tons of it. How are we fixed?" Tomlinson asked quietly, with Day standing by him.

"We'll just have to squeeze it in with the rest of the ship's supply. Any surplus, then its roast dinners all round until it gets consumed. Alternatively, if you took on say half of it, and put everybody on ration then you'd manage Fiji without trouble. I'm saying that Joe, because the main fridge is already on overload and can't take much more. Mind you I'm talking about deep frozen stuff, but if the islanders offer you a few of their prized pot-bellied pigs and a couple of barrels of live fish as cargo to eat on the way, then that's a different story. That, however would be a great step back in time to go back to the old days of sailing ships, of rum, bum and baccy, and 'shiver me timbers' me old hearties, Joe me lad! " John replied in a jovial manner.

"I don't know about you, but I think that sounds about right, and you obviously agree Happy. Yes, I'll get a good 30 tons first then ask the King for his 'live' contribution for good measures.

Be ready to receive it first thing in the morning, but I'll get the first mate to supervise it all for you. Thanks for your input John " Tomlinson laughed at John's attempts of impersonating a pirate on the old Spanish main, before he left his two engineers in the now empty saloon.

"Keep going John, you're three up already, and mind me peg leg." Day said with a chuckle, as he too got into the instant mood of pretending to be pirates.

"So I'm still the outside engineer Happy? What about Blackmore, isn't he the one that should be doing the job?" John asked in puzzlement.

"No! He's still required below decks. We need an experienced officer on deck and as you're the obvious choice, you're it. But the icing on the cake is that you're now a temporary acting 2nd engineer, which attracts half of a 2nd's pay. You've got what we need John, and we will make certain that you'll be in the frame for a proper promotion when we dock in Brisbane. That is of course unless you choose not to take the challenge."

"You're talking to the wrong man if that's the case. As I've said earlier Happy, it's payback time and now I'm paying up. I always keep my word and you know that too." John said, poking Day's shoulder gently with his forefinger.

A Beach Party

Day smiled briefly, then looked into John's eyes.

"Just making certain I'm talking to the young engineer I used to know many voyages ago. See you as and when John. Keep in touch." Day concluded as he too left John.

"What was all that about John?" Larter asked suddenly appearing through a double door.

"Just been given my orders for the next leg of the voyage. I'm now officially a temporary acting 2nd engineer, and as of now, the pay to go with it, whatever that is."

"Temporary acting 2nd engineer? On the sliding scale I'd say about £10 a day more than a qualified 3rd. I know that because our pay scale is roughly on par with yours, so mine is at the same rate as you at 3rd engineer's level. Congratulations John, you'll be able to lash Andy and me up more often. Mine's a Tom Collins whilst you're at it."

"Why not, you old Scouser. And I'll be able to pay off the lump sum Tomlinson sent home for me, before we get back to Blighty again." John replied cheerfully, and ordering the drinks they sat down in comfortable chairs to take their ease.

CHAPTER XXIV
Surfing

John had completed his upper deck rounds early, and finished up on the boat deck having his usual quiet smoke in company with Larter and Evans.

"The MET boys and the scientists have had a hectic time trying to sort out the seismograph traces and the tremors felt several times during the night. 'Sparks' the Lysander radio operator, has asked us to keep an ear out for him when he takes off around the time we sail." Evans stated evenly, stubbing out the remains of his cigarette.

"Yes, there've been a few rumbles from that volcano which seem to have upset a some others way to the west of us. There's a large fracture zone only a thousand miles to our west and it's been playing up too, lets hope for these people's sake this one doesn't start performing, or we'll all be in the proverbial dung heap." Larter added with a frown and a worried look on his face.

"Shouldn't bother us, because we're due to sail south from here, at least according to your large map. No, this group of islands are safe enough." John responded in a more positive manner, which seemed to uplift the mood of the conversation that flowed slowly and quietly as the early morning sunrise.

"Must go now and take my cargo 'temp' reading before I report to the captain. He must have charmed King Phatt for him to get all that extra frozen stuff on board. The after cargo deck is like a zoo now with all those aminals stowed on it, and I don't mean drunken sailors sleeping off a night of debauchery either." John said quietly.

"Yes it's been one good run ashore here. Hope we get a return trip sometime, as I fancy setting up a beach bar to replace the one that got lost." Larter replied and looked shore side at the last of the lights being switched off from their night duties.

"We'll drink a pint to all that, next time we get one." Evans nodded in agreement, as the little meeting broke up and they went their separate ways.

A Beach Party

John watched the smaller research vessel make its way slowly out of the harbour, before his ship started to follow closely behind.

'Maoi I'ti Princess, is an apt name for her as she's looking pretty good in the water. Just as well we're going slow or we'd give her something she'd always remember us by.' John mused, feeling the ship vibrate with the power of the engines.

Both ships moved slowly into the lagoon and slipped out through the narrow channel of the coral reefs and into the relatively deeper water of the plateau.

John left his favourite spot on the foc'sle, made his way up to the bridge to make his initial report, but decided to check with Sinclair if STAN was ready.

"Aye it's ready. Give me a minute." Sinclair started to say when Tomlinson called to them.

"Not just now 2nd, the bosun is in the middle of a tricky manoeuvre." he ordered.

"Aye aye captain!" John responded and stood by Sinclair to watch the 2 ships pirouetting neatly around each other.

"What was the idea of the smaller ship going before us, when we've got a deeper draught, Andy?" John whispered aside.

"She had to clear the harbour and the channel to get out of our way. But she had to be quick, because there's a short high tide of only half an hour. We've just cleared the channel and sorted ourselves out for our own courses. Won't be long now to get STAN connected up, so wait a moment John." Sinclair whispered back.

"Thank you captain, its not often I get escorted by a fair princess. Good hunting, over." Tomlinson said into the radio microphone, and waited for the response from the research vessel.

"Roger that, except we seem to have picked up a few gremlins in our engines. My chief engineer informs me that our *Princess* has had her drink spiked and doesn't like it. Wrong drink for our engines I'm afraid. We need to return to harbour and get the system cleared before the tide turns against us. Over!"

"Both tugs are out of the area now, so I suggest we wait here until the next high tide and I'll tow or push you back. Over!" Tomlinson replied calmly.

"Yes that will be fine. I've got a small manoeuvring engine to get us alongside after that. Over!"

"Well at least you'll be able to keep the way on the ship unless you care to come alongside until then? Over!"

"No that will not be necessary, just as long as we get into position with plenty of fenders, ready for you to give us a shove, that will suit me. Over!"

"As I'm sailing light by at least half a fathom, we won't have to wait until the full tide again. I make that in about two hours from now. Over!"

"Thank you Tomlinson, that is a good idea. I'll hold my position here for you to line up on me. We'll use megaphones when we're in close quarters. Over!"

Evans came onto the bridge and told Tomlinson that he should tell the other ship's captain to listen out on an aircraft frequency, which Tomlinson did.

Evans then switched the frequency over for Tomlinson to listen to.

"Hello Base, this is Sandy. Radio check! Over!" came the crackling voice.

"This is Base, hearing you loud and clear Sandy. Over!"

"The *Inverlogie* pit stops are working a treat. Have just picked up my outer fuel pods and will be making one sweep around Mulani before heading back. No ships or fishing craft sighted so far. Will return on my pre-flight plans. Over!"

"Message received Sandy. Make a little detour and give our two friends a little fly past before you return. They should be clear of the lagoon by now. Over!"

The usual static from the radio crackled when Sandy spoke, but there was a clear signal from the base.

A Beach Party

"Roger that!" came the voice which was followed closely by a loud rumbling noise followed by a series of explosions

"What the fuckin' hell was that? Quick pilot! Get us out of here, preferably onto the water." the voice shouted out alarmingly.

"Did you get that base? Mulani has just erupted and by the look of it she is about to blow herself to smithereens. She's sent a couple of fairly high waves towards us, about 70 feet high. We've got to try and beat them before they sink our pit stops, else we'll be paddling home. Over!"

"Hello Sandy this is the *Maoi I'ti Princess*. Professor Chandler speaking. You've got to beat 200knots to outrun the waves. Be careful and make sure that you're on water if Mulani does explode else you'll be swatted out of the air with the blast shock waves. Over!"

"Hello *Princess*. Thanks for your tip. We can't do more than 70knots even if we're outside pushing it. The pilot has just landed us onto the last wave. The plan is to surf on it until we reach the atoll, but for you to know, according to our altimeter, the waves are steady around 70 feet."

Before Sandy had the chance to finish his transmission, everybody heard an enormous bang and several screams of panic and fear coming from the plane.

"Oh my god! Mulani has just blown itself apart. There're dirty great boulders the size of icebergs coming our way. There's some sort of a black ribbon-shaped cloud that just passed us and bit off our starboard wing tip. And I'm seeing red hot lava pouring into the sea like a river. Scratch one boil in the ocean. There's just a great big hole where the pyramid used to be, and it's swallowing most of the ocean around it as it's falling down into it like the Niagara. The pilot has been knocked unconscious, and the navigator is bleeding from his ears and is trying to keep us flying. We were about 50 miles from it but the blast wave has blown us across the water towards the atoll much faster than a bloody jet engine. As long as the engine doesn't catch fire as well then we'll make it. At this rate, our ETA will be about 1 hour from now. The explosion and the cliff rock fall into the ocean, has created a dirty great MEGA TSUNAMI of a good 160 feet high I reckon. Hope the skipper wakes up to get us up over the top of it for us to surf home, as I've forgotten my flippers. We'd need a couple of parachutes to get down off it though. Hope me missus and nipper are okay. Must stock up the beach bar when we get back, bad for tourists when there's no beer in the bar.

I wish this bloody aileron would work properly. Maybe the aircrew will do a proper job next time. Come to think of it, we'll be needing a new fuselage, as this one is now more holy than righteous. For fuck sake navigator, get us up over that bloody great wave. It doesn't matter if we don't reach our flight plan heights just get us up-up-up-up up C'mon navigator, up-up-up. That's it, a little more a little more-more-more!

It's just past underneath us, now get us back down again, it'll give us a piggyback home. Down-down-down. That's it. Now just sit back and enjoy the ride. We're probably travelling faster than any airliner. Maybe we've got a rocket shoved up our arses. The engine has just conked out, now we're just a bunch of tourists on a surfers holiday." Sandy ranted in a delirious manner but still kept up his running commentary.

Tomlinson had heard enough and radioed the *Princess*.

"Captain. We've got about just an hour or so to get ourselves into some shelter. I'll tow you around the back of the atoll, get yourself lashed to us when we get behind the Ilani Island. Over!"

"We've got less than that captain. Ilani is no good, suggest the back end of Wianii, as it's a good 300 feet high, or even Maoi 'Iti' as its almost protected by Kianii opposite it. I'm expecting severe gale force winds to hit us within thirty minutes and the wave shortly afterwards to be around the 200foot mark when it hits the archipelago. The splash height will be around the 250feet mark, so we need to be as close to the shore of the island as possible yet give enough room for the water to splash over the top of it. Don't forget it's not so much the height of the wave but its

A Beach Party

thickness that does all the damage. I'm turning around to get hitched onto you. We need to be at least behind Maoi I'ti before the first lot of waves and the wind hits us. Over!"

"Let's get going. I'll keep an ear out for our plane spotter. Out." Tomlinson said quickly then turned to the plane and its base station.

"Hello Base this is the *SS Inverlogie*, Captain Tomlinson speaking. Be advised that a severe storm is heading this way and should hit the atoll within thirty minutes. There are a series of short shock waves about 70 feet high, which is followed by a MEGA TSUNAMI with an estimated height of 190feet plus. I've got the disabled research vessel under tow and will be running for cover behind Wianii. Sandy, suggest that you try and position your plane so that when the wave hits the atoll, you'll be stranded on top of Wianii. If you overshoot, we'll catch you on the other side where we'll be waiting for you. Good luck. Over!"

"This is base. Thank you *Inverlogie*, King Phatt has been warned and is getting the islanders mustered on top of all islands above 300 feet. Good luck to you both. Out!"

"This is Sandy. Wave now at 190 feet, just been joined by three fishing boats that managed to get up the incline. The wave has just hit the plateau and has thickened to about half a mile and appears to be much steeper now. It's fanned out further than I can see with my binoculars. Can see the atoll in the distance. There is a second wave behind this one, but not as high, although it seems a lot quicker. The storm is hitting us now. We'll be coming around the mountain when we come, so have a soft mat for us to land on when we do. Here comes the rain, something to drink at last. Will keep on air for as long as possible." the same delirious voice shouted.

"Right then bosun, lets collect our friend and get the hell out of here. First mate tell the 5th mate to organise the passengers using standard procedure, then get yourself down onto the stern and take charge of the tow. 2nd engineer, inform the engine room what is happening. Then I need you to grab hold of the 3rd mate and go through the ship like a dose of salts and make us as watertight as you can. Report back when you've done so.

Messenger, start recording all this, word for word and in your best writing. Evans, you will maintain radio contact with the Lysander and keep me patched up with the *Princess*." Tomlinson ordered calmly to each person that was on the bridge.

A Beach Party

Chapter XXV
Geronimo

"**Ship** secured for collision and storm, captain." John reported, panting for breath due to his exertions.

"Very good 2nd. Get aft and see if the first mate needs your service. We keep parting the tow, and we've not a lot of time left to get behind the I'ti atoll. If we fail to get the *Princess* into safety then we've lost one hell of a pricey ship. Phone me direct if you need anything." Tomlinson replied tersely, taking relative bearings from the atoll and plotting it on his chart.

"Aye aye captain, on my way." John said quickly and was gone in a flash towards the stern.

"First mate. Been sent down to see if you've got towing problems." John greeted.

"Glad you turned up, we keep losing our tow even though we've got everything covered." the first mate replied anxiously.

John looked at the towing gear and over to the *Princess,* who was being dragged slowly behind them.

He rushed to a deck locker and opened it.

"First mate, get these sent over to the other ship, they'll know what to do with it." John shouted, holding up two Panama plates. The first mate ordered one of the sailors to throw a heaving line over to the *Princess*, which was successful on the 3rd attempt. Within minutes, the plates had been hauled over to the *Princess,* before the heaving line was sent back.

An officer from the *Princess* called over using his megaphone, stating that the plates were just the thing and that they were now in position.

The first mate acknowledged this with his own megaphone, before going over to a sound telephone and speaking to the bridge, then coming back to where John was standing.

"Now that the tow is secure, we can increase speed. I've got an extra cable around the after capstan in case of the main tow snapping. But we should be okay now Grey."

"The captain will be slapping his anchors on when we get in behind Wianii, so I suggest that you and your opposite number on the *Princess* prepare for a collision aft." John said almost absentmindedly, watching the research vessel following along behind its much bigger sister, seemingly only a few feet astern, yet in fact it was a good 50 yards.

"Yes, I've already got that in hand. But that was a good bit of thinking Grey, even though you are only engine room staff." The first mate said arrogantly.

"It just goes to prove that we're not just 'oily rags' then first mate." John responded and leaving the poop deck to report back to the bridge, managed to get into the bridge before a howling gale suddenly hit the ship, causing her it to lean over to port at an alarming angle.

Most everybody on the bridge was sent hurtling towards the port side before the ship managed to right herself again.

"That, gentlemen, is the weather for the next few days. One down, and about six to go, so get yourselves lashed onto something or somebody will get seriously injured." Tomlinson said calmly, struggling to get himself back to the navigation chart on the other side of the bridge.

"Starboard 10. Make speed 10 knots. We've got to clear the open bit of the atoll before the first lot of waves hit us." Tomlinson ordered the grabbed the radio mike.

"Hello *Princess*. Making speed 10 knots, just hang on to my nylons and try not to stretch them. Estimated time for the first series of waves to hit is ten minutes. Once we've cleared the second open stretch between Maoi and Wianii we'll be stopping engines and putting the island to my starboard side for you to steer to port and come along the lee side of me.

When I give you the word, release both bow and stern anchors. Get as much nylons and ropes as possible lashed onto me when you come alongside. Don't forget the fenders, that way we'll be like a large raft. We'll probably have a swarm of fishing

A Beach Party

boats around us, so have the occupants taken on board, animals included if they've got any. Over!"

"Roger that *Inverlogie*. Our towline has been secured thanks to your Panama plate fitments. Without them we would have parted our tow yet again and would probably have floundered when the storm hit us. We estimate the Mega Tsunami to hit the atoll in about 15 minutes. Awaiting your instructions. Out."

"Hello *Inverlogie*, remember us? Oh we're just sailing along on a crest of a wave, tayatti ti tatti dee." Sandy sang.

"We're nearly on our way in and our altimeter is showing the height of 200 feet. Skipper okay now. Could do with a large mug of cocoa and a suggestive biscuit to dunk We've just been joined by several more fishing boats and got ourselves lashed together to help keep each other afloat. Mind you, once the ocean has gone we're in for a heavy landing. Must go now. Keep listening." the delirious Sandy said in a much calmer voice

"Hello Sandy. We're listening and waiting for you. Storm has just hit us. The first lot of waves are about to arrive any minute. The smaller islands have been evacuated, and the atoll has been sealed off. We'll be behind Wianii waiting for you. *Princess* estimates your travelling at around 400mph and your ETA in about 10 minutes. Providing that you get carried over Kianii you should be on course for the top of I'ti. Over!" Tomlinson advised as he repeated every sentence.

"Thanks *Inverlogie*, good to know there's some bastard listening. I'll drop by and see you later. Out!"

"What a brave man he is." Tomlinson said humbly and replaced the radio mike.

"Wianii cove on green 10 captain." Sinclair announced.

"Very good bosun. Prepare to stop engines when I give the 'Mark' signal, bosun."

"*Princess*, am about to stop engines in two minutes. Prepare to turn to port on my mark. Over!" Tomlinson ordered over the radio.

"Standing by." Came the reply

Tomlinson looked at his stopwatch and shouted, "Mark!"

"2nd engineer. Let me know when you see the bows of the *Princess* come around my stern."

John did as he was ordered.

"She's coming nicely around the stern in an arc. The first mate has only got 5 chains of tow line captain." John advised.

"Very good 2nd. Starboard 10. Slow astern. That should give us a little bit more sea room." Tomlinson replied, then grabbed the ships tannoy system microphone.

"Second mate, standby port side with all fenders. Get ready to grab her as she comes alongside. First mate, secure the stern towline then drop the stern anchor on my mark. 3rd mate, make ready with the bow towline and get it over to her quickly. Then drop the for'ard anchor on my mark." Tomlinson ordered in rapid succession before he turned his attentions back to the bridge.

"Mid ships. Stop engines. When the ship has started to lose way port your helm to 15 degrees."

"*Princess*. Stand by to drop your anchors on my mark. Over!"

"Roger that! But we've only one for'ard anchor on board. Over!"

"That's fine *Princess*. You're coming alongside nicely. Prepare to receive my heaving lines and heavy nylons. Double up with yours once secured. Out!"

John stood on the bridge wing and watched the *Princess* who was almost half the size, come neatly alongside the much bigger ship then observed the several ropes snaking across the ever decreasing gap between them, before there was a slight nudge as both ships bumped into each other.

The sailors were working at a furious pace to get both ships secured together as the bad weather hampered their efforts. After a little while when all the ropes were neatly tied and secured the waist gangway was slid into place for cross ship access.

Tomlinson stood by John and observed the same, before he ordered his mark.

The two ships were now anchored in the little cove of Wianii, sheltering from the fierce winds, and the imminent onslaught of the mega tsunami rapidly approaching their fragile wall of rock.

The first mate came rushing onto the bridge to report when the loud sloshing noises of the first lot of waves smacked into the island.

Everybody who was on deck saw the waves rush past their cove and out into the ocean again, and realised that they were only baby ones in comparison to what they were expecting.

"Both ships secured. Have got a double anchor watch, but we're now being plagued with small fishing boats, captain." The first mate reported.

"Tell them to secure alongside the *Princess*, then come aboard us. If they've got animals, have them winched on board a.s.a.p." Tomlinson ordered calmly.

"It looks as if we're the duty Noah's Ark Bosun." Tomlinson joked.

"Aye captain. If we go then so does everybody else. How long for the impact?" Sinclair asked after a moment of watching the busy scene on both ships decks.

Tomlinson took the tannoy microphone again and announced that the mega tsunami was due to strike in two minutes, and that all personnel should get off the upper deck but be ready in case of a quick exit from the cove.

"Better tell the engine room what's happening 2nd." Tomlinson said loudly over the noise of the howling winds.

But suddenly, there was an eerie silence that fell over the place with not even a breath of air, nor a spot of rain to break it. That silence was broken by a raucous voice of Sandy

"Hello *Inverlogie!* That's a Scotch name, so hello you Scotch bastards! Look out! Gangway! Gangway for a lady with a baby!" came the panicky voice, which fell silent for a few seconds followed by a faint whispering sound, which got louder by the second until there was just a great howling noise approaching. Everybody looked up to the towering rock formation of the island, with baited breath.

"We've just steamrollered our way over the outer islands. Those poor bastards didn't stand a chance, and we're about to hit the main islands. Look out! Look out! Gangway! Here we come!

"G-E-R-O-N-I-M-O!" Sandy shouted over his microphone, which was immediately followed by a very loud crashing and slopping sound, followed by several curses and swearing from him which was drowned out by the static and crackling from the radio until that too fell silent.

Tomlinson blew the ship siren, which was drowned out by the thunderous noises on the other side of the island. A large slap was heard, before the island started to tremble and groan with the enormous weight of water that was engulfing it.

The wave in front of the island had been stopped, but the rest of the massive juggernaut just rolled by on each side of it and created a large vortex of water almost within reach of the two sheltering ships. The wave just steamrollered its way right over the lower parts of the island and swept away anything in its path.

Everybody saw how it literally towered above the *Inverlogie* let alone the *Princess,* as it rushed past their shelter, and they dared not to look too much in case it spotted them and came back to complete its destruction.

"Bloody hell Andy! The last wave we sheltered from was a mere baby compared with this one. Look! The water has slopped right over that part of the island and is coming down this side at us with large boulders in its teeth. Look at all the debris raining down onto the foreshore. Look…!" John shouted and pointing to the waterfall coming their way.

"The water is overlapping, must get down on deck, Andy for god sake follow me, never mind the helm. Joe, I'm borrowing your bosun. Look there!" John shouted and gesticulating to what he saw.

Tomlinson looked to where John was pointing but just stood there smoking his cigarette.

"We're safe from that deluge John, as we're a good two sea miles from its drop zone and the beach. It's the actual island that's worrying me. It's made of solid stone but if it gives way before the wave has passed then we're in shit-street." Tomlinson replied, but saw John and Sinclair disappear off the bridge and arrive onto the for'ard cargo deck.

"Quick Andy, grab that length of rope, call that man on the *Princess* and throw it to him. Tell him to secure it to somewhere sound, whilst I wrap it around our cargo winch. See that other rope; tell him also to wrap it around another point.

I'll get the first one onto the cargo winch and the second one around the base of the central derrick mast." John shouted, pointing to the objects before he grabbed hold of the first rope and tied it securely around a stanchion on the *Inverlogie*, then went and wrapped the second rope around the winch before starting it up to take the slack from the rope. He left the engine running on the winch and raced up onto the foc'sle, to spike the anchor cable that was slipping away out of its capstan.

Just as the man on the *Princess* managed to secure the rope when the vortex of the wave shifted, and began to try and drag the smaller ship away from the bigger one, and then trying to pull both of them from their moorings. Most of the outer fishing vessels that were lashed against the *Princess* got torn away and disappeared into the maelstrom of the wave as it continued to steamroller itself swiftly away from the island.

Both ships were slammed against each other, with their anchor capstans screaming with the strain of trying to keep the ships held onto the rocks as the main bulk of the wave did its best to suck them into its death trap. Large boulders and solid debris kept hitting the bows and sides of the *Inverlogie*, as she protected the *Princess* from the onslaught. Whole trees were being hurled around like javelins with several landing onto the *Inverlogie's* deck and causing deep dents or holes where they landed.

"For God sake Andy, keep your ruddy head down. Look at the holes in the deck they're making, some of them are big enough to throw the proverbial kitchen sink through. Any more damage to our hull and we'll end up like a flippin' colander!" John shouted, and ducked yet another large piece of rock coming his way.

"Is there any more rope we can use? Only some of them holding us together are snapping like cotton." Sinclair shouted back.

John raced over to a deck locker and dragging out water hoses threw them to him.

"Couple them up and throw them over to the *Princess*, and tell the man you see hiding below their foc'sle brow, to tie them onto his winches and any other solid stanchion or whatever. It might not be much but it's all we've got left." He ordered and proceeded to wrap his end of the hoses onto the base of the for'ard derrick.

The person on the *Princess* understood what was wanted and with frantic haste managed to secure the hose line before some more of the securing ropes started to snap and whip backwards like an angry snake striking its attacker.

Tomlinson saw what John and his helpers were doing and grabbed the ships wheel to keep the ship almost hovering over it's anchorage by keeping the ships engines moving, with the ship straining against its tether of the anchors that tied her down. But it was Mother Natures much more powerful actions she fought against as the vortex of water tried its hardest to snatch them as yet another morsel of a few ships to devour.

Against all the odds, she managed to hang on to her little shelter, before the giant wave finally passed the archipelago. It seemed to leave with increasing anger as if it was not quite satiated enough just to swallow a whole host of islands that were erstwhile enjoying themselves in the cosy life of an archipelago that even man had ignored for centuries past.

"We're not exactly in the clear yet captain. Because it will take the wave a good two minutes to clear the area." Chandler said, as he appeared onto the bridge.

"Hello Chandler. Glad you came over to join us. How's the *Princess*' captain doing? Beginning to wonder if the plan was working or not. Still, we had a dummy run at the start of our voyage across the pond, for us to know what to look out for." Tomlinson replied with a grin.

Both men looked down over the front part of their ships and saw the three men involved in a heroic struggle to try and save

A Beach Party

the two ships from parting and being swept away into the maelstrom of the wave.

"There are three more heroes to write home about when it's all over. But then I expect that sort of thing from my officers." Tomlinson said with quiet satisfaction, as Chandler surveyed the scene.

"We were forced to hide behind some small island on the other side of the Pacific. The one we hid behind was almost wiped off the map. So heaven help these in the archipelago." Tomlinson informed.

"We must have missed that as we were down on the Galapagos Islands before coming here." Chandler replied, then looked at his watch.

"3, 2, 1... The wave should be flattening down now as it passes us. It was much bigger and thicker than we anticipated, still it was an interesting project." Chandler added.

"Project? Do you mean to tell us that you were expecting this bloody monster, and didn't let on to the rest of us?" Tomlinson exploded angrily.

"We had an idea something was up but couldn't pin it down to this exact hour, day or even year. Still now that it's happened, we know what to expect if there's a next time. You chose your shelter well captain, but we're keen to see what has happened to the rest of the archipelago, especially Maoi's volcano." Chandler responded, still unperturbed by the momentous event as performed by Mother Nature.

"We're still not out of the woods yet Chandler, as the aircraft has reported a second wave." Tomlinson said swiftly, then added.

"They were three very brave men in that Lysander, that reported the second wave, Chandler. They say its probably about another five minutes behind that big one."

"Ah yes, the second one. According to our calculations and our radar reports, it's only half the size, but is due any minute now. That's the one I've come onto your ship to watch."

"Well here it is gentlemen. Look, it's coming a round the corners of the lower half of the island." John said, arriving onto the bridge to give a damage report, then watched with mouth agape this second killer wave that swept past their little cove in its race to catch up with its bigger one in front.

"All stations, all stations. This is Maoi I'ti Radio. Maoi I'ti radio calling any station. Over!"

Tomlinson walked swiftly over to the radio mike and answered calmly.

"Base this is *SS Inverlogie*, with *MV Maoi I'ti Princess* in company. We're still behind Wianii Island. How's life on the islands? Over!"

"Bloody hell *Inverlogie!* Well done. Thank God you survived. We're still getting reports in but apart from the two Maoi's, Wianii, Ilani, and Kianii have survived because they're above the wave height. But the rest have been totally destroyed, and either gone or reduced to a mere stump. Over!"

"At least the main islands have survived and I'm glad you're okay. We're on our way just as soon as we find somewhere to park. Please advise on the runway structure, as it's probably the best place, if given that the harbour is now no longer navigable. Over!"

Before the base answered there was a loud but triumphant voice that broke through the transmission.

"Hah Hah! There you are *Inverlogie!*. Remember me? Oi you bastard birdbrain! Cooook Hoooo! Oi! Yooo Hooo! Hello *Inverlogie* you Scotch haggis yafflin' bastards! Never mind scratching your bollocks and picking your fuckin' nose, we're stuck up here on the top of this pile of rock. Can't land due to lack of water. In fact we've got no fuckin' plane 'cept this piece of junk I'm talking into. Somebody send a ladder for us. And make it a bloody great one at that. Hello you slope headed bastards! Speak to me! For fuck sake come and get me. Yooo hoo! Hello! Hello! *Inverlogie,* speak to me you bagpipe blowing bastards!" shouted the almost unrecognisable voice of Sandy.

"Hello you bastards! I can see you. For fuck sake come and get us." the crazed voice shouted.

A Beach Party

Everybody on the bridge gasped at this loud interruption, and were very glad that the men on the Lysander had managed to survive their somewhat roller coaster of a ride.

"Hello Sandy, you skiving gits! Keep regulation transmission at all times. Get yourselves back to base and make your debriefing in a proper manner, you dopey sods. We want your name rank and number, don't forget." the base answered calmly but with a hint of relief in its voice.

"You stupid bastards, why didn't you tell us we had a date with a fuckin' great box of explosives! No way are we gonna pay for the damage to this crate. We've been bloody lucky we're not wearing wings and playing a woofters guitar."[*]

"Hello Sandy, this is the *Inverlogie*, captain Tomlinson speaking. Glad you made it old son. We can see you above your base, and will come and get you as soon as we get a team together. Don't fly off now will you. We've got plenty of cocoa and dunking biscuits waiting for you. Give us about an hour, we'll have the red carpet ready for you."

"A bleedin' hour? We can't stay up here that bleedin' long like ruddy stuffed chickens. We've got a flight debriefing to hand in. Fuck the cocoa and biscuits, make it a gallon of the amber nectar and a few bottles of the hard stuff all round and we might just consider it."

Tomlinson started to laugh as did the rest of the men on the bridge, with gladness and relief that those three brave men had managed to survive all what they had gone through.

"Fair enough Sandy, we'll make sure you've got a good measure of Nelson's blood. On our way! Tomlinson. Out."

"*Inverlogie,* this is base. We're still getting reports in, but the atoll has been flooded up to level 5, which is at 200 feet. All people within that area are suspected as having been drowned. From all accounts there is an estimated loss of life throughout the archipelago at around 70%. We have confirmed reports that most

---

[*] An expression to describe the musical instrument, Lyre.

of the utilities or public works below ground have managed to survive, but as said, everything above ground up to level 5 is either destroyed or out of action. The harbour appears to be wrecked or non-workable. The atoll has been given a Mohican haircut with approx two thirds denuding of vegetation. Although strangely enough, the leeward side of the main islands managed to escape untouched. The fresh water lake has been, or is suspected of being contaminated. The big lagoon has been nearly filled in with the debris from the flattened islands. The Pink Lagoon has been filled in with debris, with all that pink sand piled up into one large dune and covering the destroyed runway. The causeway is now twice its height, and the harbour totally destroyed.

But you will find a cove directly under our control tower that has a small landing jetty, which somehow has escaped damage. The water should be around a good 5 fathoms, so you should be safe for parking alongside it. We'll send somebody down to get you tied up when you've got our boys back from their nature study lessons. Over!"

"Roger that base. Effecting rescue now. Will call you in 2 hours. Over."

"Thank you *Inverlogie*. This is my last transmission due to the lack of generator power. Will keep a listening watch only. Kindly use the 4 or 8 Megacycle frequency to inform my own contact of the situation. Use any callsign with GYA or GBZ. Over!"

"Roger that base, GYS or GBZ. Hope to see you soon once we've rescued our intrepid friends. Out!" Tomlinson replied, before he started to issue a series of orders.

"Mr Chandler, ask your captain to weigh anchors. We shall be moving with him alongside, and intend to anchor alongside the I'ti side of the runway embankment. Just call over with your megaphone when it comes to the close manoeuvres. In the meantime, get your team of expert rock climbers kitted up and fetch those poor men down from their little perch." Tomlinson remarked, which sent Chandler scurrying out of the bridge and onto his own ship.

A Beach Party

"First mate, check and see that the bows are seaworthy, then inform your opposite number to weigh anchors. Tell the 2nd mate to ensure any surviving fishing vessels remain secured alongside the *Princess*. 3rd mate, accompany the 2nd engineer and inspect my ship from stem to stern, starting with the bow section. I have got a damage control team already working in the for'ard hold, but make a quick survey and report back. Messenger, tell the engine room to obey telegraphs." Tomlinson ordered in a calm but stern tone of voice.

Soon the battered ship managed to release herself from her anchorage and left her little shelter, before she steamed slowly and awkwardly around the back of the atoll towards her 'new' harbour.

"Port 15. Slow ahead! First mate! Be on the ball to receive the heaving lines from the shore party. There's a small 'landing' jetty at the end of the island, so get ready to pay out as much nylons as possible. 2nd engineer, I need you to ensure we've got full power to my winches just in case we've got to warp ourselves alongside. Evans, call our crazy Sandy friends and tell them that JC will be sending them a lift to bring them back down to earth again, just as soon as somebody puts a shilling in the electric meter." Tomlinson ordered automatically, taking rapid bearings of the island so that he could fix his transit from the cove to the 'docking' area.

The ship moved almost crablike with her smaller sister holding onto the one side, and a veritable raft of flotsam clamped on her other side.

"3rd Mate, start to fend off the flotsam as we pass the runway. When done so, get ready with the fenders onto and around our bow just in case we bump into anything that will make more holes in it. Stop engines. Starboard your helm bosun and watch her as she comes alongside those markers the shore party have given us. First mate, get the gangway rigged up and ready for slinging over to the landing area you see at the end of the island"

Tomlinson shouted out, keeping a close eye on the rapid encounter between ship and the islands.

"Stop engines. Get the heaving lines ashore quickly and get those fenders out now. Slow astern. Bosun as soon as we get almost alongside, midships your wheel, then stop engines."

John was at his usual place, and on hand to help some of the sailors to get fenders over the side just before there was a heavy bump and a loud clank which reverberated through out the ship, which told everybody that the ship hit solid land.

"Bloody hell. That sounds as if we've just lost our propeller." John shouted over to the harassed man.

"Yes 2nd engineer, and we've got to be swift to reel in the nylons else we'll bounce off the rocks again." The 3rd mate admitted, giving John an anxious look.

John didn't say anything, but ran across the deck and spoke to a sailor on the *Princess*.

"Quick, get your skipper to use his little manoeuvring engine to push us against the dock wall." he shouted.

Within moments John could feel the sideways thrust of the *Princess* pushing her bigger sister towards the docking area that was prepared for them.

Before long, both ships were nestling alongside their new berth, with people and their animals streaming ashore over the two gangways that had been hoisted into position.

"Look at that 3rd mate. Talk about Noah's Ark and all that. What you see is what is left of virtually an entire existence from these islands. What price the joint of pork now, I wonder? More to the point, what price of a new propeller." John said softly as both he and the 3rd mate stood side-by-side witnessing the exodus of life.

"Judging by what's left of the vegetation, there's not enough to feed a bloody parrot. The island is totally beaten up and it looks as if we're the only game in town for quite a while, 2nd!"

John looked at the carnage and destruction the wave had caused the atoll, and agreed with the statement.

A Beach Party

"Yes 3rd mate, we've been lucky not have been sunk along with this bloody island. This atoll will never be the same for at least another 10 years, by the looks of things. The fresh water lake has been contaminated. Although the main turbine citadel survived, there's no steam to drive the turbines for the electricity or even any power to pump out the flooded caverns.

If my memory serves me correct, the main fridges and larder storage system were on level 2 which has been wiped out, which also means that apart from tinned stuff, there's no food for the people to eat. All those animals will be eaten within one day given the appetites of these Phatt people. Just as well they're not cannibals or we'd all have to look out." John said slowly, looking slowly around the derelict place.

"For god sake 2nd! Stop giving me the heebie jeebies, will you. We won't be long here now that the wave has gone, so let's hope the skipper will put his skates on and get us off this bloody place." The 3rd mate moaned.

"King Phattie and his gang will prevent us from leaving until such times as we've restored some sort of order. So best you are on your best behaviour and volunteer as much of your time as possible to help these people, or you'll be one of the first people to end up in the hot tub, so to speak. Besides, we've got a propeller problem to sort out before we even think of leaving." John replied jokingly as if to further wind up the already agitated 3rd mate.

"Now listen here Grey, stop that or I'll be forced to thump you. I don't take kindly to talk like that."

"Thump me 3rd? Why me? I'm only surmising what might happen if we don't get away from here. Our propeller and bows will probably see to all that." John persisted, but stood way back in case the man tried to re-enforce his statement.

The 3rd mate looked angrily at John, but merely left angrily and muttering to himself about all engineers were queer and as nutty as a fruitcake.

John looked at the damaged ship and wondered if Tomlinson would risk sailing across the largest ocean on a sieve for a ship.

A Beach Party

Chapter XXVI
Recovery

John stood on the bridge talking to Sinclair watching the rescue and the return of the three airmen, who landed on the for'ard cargo hatch.

"Whey Heyyy! And about fuckin' time too." Sandy shouted as he landed onto the ship and promptly kissed the steel deck.

"Wait 'till I get hold of my missus, I'm going to fuck her until her fanny drops off. It'll even be coming out of her earholes when I've fucked some sense into her. Hello sailor! Seen the golden rivet yet? Mind the skipper he's got a bad head. Mind the navigator, he's got half a tree stuck up his arse when we landed. Oi Jack! Watch where you're putting your fuckin' hands, unless you give us a big kiss on my hardy." he shouted lewdly but hoarsely, as he stood by and watched his other two comrades arrive on deck.

All three airmen were young men, but outwardly they looked like little old men. Their hair was totally white, and the wild expression in their eyes told of the fear that they had endured, still clutching on to whatever was in their hands. Sandy still had his earphones on his head, and his radio microphone almost inside his mouth, and every time he spoke it was to curse and shout abuse at anybody within earshot of him.

The ship's doctor rushed to check them over, and after a short while declared them all temporarily deaf and in catatonic shock. He gave them a sedative to help them relax which soon began to take effect upon them. Except for Sandy who was still in automatic communications mode, which was the saving point for them all, as his delayed shock had not kicked in until he actually realised that they had been saved after all.

Soon all three were put onto stretchers and carried gently across the gangway to be taken away to their base, with the full effect of their jabs taking hold and sending them to sleep. Sandy was murmuring drowsily but still swearing and shouting the odds, until finally he too succumbed to the injections.

"He must be one hell of a character, Andy! Still shouting the odds even as he fell asleep." John stated.

"Yes. Some people seem to excel in situations like that, whereas most of the rest keep a low profile and try to recoup from their injuries. That's what makes heroes of the seemingly most unlikely people, which we, the British Islanders seem to have in abundance.

The Krauts found that out and even admitted to it some years ago, despite the big mouthed Yanks bragging about what they did or did not do, and tried to steal our thunder from day one of them joining us." Sinclair said bitterly, watching the stretchers being taken off the ship and towards the lift that was waiting to take them up to the base.

"John, I need you to bring a large bag of tools with you. Tomlinson and the captain of the *Princess* have joined forces for both ships crews to team up and get some sort of semblance of order back onto the atoll. The 2nd will be going to see if he can fix our bows and our prop. In the meantime we can get some of those steam engines working, get some electricity going, fresh water organised, recovery of bodies and the like." Day stated, when he joined them on the bridge.

"Happy to oblige and all that, but who's going to look after the ship. What's the score with the propeller?" John responded eagerly.

"We've bent the prop shaft and probably a couple of our propeller blades have been snapped off. Fortunately we carry a spare prop-shaft but not a spare prop. The *Princess's* 2nd will get a diving team together to help me sort it out. Blackmore will be looking after both ships until I'm finished."

"Suggest that the ships provide temporary electricity and get some fresh water pumped ashore just to tide things over, Happy."

"That will be arranged soon enough, but I need you to take a team of stokers to go over to the contaminated fresh water lake and get some sort of pumping going. We can always desalinate the water as it comes through your filter system. Once you've got that organised, leave the stokers there to take care of the situation, I need you over this side to team up with Moore and his gang who are going to try and rescue any of the deep store provisions that may still be usable. Without them we'll all starve."

"Not as bad as that Happy. We can always use the cargo that we're supposed to be taking to Fiji, Port Moresby or even Brisbane. We've got plenty of fresh animals to go on with, at least." John said stoically.

"Each rescue team will have a scientist as an advisor, so we don't stray too far from what is required." Day said sternly.

"If we're going into flooded areas, then we'll need a qualified diver to accompany us. If, and I'm only surmising, that if I'm allocated the food cavern, then I'll definitely need someone who can use breathing apparatus, apart from a fire-fighter that is."

"I've got the main bulk of the divers lined up from the ships' company, as I need at least four for the prop shaft replacement. But you've got somebody who is nearest and dearest to you." Day said with a smile.

A man came wandering over to John, wearing a diving suit and goggles. When he stood next to John he took off his goggles and revealed himself.

Happy chuckled at the expletives John gave as he saw just who it was.

"Cheers Happy, you certainly know how to ruin a man's day, by giving him a piece of shit to work with." John responded over the protestations from Moore.

"He loves you really. Just let him show you he's not such an asshole."

John looked angrily towards Moore but turned back to Day.

"If you sure he's up to it, then it's game on. Give me your instructions and I'll get on with it."

Day nodded his head and gave John detailed instructions, many of which John had already guessed.

John flicked through the instruction sheets and the tasks needed to be done, then stated he was already on his way.

"See you later John, but keep in touch even if it's by a runner. We've got until sundown tomorrow to get organised before the King Phatt and his gang descend upon us." Day concluded, and left the bridge.

The combined crews of the *Inverlogie* and the *Princess,* and even most of the would-be passengers pitched in and worked hard for several days just to get some semblance of order on the now very new shape of the archipelago, before they had a chance to see to their own wounds and defects.

The engineers sorted out the lifelines of the atoll, leaving the sailors to the general clean up operations. Whilst the islanders, under the direct guidance from their King and Queen, tended to the injured and gathered up the increasing number of bodies littered everywhere. It was the Islanders unhappy duty to dispose of them, which gave off a stench that was in direct competition to the new smells now given off the Maoi volcano.

John and his team had already sorted out the reclaiming of the fresh water just as he did off the *Inverlaggan,* and was in the process of trying to rescue what was left of the 'State' larder.

It was found that whilst most of the 'live' provisions managed to survive, due to their protective wrappings and the like, in fact it was virtually all of the 'dead' provisions that perished.

"Sorry Grey, but even though we've managed to clear the water from the vault, it appears that not even a revamped chiller system could rescue it." Moore said glumly, taking off his diving mask.

John looked slowly around the place and although he did not like it, he had to agree with Moore.

"It's just as well I've still a working example on board the *Inverlogie,* then." John replied with sarcasm.

"For what it's worth Grey, we need to work together and try to get some of these new freezer units back into commission, even though we've nothing to keep it working for." Moore said flatly.

A Beach Party

"Yes, well, Moore. It looks as if the only things worth eating on this island turn out to be humans, and what's left of the vegetation for afters. Maybe you'll be the first one into the pot. Yes?"

Moore gasped at John's statement.

"Now look here Grey. I don't give a monkey's what you can or can't do, but we've got a specific job to do whether you like it or not. You might be a marine engineer, but I'm the scientist between us, and as such I'm the one in charge. So unless you climb down off your high horse and start coming up with some ideas, I'll make certain that Chandler hears of this." Moore said angrily.

"Me? Come up with ideas? You're the so-called boffin, so you come up with them. I'm going back to the ship, to do some real work." John responded angrily leaving Moore totally aghast and stuttering to utter a suitable reply, then strode out of the cavern and made his way back to the ship, meeting up with Sinclair and a couple of the sailors.

"Hello Andy, what have you been up to?"

"Helping the locals to recover their dead and clearing the living areas of the atoll. You should see what the tidal wave's done to the place. The entire Darnier Atoll has been devastated with all the outer islands and most of the barrier reef has been washed away and dumped into the lagoon to form a barrier against the 5 remaining islands, so that its almost one big island now. As you can see, the Pink Lagoon has also been almost filled in and all its fine sand piled up like a sand bar across where that new runway was. Mother Natures way of reclaiming the land I suppose. The causeway has been built up to twice its height, and the harbour filled in as well." Sinclair informed grimly, pointing to the devastation that surrounded them.

"Yes, we're certainly glad to survive it Andy, but without food we'll starve to death before another ship can reach us. Just as well the Phatties aren't cannibals or we sailors would end up in their pots."

"Let them try John. Besides, haven't we got enough on board to share out? I mean, you've got your new-fangled fridge working to see to that until a relief ship arrives? There're only about 250 or so surviving islanders left, and we've got several tons of the stuff just sitting around going nowhere fast. But as it turns out, this is one occasion where we visitors on board outnumber the locals so we come first, so to speak."

"Yes, but once King of the Phatties decides that it really belongs to him and his natives get hold of it, they'd scoff the lot in a couple of days. Maybe I'll recommend that you and a gang of well armed men be assigned to guard it, and see that it's dished out properly."

"Well thank you very much. And here's me thinking you were a mate of mine."

"There's no need to thank me yet Andy, just keep yourself available in case the locals mutiny and come demanding their food back." John said, offering Sinclair and the other sailors a cigarette, which they promptly took and commenced to enjoy a long awaited smoke.

"Got to go now Andy. See you later." John concluded, leaving his friend.

A Beach Party

Chapter XXVII
Saving Grace

It was on day four after the wave struck, when Tomlinson and the *Princess'* captain called the officers together for a meeting, to discuss their departure from the island.

"There is an international relief convoy being sent out to us and the other archipelagos that were affected by the Mega Tsunami. As we bore the brunt of it all and crucially, stopped the tsunami in its tracks, they'll call on us first. In the meantime, the *Princess* is getting ready to put to sea again to survey the damage done in the area. But unfortunately, like us they are unable to do so as we've got the only food left on the island, apart from the local off shore fish that is. If we offload it, it will perish within a day, let alone eaten before it even gets landed ashore. For that reason, the decision was made to remain here and act as a grocery store for the islanders, until the convoy arrives in about another four days or so." Tomlinson informed them, and continued to outline what he and the scientists intended to do in the meantime. When he had finished he had his customary question and answer session, giving anybody the chance to offer any suggestions or observations to the notice of the rest.

"Now that the island has a reasonable level of self –sufficiency by providing their own electricity and fresh water, perhaps if the captain would care offer a diplomatic solution to King Phattolei and his people. Arrange for my cargo hold fridge units to be unshipped and re-assembled ashore in some appropriate place. Once this is done, they can have back all the food that is now needed here and not taken to some other port. That way, when the next ship arrives, their cargo can be offloaded straight into the cold store without having the same problems as we faced when we arrived. This is my answer to the storage facility that is still noticeable by its absence, despite the efforts of the boffin in charge of this project." John stated calmly but giving Moore a stern look.

Tomlinson and Chandler nodded in agreement and discussed briefly the merits of John's proposal before they finally consented to it.

Moore complained about the negative attitude John was showing towards his project and started to protest vigorously about them siding with John and not him.

Chandler spoke crossly to Moore, and ordered him to assist John with the transfer, telling him that he might learn something from an engineer instead of out of date ideas from out of date books.

"Now that we've got that sorted out we can start taking the time to make the rest of the ship repairs needed to make our return trip. You are reminded that we're still guests of King Phatt and his depleted subjects. Therefore, even though most of the atoll has been devastated, everybody must still comply with local laws and such like." Tomlinson concluded.

When the officers filed out of the *Inverlogie's* saloon, John was called over by the captain of the *Princess*.

"Excuse me engineer! I understand that it was you who helped my sailors to secure the ship during the tidal wave onslaught? Also that it was you that sent over some Panama plates to effect our tow to safety?"

John looked at the much-freckled face of the ginger haired man and nodded, but said nothing.

"It appears that you have a shy hero here, Tomlinson. He had saved my ship twice in the matter of about 30 minutes, you know."

Tomlinson made a brief introduction for both of them, before John replied.

"All I did was to appreciate the situation and offer assistance as I saw fit, that's all." he responded civilly and with modesty.

"John was our trials officer but as his trials have finished, he is now almost a passenger. It's his invention on board that's going to be the saving grace for the local islanders." Tomlinson said in support.

"Well Tomlinson, you're a lucky man to have him. Thank you Grey, I shall see that your name is mentioned in the ship's log under my own column. Well done." the captain said and shook John's hand firmly but gently.

Before John had the chance to excuse himself, Chandler arrived to speak with him.

"It seems you've upset our Mr Moore again, Grey. I wish you wouldn't keep doing that, as it's bad for morale. It's taken me days to get him to stop throwing his toys out of his pram and he blames it all on you. For the sake of unity I request that you go easy on him." Chandler said glumly.

"Sorry about all that Chandler, but that man gets right up my nose. He's supposed to be the boffin and the one to sort out the fridge problem, not me. According to him I'm just an oily rag, yet it's me that's come up with the solution that he should have solved in the first place. I happen to be a fully qualified marine engineer, in case you've forgotten." John said with rising anger.

"I'm on your side Grey, so please don't have a go at me. Sufficient to say, you'll be the overseer for the transfer, whereas Moore will be doing all the grafting. Just let me know when you're ready to start and I'll get a few of the other scientists help out too, you deserve this one at least." Chandler replied in a conciliatory voice.

"That's settled then. I'll go and tell the King what we intend, perhaps he'll get some of his people to help offloading the food. That should put them into a good mood at least. Catch up with you later John, but see the chief before you do start." Tomlinson concluded, which broke up the little meeting.

John worked hard with his own team of men who were working in tandem with two other teams that were responsible for the removal of John's creation on board and its re-assembly into a recently cleared cavern that would take the off loaded cargo from the ship.

It was during a lull in the proceedings that Larter came along and spoke to him.

"Hello John. Keep this under your hat, but I've just received a signal that states the relief convoy got held up due to stormy weather, but should arrive within the week. It's a convoy of two freighters, two tankers and an ocean going tug. Due to the fuel storage tanks being destroyed, one the tankers that's arriving will be moored permanently until such times as new bunkers can be rebuilt. But the one that's more in line with our lot, is one of the freighters which is a 15,000 ton fridge ship similar to us that is loaded to the gunnels with frozen goods. So reading between the lines John, we'll be sailing home just as soon as they discharge their cargoes. Mind you it will mean extra work to provide for its handling ashore." Larter said and handed the signal pad for John to read.

After a few moments to read the lengthy signal, John handed it back.

"Thank god for that Bruce, and here's me thinking we'd be ending up in the cooking pots of these Phatt people. As far as the problem of storage ashore, it will be all down to that idiot Moore, and bloody good luck to the bastard. Anyway, let's hope they bring some mail for us too." John said with relief.

"Andy has told me that there's going to be a big bash on the island tomorrow, which is something to do with King Phattie and his gang celebrating their survival of the 'great wave'. He says that the last of the live animals will be slaughtered as an offering to their ancient gods, but he also says that it will all go into one big barbeque. So, providing that you can pull off your magic tricks and live up to your nickname of 'The Iceman', we'll all stand to have a bloody good nosh up." Larter informed him.

"Providing that that useless, so called boffin by the name of Moore can do as he's told, then all is well." John replied modestly.

"Just keep faith John. Oh and by the way, all officers will be required to attend a special meeting first thing in the morning after breakfast, that is. The steward will advise you, but until then, I'll see you later in the saloon, perhaps. In the meantime, I've got some serious signal traffic to deal with. See you then."

"Thanks Bruce. If you see Andy on your travels, ask him to meet up with us then. See you!" John answered as Larter left him.

A Beach Party

* * *

It was almost dark when the final load had been taken away into the new cavern storage area and for John to hand the clearing up and the myriad of other jobs to be done to the 3rd mate.

"Suggest you just clean and clear away 3rd, as there'll be no further cargo coming aboard this vessel until we hit Aussie land. We've got plenty of beer on board for you to offer the men a couple of cans each for their endeavours. But I expect I'll see you in the saloon later for a well-earned drink. See you later if you care for one." John said, and started to leave the deck and head for his much-needed cool shower.

On the way he met Day, who was coming out of his cabin.

"Hello John. We've got a special 'Captains' meeting in the morning to discuss our situation here on the island. In the meantime, you will provide me with a special report on the cold store situation, so as to present it to Chandler and his gang, who will be there as well. Nothing too elaborate so as to baffle them with science, but something straight forward."

"Hello Happy. As a matter of fact, I've got it almost written down. Sufficient to tell you from the outset, that all is well and within the test guidelines and parameters. That is despite the shambles the so-called expert tried to produce.

Maybe if the relief freighter can provide a back up to our Heath-Robinson affair, then we can get from this bloody place sooner than later. For the by and by, how's Blackmore getting on?"

"My sentiments entirely John! Blackmore is doing very well and holding his own. Anyway, hope to see you in the saloon later." Day said crisply and departed from John's company.

The following morning was the start of yet another beautiful tropical day, as Mother Nature was trying her best to try and heal the wounds and scars that the tsunami left behind.

John had completed his final early morning rounds and because he had no monitoring of the cargo to conduct, he found plenty of time on his hands just to sit on the boat deck and have his pre-breakfast cigarette in peace.

"Morning John! Figured I'd find you up here, where's Bruce?" Sinclair asked quietly as if not to disturb the silence of the morning.

"Hello Andy! Bruce is still probably turned in, but what brings you up here?"

"One of the lads got involved in a fight with a local man last night, who claimed that he had raped his daughter. If that's not bad enough, it turns out that the local man was found this morning dead with stab wounds to his belly and that our man has been accused of doing it. I was hoping to ask Bruce to see what he is able to do to prove our man innocent of both crimes. Both carry the death penalty if found guilty, John." Sinclair stated glumly.

"The very first question is obvious, but did he get to stab the father?"

"The way I see it, he's not guilty of the first crime, and from the size of the father, there's no way anybody could have attacked him in the manner claimed. I mean, my man is only a 7 stone weakling compared to this hulking great mountain of lard."

"One thing is for sure Andy. The captain will find out the truth of who did what, even before Bruce has a chance to look through his law books. Have no fear Andy, all will be well."

"All what will be well?" Larter asked, as he joined them.

When Sinclair repeated what he had told John, Larter told him that it was up to the captain to sort these matters out, as it involved political and diplomatic jurisdiction. He also pointed out that the sailor would probably not be punished due to the recent brave acts the ships crew had performed in the rescue of the King's Island and its people. He also said that it was up to the girl to cast the accusation directly to the sailor, if not then the girl would have to remain silent in case she got punished for false accusations. The stabbing would be determined by just what weapon it was and who owned it.

A Beach Party

"In short Andy, your sailor should be in the clear. But it would be up to Phattman to give the final verdict. Usually death by fire and brimstone as the person gets hurled down the abyss of the volcano."

"If I tell him that, it will cheer him up no end. Just as long as he's in the clear as he keeps telling us."

"Well Andy, that's all I can advise." Larter concluded, and the friends break up their little meeting and went on their separate ways.

Chapter XXVIII
Blazing Torches

"**G**ood morning gentlemen. Today, we have several things to do prior to us finally getting on our way again, providing we get a new propeller that is. The first thing is of a very serious nature in that we've got a problem on our hands concerning the welfare of one of our sailors." Tomlinson stated, before commencing with his agenda.

He briefed the officers on that very serious matter before going through the rest of his agenda, ending on the note that if all went well, the big bash to mark the ship's sailing would be a giant barbeque on the beach.

There was no question or answer session that usually followed such meetings, which ended the meeting quickly, and quietly, as each officer was contemplated the outcome of the sailor's fate.

The only topic of conversation and interest created on the ship was the rape by one of the men, which, according to the rumours, would blight the ship forever. Even the entire crew of the *Princess* got to know of the problem, and came across expressing their support to the accused sailor

"The captain will have it sussed out, mark my words. He's been here before, and already knows the ways of these people." Chandler assured.

"We though he had, by the way he was greeted ashore when we arrived. Must have been in some other shipping line." Sinclair responded, listening to the deliberations as each of the scientists voiced their opinion on the matter.

John said nothing, but remembered what McPhee had told him some years ago when Tomlinson and he were on the SFD2. That way, he would not be accused of adding to the plot, nor the wild rumours that were in abundance.

A Beach Party

The working day finally come to an end, for everybody to get themselves ready for the promised big show ashore later on in the evening. Although there was almost nothing to go ashore for, given that the island was almost denuded by the tidal wave, and the only food left was fish from the sea and whatever was sent back onto the island.

John and Larter were having a quiet drink in the saloon, when the ship's tannoy announced that everybody was to muster at the gangway.

"This is what I've been waiting for John! Let's get to the gangway before the rest arrive, and have a good view of the proceedings." Larter said quickly, gulping down his drink.

The two friends hurried down onto the gangway just as the rest of the crew were arrived, and saw a big gathering of local islanders standing around in a large circle which was lit by several blazing torches.

Tomlinson pushed his way through the crew to appear at the top of the gangway, wearing his ermine robes, just as he had when the ship first arrived.

The cacophony of sound coming from the drums, horn blowing and the chanting from the islanders stopped abruptly, as King Phatt came forward and stood in the middle of the large circle of Islanders.

When Phatt lifted his ivory baton into the air, a man who was shoved towards him from the circle, staggered and stumbled across the ground to kneel at Phatt's feet.

Tomlinson pointed to Sinclair who with another bosun, brought the accused sailor across the gangway and left standing alone near Phatt.

The circle of torches seem to shrink as the bearers came in closer to Phatt, who held up his arms to stop them coming any further.

Another Islander came through the cordon of torchbearers, dressed in a long white robe, and carrying a long spear that was adorned with coloured feathers.

King Phatt spoke for a moment in his native tongue, whilst pointing to both the sailor and the cringing islander, before he spoke in Pidgin English.

"Bring the woman accuser forward." he demanded.

Three women dressed in colourful costumes dragged a naked young woman into the arena.

King Phatt spoke again in his own language whilst he walked around the three people. Once he stopped, the man in the white robe signalled a group of very large men to enter the ring, who proceeded to strip the prisoners naked. Phatt started to poke their anatomies with his cane before he gave another signal.

It was Queen Phatt this time, who almost rolled across the ground, because she was just as round as she was tall.

She bent down and examined the girl then went onto give a close examination of the men's genitals before slapping the sailor hard on each side of his face. She pointed to the islander then went and stood next to King Phatt.

Phatt pointed to the girl who was brought screaming towards him, as was the islander who was brought to him in similar fashion, whilst the sailor was re-dressed by the large men.

The girl and the islander were held firmly in a star fashion for the man in the white cloak, who brought out a small club and thrust it roughly right up into the girl's privates, which made her scream in agony before fainting. The islander was begging for mercy, when the man placed a bucket between the offender's legs, then produced a large curved dagger and positioned it under the offender's genitals. The begs for mercy from the islander was replaced with a large scream of pain, as with one swift flick from the man's wrist, he slashed the islanders genitals off him to land onto the ground, with his life-blood pumping out of him in spurts until there was no more. The man picked up the set of genitals and dropped them onto the upturned face of the fainted girl then turned to the King and waved his large spear as if to signal the end of the matter. With that, both the dead islander and the still unconscious girl were dragged away while the King

A Beach Party

declared that this was a timely reminder that the King's laws were to be observed at all times by everybody, and that this was his decreed punishment for such offenders who would suffer the same consequences.

With another wave of Phatt's baton, the drums and the horn blowing commenced once more, and the circle of torches to vanish into the night.

There was a brief silence as Phatt and his Queen stood alone with the man in the white cloak and two torchbearers.

When Tomlinson walked down the gangway and arrived alongside them, Phatt embraced him for a moment before he waved his arm aloft again.

As if from nowhere, several torches were lit and a melodious song was heard from a troupe of girls who had garlands of flowers around their shoulders. Instead of the raucous sound of the drums and horns, soft and gentle music coming from a group of men who were playing their instruments.

"Where do you suppose they got those flowers Bruce?" John whispered, as he and all the rest of the crew stood goggle-eyed at the spectacle unfolding in front of their very eyes.

"Phatty's own garden I suspect. His palace and gardens are on the plateau which survived." Larter replied in an equally hushed manner.

Tomlinson turned to his crew, who had lined themselves along the ship's side, waving his arm as the signal command to come and join him. Without further ado the men surged ashore and mustered around him.

Each crewman was paired off with one of the island girls, as the procession snaked itself away from the ships and towards the pink coral sands of the newly formed beach.

When they got there, they arrived into a large arena of brightly burning torches with several large open fires that were crackling with slaughtered animals turning on spits as they were being roasted.

Chapter XXIX
Chief Taster

The moon was up and full bathing the island in a silver sheen, and the smell of the animals being cooked was competing with the fragrance of the flowers that were gathered in great bunches along small sand dunes. There were log tables loaded with fresh fruit and other food items, but what pleased the crew most, were the large barrels of water, full of bottles of beer keeping them nice and cool.

King Phatt had a big rattan mat on the sand where he and his Queen went to sit, followed by Tomlinson, the captain of the *Princess*, and Chandler.

John and the other officers were placed facing in a semi-circle around them, with the crew arranged behind them in a bigger semi-circle, as the evening of feasting began.

John looked discreetly around and discovered that behind him were the rest of the surviving Islanders, made up of mostly women-folk and a few children, but hardly any of the men-folk.

"Look at the Islanders around you Bruce, there's hardly any men. What happened there do you suppose?"

"Don't know John, but I suspect it's all to do with the virtual wipe out. What you see are those that survived. Don't forget John, most of the men perished trying to save the islands and their farms or whatever."

"I just have the feeling that maybe these Islanders are trying to press-gang us into their system so as to make up their numbers."

"Whatever John, but this looks like some whale of A Beach Party, that will end up with only one outcome."

"I hate surprises Bruce, so what would that be?" John asked, but a crescendo of music, that seemed to announce some sort of moment in the proceedings, drowned his voice.

After little while, the main course of the evening was brought forward for King Phatt to approve.

A Beach Party

He stood up, drew a magnificent sword from his colourful flowing robes, and with one swipe, decapitated the roasted pig. It fell off the carcass and was caught by one of the cooks, who promptly offered it to the king.

With a nod, he took the 'prize', held it aloft, and spoke a few words of his own language before he spoke in Pidgin English.

"We of the Taranitians give thanks to our eastern friends for providing the food for bellies, and the fresh waters that we drink. And for the electricity that now shines in our homes." he commenced, then went on to describe the events of the mega tsunami, its aftermath, and mentioned various individuals as to their part in the survival of the atoll.

John was singled out for his work in providing the fresh water, calling him Mr Iceman for the cold store where they were able to keep their food fresh again.

He was asked to come and sit next to Queen Phattie. So with much approval and encouragement from Tomlinson, he accepted an ovation from the rest of the crew and did as he was commanded.

No sooner had he sat down, when Queen Phattie came and sat on his lap, causing his leg to be buried several inches down into the soft sand.

She was all of 35 stone, but not quite as heavy as her King, of almost 45 stone. She had a pretty face, and enough bosom to suffocate any man if he got caught between them.

This was the pride of the island nation, where big was beautiful, anything under standard was called many things, with the word 'puny' being amongst their favourite yet less insulting words, and akin to wiggling a bent little finger.

John winced at the pain, as her weight was pushing his legs right into the soft sand, almost burying them, but kept his decorum as the Queen was obviously taking a shine to him.

"You like pretty women then Mr Iceman?" she asked in pidgin English, as she offered to feed him a very large slice of pineapple that was wedged between her enormous breasts, each one the size of a medicine ball.

John could not answer as her stinking breath almost choked him, and his leg was starting to go numb with all the weight. He merely nodded, gave a smile, and started to eat from her offered fruit.

She must have taken pity on him as she did not prolong his agony, when she said.

"But you eastern men are so skinny and puny, not like our men all nice and big." She rasped and finally got off his leg, then crooked her little finger.

"As you're puny I will give you my number One daughter to see if you are a man to measure up." she added, and clapped her hands whereupon a large girl only half the size of Queenie, pounced onto his lap.

John managed to drag his leg from the sand to accommodate this semi-naked young woman whose breasts were full and pendulant as she settled into his lap, and started to cover his face with her breasts, then began to jiggle them.

She rubbed her breasts into John's face, inviting him to feed from the fruit that was held between them. He managed to understand what was to happen and started to eat the offered fruit, all of which drew a tremendous laugh and clapping from the rest of the Islanders, but cheeky banter from his fellow officers.

The feast was taken in several courses, each with their own 'thirst quencher' as the evening slipped into the night, and steadily towards the early morning.

As each course was devoured, the islanders put on a pageant that was an enactment of the deeds that were done by them during the past week or so.

"Each one a good drama player, Joe!" John stated, managing to catch Tomlinson's eye.

"Yes John. The next one will be about you, so be alert. Just go with the tide, that's all."

"Cheers Joe! But what am I supposed to do with this large

A Beach Party

piece of female on my lap. She's already starting to find her way into my pants."

"For your sake John, let her find you, and just hope that you make her smile. If she likes what she finds, then you're okay, but if she finds you lacking, then she'll slap you and leave. If that happens get up immediately and go sit amongst your fellow officers, and never mind the laughs and jeers from Queenie." Tomlinson advised.

"So that's how the sailor was found innocent? Too small a part to be of service?"

"Yes! If he had been well endowed, it would have been him and not the Islander that got separated from his tackle. Its their simple but effective logic none the less. The accuser was given something to cry about, and although she has been banned from sex until she dies, she will be treated like an off Islander, and at least she is the one still alive."

"So if somebody takes anything without the knowledge of the owner, they get their hand chopped off, like an eye for an eye?"

"Something like that John. But they always smile when they take, as without that smile then it would be theft, and that is also a big no-no. Whatever happens now John, just enjoy the experience and show the King that you're a British Officer. Stiff upper lip and anything else you can think of."

"Bloody hell Joe, just what is expected of me now?"

"From my own experience John, this is not just a beach party full of beer and food. Just enjoy yourself, and if all is well, you will be rewarded. As your captain, just trust me on this one. Good luck to you. Remember to smile when she does. For the sake of harmony, tell all your friends what I've just told you, if only for their own safety sake. One last thing, she is the chief 'taster' in all things. If she finds you palatable, then you will reap that reward I was telling you about."

Before John could ask yet another of his questions, he found a new and much lighter female nestling down onto his lap.

John watched the little plays to keep his mind off the probing fingers of this woman, but it was to no avail, as she finally found him and started to fondle him very gently.

John looked into the woman's face the very moment when he knew she had finally made him fully erect.

She gazed into his face and gave him a big smile as she began to rub him as if milking a cow. He smiled not only as what was suggested of him, but it had been such a long time since he was with his Helena, and the old urges started to bring him to perform what those teasing hands demanded.

She giggled and said something in her own language, which made Queen Phattie look towards him and gave him a big smile too.

"You are so skinny yet you can please my No1 daughter. You are a good man Mr Iceman." She said before she whispered into King Phatts ear, who in turn expressed his delight that John was found to be a 'man'.

The teasing fingers of the girl became too much for him especially as her breasts were swaying gently in his face. Soon she squealed with delight and held him to her breasts, when she felt his semen flood into her hand. She took her hand out slowly, looked at it, and then tasted what she found before she put her hand between her legs and pleasured herself for a moment.

In the meantime Queenie watched John closely during all this time, as did the three other younger daughters of the king, whilst her eldest daughter performed her ritual.

Only when the eldest daughter gave a shudder and an orgasmic scream did Queenie clap her hands and chant in her native tongue, which seemed to excite the other daughters in the little group.

John felt as if he had been 'used' but was still non-plussed as to what was happening around him.

Over the commotion, he heard Tomlinson calling him, as Tomlinson approached him.

"You have just passed your physical, and have more than pleased the 'chief taster'. You will be just like me now, and become honoured by helping to, shall we say, give new life, to these people. If the rest of us can satisfy the womenfolk just as

A Beach Party

well, then we've got it made for the rest of our natural. Providing that we return every now and then." Tomlinson whispered in John's ear.

"Bloody hell Joe. What if some of our members, and sorry about the pun, can't perform, or don't become a smiling success with the rest of the womenfolk?"

"You've set the standard John, but every man jack here will get the opportunity to perform a basic natural function. It is the only way for these people to survive even though full of shall we say eastern promise. Sufficient to let you know that the next visitor you will get on your lap, will be the youngest of the sisters. It might be against our upbringing John, but for God's sake, let her satisfy herself, even though she is only 14 years old. These people have no 'age' morals as any Islander capable of procreating would be encouraged to do so, if only to increase the population of these islands. Their infant mortality is very high, and their longevity is about the 50 years mark. On top of that most of their men were killed in the big wave. So we have an obligation to these people to help them survive."

"Bloody hell Joe! She's only 14 years old, but how the heck do you know that?"

Tomlinson looked across to and pointed out to one of the girls sitting and giggling amongst themselves then turned to John.

"As I've told you before John, I've been here and performed just like you will have tonight. That girl is around 14 years old and her name is the one I gave her. Telani. Judging by her Lei garland, she is still without the knowledge of men, despite what her elder sisters have told her. It will be up to Queenie who decides which one you get, but if it is Telani, then please be gentle with her." He said quietly and with pleading in his voice.

"Joe! I'd rather not do this thing. What are my own personal rights, in regard to stealing, shall we say, my essence?"

"We are at the mercy of the King and his court, without any external court of appeal, as he'd be acting on behalf of our own Monarch. I am ashore and out of the captaincy jurisdiction that I would have on board, so we've got to pander to the local laws, as our diplomatic entity stops at the end of the gangway. Just 'render unto Caesar' as the expression goes, and hopefully we can all go home in one piece. Our scientific friends knew the score all along, but did not dream of becoming involved too. They can put it all down to 'furthering the science of man'.

Whereas we sailors could put it all down to one good shack up ashore. Anyway John enough of the moralisation, just do what is expected of you and put it all down to life's experiences."

"Joe, you are a good friend of mine, and I would not even think of dishonouring any member of your family. I feel this is one moral dilemma that I shall have to square with my own conscience, so if I happen to refuse, then please do not condemn me for it. I'd rather hold decency and honour than for the sake of 'furthering the cause of mankind'." John said glumly.

Tomlinson looked into John's troubled face and gently patted his shoulder as if in sympathy.

"Your refusal to do your duty, and without sounding stupid about it, your duty on behalf of the British Commonwealth, would go down as a massive diplomatic blunder, and one that even our new Monarch would not be amused with. If you want to be coy about it, just think of your girlfriend whilst she performs, but for heavens sake smile when she's helping herself to you. Just one more thing John, when it's all over whisper her name in her ear, then pluck one of the flowers off her garland and put it into her right ear." Tomlinson stated as the noise of the party started to drown out his voice.

A Beach Party

Chapter XXX
Sausages and Pies

The party became much less inhibited, as the alcohol and the raunchy behaviour of the participants took over. There were frequent absentees in the semi-circles as couples sneaked off into the night and into the sand dunes, only to re-appear much later, with big smiles all around.

John was happy enjoying another cold beer, watching the people enjoying themselves and feeling that perhaps he had got away without having to perform his duty again. That was, until a young girl came slowly towards him, straddled his legs and sat down gently onto his lap.

She took one of the garlands from around her neck and put over his head so that both their heads were in the same loop then took his hands and placed them gently onto her young breasts.

John looked into the young girl's face, and saw that for a dark skinned girl she had the bluest of eyes that sparkled as she smiled at him.

He smiled and nodded his head slowly whilst he gently massaged her breasts, which seemed to give her the go ahead to ensure that John was at ease with what was about to happen.

He let her exploring hands release him from his shorts and fondle him to erection again before she pushed him backward then slowly and gently impaled herself upon him. He looked around to see if anybody was watching, but everybody seemed to be too engrossed in feeding or drinking to care.

The girl rocked herself slowly and rhythmically as if to the beat of the gentle music that was still being played, whilst John played and teased her breasts as they swayed gently in the early morning breeze.

Maybe it was the heady scented smell of the flowers, the sight of her mouth-watering young breasts, with the combination of the exquisite feelings he had in his loins. Maybe it was his lover's gasps and groans that spurred him on, but he could no longer resist his lovers ever demanding thrusts. With her final thrust they clutched each other in passion as they climaxed together until he finally finished pumping his seed into her. It seemed an eternity since John had experienced the pleasure of the intimacy of a woman's body, but he felt somehow refreshed and whole again, even though his experience was not with his usual sexual partner. He remembered Tomlinson's advice, as he whispered her name and put a flower in her ear. She in turn looked at him with surprise then kissed both his cheeks as she disentangled herself from him. After she had used a cloth to wipe him dry, she knelt down and took his penis into her mouth for a few moments as if to taste his last drop, before withdrawing it and kissing it gently, then stood up and stretched her arms above her head in triumph.

King Phatt and Queenie saw these final gestures, and clapped as they cheered the two sexual participants.

King Phatt commanded everybody to return to the fireside, where he proceeded to give another big speech both in his native tongue then in Pidgin English.

"Captain Tommyson visited us too, many a full season ago and brought good luck to the islands. He had promised to return one day and make good luck again. Since the big wave, he has kept his promise, and now we have had a good bonding between the Taranitians and his people from the east. We Taranitians can now ensure that our peoples will live on after the terrible big wave that has left us poor again. Captain Tommyson left behind one gift that was returned to him as we promised. That gift is my daughter TeLani, who will now bear the gift from another of his kind, and known to you as the Iceman. If TeLani bears the fruit of their union, he will be always welcome on these shores, for as long as I King Phatt, of the Taraniti tribe shall live. If any chief from amongst you denies this decree then speak now or forever hold your silence." King Phatt waited for a short while for any dissent, but instead got a cheer and a crescendo of drum rolls as his answer.

A Beach Party

"That has now been accepted by the people of Taraniti, and it is now written so. Come my friends, the party has only just begun. Bring on the food and drink!" he commanded, which brought a scurry of servants carrying yet more food-laden trays towards the ever-hungry King and his entourage.

During this time, TeLani and John had been seated together, whilst the eldest daughter served them fresh fruit and gourds of water.

Tomlinson walked over to the couple, whereupon he handed TeLani a trinket, which he took from the lining of his ermine cloak.

She looked at it then at him, before she bowed her head. He patted the top of her head, then spoke quietly to her in her language, before he asked John to stand up and place his hand on top of her head like he did. John repeated the same words as Tomlinson told him to say, before TeLani stood up and embraced them both. She took hold of one of John's hands and placed it on one of her breasts, and did the same with Tomlinson, then spoke a few words before leaving them to rejoin her sisters.

"What was all that about Joe?" John asked softly, as he saw the beautiful shape of his recent lover depart.

"Because we come from the other side of the world from them, called the big divide, and once we've sailed on our big swim again, she will probably never see us again. For me to come back was sheer luck to be able to see this unique and poignant ceremony performed all over again. So to ensure the bond between father and daughter and daughter and her lover, we promised to always remember each other as the years go by. In short John, the 'taster' woman is her mother and the girl you've just made love to, is my daughter. She said that she hoped that you'd come back one day with your friend and make her child, with child, just as the night follows the day. It also means that out of all the lovemaking that's happened tonight, from which the Taranitians hope to harvest several children as fresh blood in the tribes, it will be TeLani that will now become a tribal princess.

You have been celebrated and given a special name, so your offspring will share in that glory just as TeLani had done. The sad part of it all John, is if you never return, or don't have somebody that has proved themselves with the Islanders, then her offspring could die an old maid."

"But how was I to know it was your daughter. If I'd have known then I would not have deflowered her let alone dishonour you, protocol or not. I mean, why for god's sake? And anyway how the hell can you say it's going to be a girl baby?" John asked in total surprise and shock at this discovery.

"Queen Phatt and her womenfolk of the tribe can only produce girls, that's why they need off Islanders such as us sailors, to help them along. The other men in the tribe come from other tribes around the archipelago, and marry into it. The thing is John; it's a matriarchal system here. The men do the men thing, but it's the women decide on who gets wed or gets pregnant or not. The last time I was here, the ratio of women to men was 5 to 1. As the men were looked upon as mere sex slaves, the women were able to take their liberty with any man she fancied. But the females had to approach the males in threes to make it official and take account as to what took place, and if he protested they got the other men to deal with him. Then again, if he was under-sized, the man was treated as a second-class islander, who tended to the fishing or whatever was needed. The bigger the size of the man in every sense of the meaning, the wealthier he became and the more women he could have in his harem, King Phatt being a classic example. As I've warned you earlier John, size is all-important around this part of the world. Fortunately for you, you were able to make the club, let alone having the taste factor in your flavour as the saying goes."

"But then if that's the case why was that poor man 'de bollocked' if you pardon the expression, for a case of rape when it's the women who help themselves or decide who shags who? I mean if there's no such thing as a man raping a woman because of the other way round rule, then what?"

A Beach Party

"His punishment was not only for the refusal to the girl in question, but if she cried rape then he's done for. And anyway he was judged to be the man responsible for the murder. But as you can only kill a person once, they decided it was for the attempted rape, if only to keep the tradition going."

"Poor man! Maybe a few lessons could be learnt in our country on that score. Fancy being raped by a young 14 year old, it doesn't sound right does it? Let's hope my Helena in Amsterdam doesn't find out about all this"

"She won't know unless you tell her. Besides, if you happen to come out to the Pacific and the Orient again, you'll always encounter these goings on, and she will understand it. Providing of course you don't come back loaded up to the eyeballs with v.d., which is a no-no in anybody's language."

"Oh well, glad to be of service then Joe. Anyway, isn't it about time we all got our heads down, I'm fairly knackered, to say the least."

"We've got about another three hours yet John, until sunrise that is. Mind you, you are expected to do at least two repeat performances with TeLani before that happens, but this time in total seclusion from any prying eyes. So you'd be best advised to make the most of it because once the sun comes up, its back to being Cinderella again. She will be expecting you to do this, so make sure you give her a token this time. The one I gave her, was the one her mother gave to me, which she recognised even after all these years. I would suggest the gilt button off your epaulette or whatever. Failing that, even if it's only a fly button off your shorts. But you make it a little gift to her for her to remember you by. Anyway, enough of my preaching. I must attend to my other duties John, so hopefully I'll see you later when everything has been declared over with.

Usually by a large gong being sounded, and the Islanders running to surround their king Phatt." Tomlinson said as he yawned and made his way back to his semi-circle of merrymakers.

The gongs finally sounded as the signal for all merrymaking and fornication to stop, almost like a party pooper ruining everybody's fun. Soon all the islanders were rushing towards the central arena where the party had begun, with the off Islanders following slowly behind wondering what was to happen next.

When everybody was assembled, King Phatt and Queenie stood up and announced that the party was now at a close and brought great blessings from their ancient gods. That any union between man and woman during the night would be blessed with new life, which the islands needed to carry on their ancient traditions and customs of the tribes that had lived upon them. He mentioned the special union between Tomlinson's daughter and Mr Iceman as witnessed by him and Queen Phattie, and hoped that the special bond would bear fruit of his loins to enable the future of the islands, hopefully in many seasons to come.

He called upon Tomlinson to give a small speech, which was slow and precise in the wording of his oration. John knew that he had to speak wisely for fear of upsetting the diplomatic balances but mostly for fear in case of upsetting any female that may have had a union that was not of a 'smiling' nature.

John felt totally drained and satiated but quietly pleased within himself, as he kept looking at TeLani, who, although was surrounded by the rest of her sisters, managed to keep eye contact with him, but with a tearful and wistful smile.

'Just as well I listened to Joe. I gave her my lucky florin with the fish on the side of it, as fish is their sign of good living.' he thought, smiling and nodding back to her, then watched as she was shepherded away off the beach.

The blast of horns, gongs, and the loud throbbing of the drums brought John back to reality, as he witnessed the leaving of the Islanders, leaving the two ship's companies alone where they stood.

Tomlinson looked around at the men and summoned them to gather together and to walk proudly off the beach towards their own ship.

A Beach Party

John was feeling tired and probably looked just like the rest of the men. Tired and haggard after their King Phatt-sized night of feasting and fornication. There was a tired cheer from the men when they trooped slowly along the beach, which took them quite a while, even though both ships were nearby.

When John and the other officers of the two ships arrived, they formed ranks opposite each other and clapped each crewman as they staggered aboard.

The crewmen nodded their thanks to each officer they knew, and slipped quietly aboard for a much needed rest.

Tomlinson stood on the top of the gangway and greeted each crewman as they arrived. Then told them to go and get turned in have the sleep of the dead.

John was one of the last to reach the top of the gangway where Tomlinson was still standing, but now in company with Day.

"Well done John! King Phatt has told me that you managed to service some more of his other daughters, but TeLani twice more. Everybody will have the rest of the day off, but have a good rest and report to me in my cabin around 1400. The chief and I, plus our opposite numbers from the *Princess* will have resumed our duties by then so anything you may have for us prior to the party can wait until then. You've done us all proud, let alone the lucky damsels in distress you helped out whilst doing your duty to the monarch and the commonwealth." Tomlinson said proudly, shaking John's tired hand.

"1400 Joe? See you both then." John mumbled struggling to keep his eyes open to make his way to his darkened cabin and his bunk that seemed to call him as he entered the cabin.

"Here ye are 2nd. All nice and comfy for you. I'll call you at 1300 for you to have a nice shower and the like." Henderson said softly, helping John out of his now ragged tropical uniform, and onto his bunk.

"1300? Whatever! It's sausage and pussy pie time! Quick, taste this purple parsnip!" John mumbled on crudely but disjointedly, before he finally succumbed to his fatigue and fell onto his bunk already fast asleep.

A Beach Party

Chapter XXXI
Choices

John was on deck enjoying a cigarette but still feeling tired from his nocturnal activities, when Larter came and joined him.

"Hello John, how're you feeling today? Just like death warmed up with eyes like pissholes in the snow?" Larter asked playfully.

"Worn down to the last 'thou', Bruce. Still, as long as we carried the flag and did our duty, nobody can get us for it." John replied wearily, offering Larter a cigarette.

"That's the truth. Anyway, the good news is that those ships I told you about are due in later today, all full of supplies and goodies. No good to us mind because we've got a tug on the way to tow us to Brisbane. What's the score on the repairs?"

"The bow has had it, along with several side plates. We've got the wrong type of replacement prop shaft, even though we've got no replacement propeller parts. Unless the cavalry brings us what we need, then this ship is going absolutely nowhere."

"Just what the chief had to say. Mind you, we might be able to have a repeat performance of last night. Now that really was some beach party and a half."

"Not one being used to such things Bruce, I wouldn't know." John replied half heartedly, thinking of the prospect of yet another all night sexual performances.

"Fancy you, an officer getting too tired of the old pull and push." Larter teased.

"Done my bit for queen and country Bruce. The sooner I get away the better."

Larter chuckled at John's lack of enthusiasm, but changed the subject.

"Our Lysander friends are now okay. They certainly went through the scary mill they did, and will be relieved off their duty just as soon as the new spotter plane arrives, which I believe is on one of the tankers. One of them has several aviation tanks on board, which means that somebody is thinking of re-starting the flying boat service again."

"Flying boats? Right, that means we might be able to fly home instead of floating around the ocean waiting to be sunk whenever a decent wave hits us."

"The first mate has already been detailed off to stay on board as towing crew, so the rest will be detailed off when the captain has his speech this afternoon. I for one won't want to hang around, so I'd better go and see Andy to tell him about it. In the meantime, don't you go all heroic and volunteer, or we'll all have to stay behind. One for all and all that jazz John."

"No Bruce, I've had it up to the eyeballs with this flaming ship. The islanders can scrap it for all I care. Maybe we can get a lift back on the *Princess* seeing as they lost a couple of their crew during the big wave."

"There you go again John. Watch Bruce's lips and repeat after me. We're not going to volunteer."

"We're not going to volunteer!" John responded automatically, being too tired to do anything.

"That's the ticket. You must remember that only one engineer and two deck officers plus twelve crew are required for the tow. Anyway, must go and see Andy." Larter concluded, and left John in a hurry.

As Larter left, Blackmore arrived and sat next to John for a while.

"Hello Blackie! How've you been these last few days?"

"Hello John. Never better, especially now that I've been selected to be the chief engineer on board during the ship's tow to Brisbane." Blackmore said jovially.

"Well done Blackie! Congratulations! You'll certainly make a proper 3rd engineer after all. I've already done something similar so I know exactly what will be in store for you. If you want my advice, make sure you've got a couple of good stokers on board with you. One of them had better be a decent welder too."

"Thanks John, I knew you'd be glad for me. And thanks for the tip, as I'm about to recruit my four volunteers. What happens when we finally get there? Do we stay with the ship during its repairs, or will the company re-allocate us to another ship and bring us home?"

A Beach Party

"Don't know Blackie. But I dare say the captain will put you right on that score. Er, the steaming crew captain that is, which is the first mate."

Blackmore looked down cast at the first mate's mention.

"Don't feel too bad about that Blackie, at least you're the chief engineer on this trip, which means that it's your call every time there is an engineering decision to make. And especially as the ship would be under your control the moment you enter the ship repair yard wherever that may be. On top of that, it's the tug that will dictate the passage of the ship, all he's got to do is make sure there's somebody looking after the tow ropes."

Blackmore cheered up when he heard John's reassurances.

"Thanks for your word of comfort John, I won't forget all you've done for me. Must go now before our captain calls us for our briefing." Blackmore said in a more cheerful voice.

"Glad to be of help Blackie, see you sometime." John concluded standing up and made his way to the saloon where Tomlinson was about to hold his briefing.

"Afternoon gentlemen. First off, I have to inform you all that the ship is to be taken under tow to Brisbane, which means that we need a standby crew on board for her voyage." Tomlinson greeted, as he commenced his briefing.

During which time there were moments of total silence, which contrasted with the moments of laughing and banter, whilst Tomlinson managed to extract the would-be volunteers.

Once he had finished sorting out the 'steaming' crew he turned his attention to the other half of the equation.

"As for the rest of us, we will remain on board until such times we get our travel arrangements sorted out. That is to say, via the returning relief ships or on the next flying boat that arrives in a couple of days. For those of you that wish to return via the sea-route, see the purser who will make the necessary arrangements with whatever ship you choose to return home on. Those opting to fly back will stay on the *Princess* until the aircraft arrives. Any questions?"

"We've been seen to, but what about you captain?" John asked quietly, which seemed to cause a silence in the saloon.

"I thank you for your concern, but I shall be returning home on one of the tankers as its captain. The other tanker will remain as a temporary fuel depot until both tanker captains; their chief engineers, along with some of their crews, rebuild the islands fuel bunkers, and other things that we haven't done. For those of you going back on the freighters, you'll probably arrive home before me, if in fact you're not diverted onto another ship as crew, at the next port of call, be it Singapore, Brisbane or wherever. So be careful what method of return to the UK you choose to use."

"Christ, it's like a bloody lottery!" the 5th engineer shouted angrily, which seemed to unnerve some of the deck officers. But Tomlinson managed to settle him down and prevented a nasty situation that could have developed; given the choices the men had to take.

"Sorry and all that gentlemen, but it's company policy to utilise manpower to maximise profitability and fit in with company policies. And in case you have forgotten, each one of you volunteered to join this ship in Belfast. The company will get you home again, that is without doubt. But the time getting you all back home again is just like the proverbial piece of string and how long it was. Still, think of the bonus and back pay you'll be getting once you've arrived back in Belfast again. The last option you could take would be to sign off and remain on the island for the rest of your natural. There's plenty of good local talent to while away your days. You could always go fishing now and again, or even help out in repairing the islands' plumbing system again. Mind you, you'd have to pay your own way back from here, as and when another ship dares to wander this way again." Tomlinson said sternly, giving the officers more food for thought.

The room fell silent again, which gave Tomlinson the chance to conclude his briefing, and a final word to his officers whilst he still could.

A Beach Party

"Whatever your choice gentlemen, I wish you all Godspeed, and reach home safely again. For me it was a pleasure to have such a good set of officers on my ship, and as fine a body of men any captain could wish for. Before you leave the ship, make sure you square off your mess bills immediately you've seen the purser for your termination payment."

The officers stood and cheered Tomlinson, as he left the saloon with Day following behind him.

"That's it settled then John, us three are going home by plane. We'll be home in about three days, according to the Lysander sparks. He knows, as the Lysander crew will be going home on it too. Also according to him, we'll be going to Manila for onward flight to Blighty via Rangoon and other exotic places." Larter whispered for fear of being overheard.

"Thank god for that. But what about Dave Evans?"

"He's staying on board to get his senior radio certificate, then he hopes to remain down under for a while to visit some of this relatives there."

"I wouldn't fancy sailing with this dodgy bow, and holes in the deck its like a flippin colander. Maybe they'll get danger money or something?"

"Doubt it, more like scrap money. Providing it survives the tow that is."

"Well, the sooner we're back home again, the quicker we'll get re-assigned and earning again." John remarked sombrely.

"And so say all of us. In the meantime, we'd better square off any loose ends we might have on board, so as not to give the poor sods more work than what's necessary."

"What do you mean? All they've got to do is make sure the ship doesn't sink on them, and that the towrope is still hooked on. They'll be able to stay on board in luxury until they arrive at the other end. Almost like a cheap holiday cruise." John laughed.

"Maybe so, but I'm still going back by plane." Larter concluded, for the friends to leave the saloon.

249

Chapter XXXII
So Long

"**M**orning John. Glad I've caught up with you. You will present yourself to the captain at 1100 in his bridge cabin. Bring your logbook with you and the paperwork that you hold concerning those, shall we say adaptations of company property. Make sure you're in proper dress as befits this occasion. Just tying up loose ends that's all John, so there's nothing to worry about." Day announced.

"I'd better get cracking Happy, as you've only given me a couple of hours. You've already got my logbook, which was handed in the same time as Blackmore's. You were discussing matters with the 2nd at the time." John stated, jogging Day's memory.

Day frowned and looked up to the deckhead for a moment before answering.

"Ah yes, so I was. There's a frenetic activity going on around us at the moment, and I'm beginning to run around in circles with it all. But I still need your 'project' log and write up for the work you did with Moore or whatever his name is, as it's needed on the *Princess* by their chief boffin. I have to attend this meeting, so I'll take your logbook with me. See you later and don't be, well you know the answer to that, I'm sure John."

"Let me think. It starts with an A and ends with drift!" John chuckled recalling the very first time that expression was used on him.

"That's the one. Must go now John, million and one things to do before I join the tanker." Day said hurriedly then rushed away muttering to himself.

John made his way back to his cabin but managed to sight the 5th engineer to relay Day's message. Once the message was relayed, John dived into his cabin and started to prepare himself for this mysterious meeting with Tomlinson.

"Hello 2nd! The chief was looking for you earlier on. Here are your freshly pressed tropicals. Fancy a cuppa?" Henderson said affably.

A Beach Party

"Hello Handy! Yes thanks. It's okay; I've just been speaking with the chief. This is my last fresh set of tropicals. Is there any chance of getting another set ready for me by tomorrow morning?"

"Why not, 2nd! There's no shore leave until this evening anyway. Everybody is getting ready to move off the ship, except for the steaming crew, lucky bastards."

"What about you, how are you getting back?"

"Going back on one of the freighters, as most of us are. But according to the purser, it's bound for Singapore for a flight home or simply re-allocated to another ship's voyage. But the tanker's going back via the Panama to Venezuela for another load before arriving back to Blighty. I might just opt to go on it as I don't fancy floating around the South China Sea for months on end, as that's what's going to happen to us if we transfer off the freighter."

"Sounds a good prospect either way. At least you'll be earning all the while. As for me, I'm on the next flying boat out of here. I don't fancy staying on this island longer than necessary, even though I appear to be the flavour of the month, so to speak."

"Yes, you lucky bastard. We heard all about that floorshow you put on. Goes to show that we British are up for anything, if you get my drift." Henderson said crudely but with joviality in his voice.

"Even though she was a virgin, just as long as I'm not carrying any nasty disease I don't care. Anyway, will you help me find my pile of project books that I normally keep under my bunk?" John asked changing the subject.

Henderson crouched down, reached under the bunk and pulled out a pile of notebooks and other drawings that were folded in among them.

"Thanks! I couldn't find them the other day, must have re-stowed them and forgotten."

"No 2nd, it was me that shifted them, because there's a dirty great dent in the side of the ship where your cabin is located.

I managed to get them shifted before the welder got to work in patching it up."

"Well thanks again, and that was a good fire safety move on your behalf."

Henderson left John to get himself organised, but popped back shortly afterwards and gave him his cup of tea and a handful of mail that had arrived off the freighter.

John took the mail gratefully and whilst he drunk his tea, read through a letter he had from Helena. He didn't have time to read the others from home, but vowed he would once his meeting was over.

'I must try and get a coastal tanker going between Britain and Holland, that way I could have a few days off with Helena, in between each cargo discharge.' he said quietly to himself, holding up a new photo that she sent him. He kissed the photo and put it into the top pocket of his tunic, then readied himself for his appointment with Tomlinson.

"Morning John, glad you came on time as I'm running behind my schedule. Good, glad to see you've brought your, shall we say, homework, with you." Tomlinson said politely, taking the pile of paper work from him.

"That's the bane of this shipping company, more and more paperwork." Day remarked, placing John's logbook on top of the pile.

"You don't know these two engineer officers off the freighter, but you certainly know Mr McIntyre and Mr Chandler. They have been asked to witness this meeting today.

Tomlinson explained the reason why John was there, which was a pleasant surprise to him considering he had clean forgotten all about the promise he was given when the ship left the Panama.

The two guest engineer officers posed several questions to John, who answered in a clear and concise manner, before Day and Tomlinson called the meeting to a close.

A Beach Party

"It is our pleasure to endorse your work which has been of outstanding value to the shipping world.

Your project notes and logbooks do you credit, as no doubt your peers here this morning will testify. Your name will now be entered into company records as having achieved your next step up the Promotions ladder, and not before time I might add.

3rd engineer John Grey, formerly off the SS *Inverlogie*, I do hereby promote you to acting 2nd Engineer, and as of this day you will draw the appropriate salary that befits your new status. Congratulations!" Tomlinson announced with a smile and shook John's hand firmly but gently.

Day and the other officers did the same, with John basking in their well wishes and congratulations.

Tomlinson thanked the guests for their time, and the generous tributes they gave John, before announcing that it was time to get on with the more mundane matters of the day.

He stated that there would be a short session in the saloon to mark the occasion, and no doubt the new 2nd engineer would see that the whiskey bottle would be passed around fairly. This brought cheers and mild banter from the men, with John merely shaking his head in accepting his lot.

"That will certainly knock my mess bill up somewhat. Must try and get it on the slate this time." John said quietly into Day's ear, who merely laughed at the suggestion and slapped John's back gently as they left Tomlinson's cabin.

The get-together with all the officers, including all those from the relief ships and the *Princess*, even all the crew from the two tugs that had just arrived joined and in, was a riotous affair as everybody knew that the following day was departure day for everybody.

"Just as well we had a generous donation of booze from the tanker boys, otherwise we'd all be using straws from the same bottle!" John said in Day's ear and handed him another drink.
"Yes, we drank the island and the ships dry at the beach party. Just as well Larter sent his stores signal early before the freighters

loaded up and sailed. Although tins of Mackeson and bottles of Newcastle don't exactly mix, but this single malt tastes grand, even with the mountain of ice cubes you normally get." Day replied, holding up his glass and looking at the cubes of ice swirling around the amber nectar.

Tomlinson came over and chatted with Day as John sat down again next to Larter.

"Pity Andy's not here, he'd love the pop they serve." John said loudly over the noise of the party.

"Oh yes I am! The entire crew had been invited to this bash by the skipper, but only a few of us remain on board to do so. Anyway, who's got the fags this time?" Sinclair replied from behind John's back, making him flinch in surprise.

"Bloody hell Andy. Wish you'd stop doing that, you old Scotch egg!" John said handing Sinclair a drink and a cigarette.

The party went on for a while, before Tomlinson rang the bell at the bar to silence everybody.

When he had everybody's attention, he called for them to raise their glasses in a toast.

"To all the crew of the *Inverlogie*. Without them we would have been in a right bloody mess long before now. To the captain of the *Princess*, and his gathering of scientists who put their brains together and helped us to claim the Islanders land for them. To the captain and officers of the relief ships, whose beer and whiskey we're now slurping.

And last but by no means least, to the tug's captain and his crew who have the unenviable task of towing my ship all the way to Oz land not knowing if she will make it or not. To all seafarers that have gathered here tonight I bid you all farewell, so long, adios, sayonara, or whatever your language uses on this occasion."

Everybody replied with their glasses held high, and with one word, they said 'CHEERS!' in a loud and solemn manner.

Somebody broke the silence by saying.

"Last one down the gangway, switch off the lights, and don't forget to bring the moggie with you." which brought laughter, life

A Beach Party

and soul back into the party that was temporarily halted by the hush of the speech that Tomlinson had delivered.

Soon after the speech and toast, everybody started to drift away to their own ships or cabins, leaving John, Larter and Sinclair in a huddle in the corner by the bar.

John remembered his new photo of Helena in his pocket and showed it to his friends.

"Bloody hell John. If she ever finds out that you've shagged the arse off a Kings youngest daughter, then you'll be under stoppage for quite a long while!" Sinclair said whistling with appreciation when he saw the picture.

"Not if I know continental women, he won't. She'll probably get him to make a repeat performance on her, then forget it." Larter said knowingly, handing back the picture.

"Mind you, you've got to hand it to John. He doesn't do things by halves. Not everybody gets to shag a harem of princesses." Larter added.

John didn't let on the truth of the matter that the woman that first sat in his lap and fondled him was the mother of Tomlinson's daughter who was the young girl that had made love to him publicly, during the party.

He just sat there, to grin and bear the good natured banter he received from his two close friends, until they finally gave in to their fatigue and got turned in for a well earned sleep.

"Here we are for the last time, look our plane has just landed. Bagsy a seat by the window!" the Lysander sparker shouted in excitement as he pointed to the giant Saunders Roe flying boat that glided to a halt next to a hastily prepared pontoon jetty.

John and his friends along with the other flight passengers stood and watched as uniformed people stepped out onto the pontoon and made their way towards them.

When the co-pilot and the pretty stewardess came forward to take everybody's names, for passenger records, Sandy wolf whistled and made a bawdy suggestion, which made the stewardess shy away from him.

A woman next to Sandy, who must have been his wife, swiped him around the ear and told him to behave, before apologising to the stewardess.

She explained that he was suffering from shock and his mind had been affected by it, so she was not to take any notice. The stewardess nodded her head but told her that he would have to be sedated if he upset the passengers or worse still, had a fit during the flight.

Larter went over and told them that he was a Radio Officer and offered to look after the man whilst flying.

"Thank you, but that won't be necessary. We've got a Neil Robinson stretcher on board for use in these occasions." the co-pilot stated, which put an end to it.

Before John and his two friends had a chance to gather up their belongings and walk the short distance to the pontoon, they saw and heard a crowd of islanders swiftly approaching them.

"Look out everybody, its Phatt Man and his robbin' bastards comin' after us! Ooooh! Singin' rum and co-co-o-lah, up his fat-ass-o-lah, as they're working for the Yankee doll-lah" Sandy sang, just as the crowd arrived.

King Phatt and Queenie, with their daughters following closely behind came up to John and announced in a booming voice.

"Let it be known that Mr Iceman will be welcome any time he or his kin chooses to visit our islands." Then waved his ivory baton a couple of times over his head then pointed it at the daughters.

TeLani came slowly forward, followed by all the others, who in turn, placed a flower garland around John's neck and kissed him on both cheeks. Whilst this was going on, Sinclair, Larter and all the others were each given a single flower and all accompanied by soft music and singing from the rest of the Islanders.

For once, Sandy said nothing, nor did he act up. He looked slowly around at the Islanders and burst into tears then clutching his wife sobbed bitterly onto her breast.

A Beach Party

It was at this moment when his mind started to heal itself from the terrible dangers he went through in two short hours of one day.

But this was the moment of truth and the sad parting of the ways between two sets of people who were a whole a world apart. John looked at TeLani standing by her sisters looking at him, smiling and gently patting her tummy. He returned her smile with a slow nod of his head, then turned to King Phatt and said quietly and passionately.

"My name is Engineer John Grey, who has come on the great swim with you back to your islands. My work is now done so I must leave you and return to my own people, but I do so with a heavy heart at leaving you all. My fellow officers and I hope that your kingdom will flourish and prosper once more. Nobody can tell when the next wind will blow, or when the next bloom of fish will arrive to fill your nets once more. For I cannot tell you when I shall return to see the fruit of my loins. But always remember this time and forever. May your gods go with you and keep you all from harm."

Queenie came up to John and whispered in his ear.

"You good man. You always be remembered. TeLani and my daughters will know as they pass their child from their bellies." she said, kissing him on both cheeks.

King Phatt gave a command in his own language, pointed his baton towards the islands again and led his crowd away, slowly, and in tune to the fading music they disappeared along the rock-strewn bed of the old Pink Lagoon.

Everybody stood speechless and silent for several moments before the co-pilot coughed politely and asked them all to make their way onto the plane.

The stewardess wiped the tears from her cheeks with a spotless hankie before putting a brave face on and escorting the passengers towards the waiting plane.

"Bloody hell John. How come you got all the attention!" Sinclair asked in puzzlement.

"I've no idea Andy. All I did was to make their fresh water and save their food from rotting by making a temporary fridge for them. I mean, it was you who helped to rescue and recover several of the Islanders, and you Bruce helped out with the administration. No if it were my choice, I would have chosen the crew of the Lysander. It was them who gave the Islanders an early warning, to prepare for that massive tidal wave which wrecked the place. They are the real heroes not me." John replied modestly.

"We always knew there was something about you John, and we don't mean about you talking to yourself either. You seem to forget that you've just been promoted to acting 2nd engineer, let alone becoming an honorary member of the Phatt tribe by managing to fill his daughters bellies full of arms and legs." Sinclair chuckled.

"It's too soon to know about that Andy. But we must not speak about it for fear of starting an uprising, if you pardon the expression. I mean, imagine our own Queen summoning us to her court and demanding to know who the dirty bastard was that put all her womenfolk up the duff." Larter said with a chuckle, which started a cross banter between them.

"This is your captain speaking. Welcome aboard the North West Orient Airlines Clipper service. We shall flying at an altitude of 15,000 feet. Our land speed will be around 350knots. There is a lounge and bar in the lower deck for those of you wishing to refresh yourselves. We have a change of flight plans and I hope to arrive Oahu Bay around 2100 GMT. Should we experience severe air turbulence then you will be requested to return to your seats. Thank you." the pleasant and well-spoken voice announced over the tannoy system.

"That's more like it. A perfect island with plenty of nightlife I'm told, with the prospect of the delights of the good 'ol U.S of A' still to come. I don't know about the rest of the stops on the way, change of crew and replenishments, but I reckon we should

A Beach Party

land in Blighty in about two days time." Larter said, looking out of the small window next to him.

"We might as well enjoy the flight so lets get a wet down us, I'm thirsty as hell!" Sinclair suggested, but John remained sitting as he looked at the devastated atoll way below him, and watched it slowly disappear away over the horizon. He sighed gently then took the several layers of garlands from around his neck and placed them on his seat, before joining the others.

The three friends sat together whilst a stewardess served them drinks.

"Erm! Who's got the cigars to go with this?" John asked quickly.

"They're on their way John. So here's to us. May we have a proper voyage next time." Sinclair stated, as the friends clinked their ice filled whiskey glasses together and commenced to commit their recent events to memory.

'I wonder where the next time will take us?' John thought, and drained his glass leaving only the half melted ice cubes rattling around the bottom of it.

Frederick A Read

A Beach Party is the fifth book within the epic *Adventures of John Grey* series, which comprises of:

A Fatal Encounter
The Black Rose
The Lost Legion
Fresh Water
A Beach Party
Ice Mountains
Perfumed Dragons
The Repulse Bay
Silver Oak leaves
Future Homes

All published by www.guaranteedbooks.net

Ice Mountains is due in November 2009.